W9-BLW-637

Poisoned Pages

Berkley Prime Crime titles by Lorna Barrett

MURDER IS BINDING

BOOKMARKED FOR DEATH

BOOKPLATE SPECIAL

CHAPTER & HEARSE

SENTENCED TO DEATH

MURDER ON THE HALF SHELF

NOT THE KILLING TYPE

BOOK CLUBBED

A FATAL CHAPTER

TITLE WAVE

A JUST CLAUSE

POISONED PAGES

Anthologies

MURDER IN THREE VOLUMES

Poisoned Pages

Lorna Barrett

BERKLEY PRIME CRIME
New York

BERKLEY PRIME CRIME
Published by Berkley
An imprint of Penguin Random House LLC
375 Hudson Street, New York, New York 10014

Library of Congress Cataloging-in-Publication Data

Names: Barrett, Lorna, author.
Title: Poisoned pages / Lorna Barrett.
Description: First edition. | New York : Berkley Prime Crime, 2018. | Series: A booktown mystery ; 12
Identifiers: LCCN 2018004283 | ISBN 9780451489838 (hardcover) | ISBN 9780451489845 (ebook)
Subjects: LCSH: Miles, Tricia (Fictitious character)—Fiction. | Murder—Investigation—Fiction. | Women booksellers—Fiction. | BISAC: FICTION / Mystery & Detective / Women Sleuths. | GSAFD: Mystery fiction.
Classification: LCC PS3602.A83955 P65 2018 | DDC 813/.6—dc23
LC record available at https://lccn.loc.gov/2018004283

First Edition: July 2018

Printed in the United States of America
1 3 5 7 9 10 8 6 4 2

Cover art by Teresa Fasolino
Cover design by Steve Meditz
Book design by Laura K. Corless

For Fred and Chester

Acknowledgments

My thanks to Linda Kuzminczuk and Mary Kennedy for being my first readers and sharing their eagle eyes and insights.

Cast of Characters

Tricia Miles, owner of Haven't Got a Clue vintage mystery bookstore

Angelica Miles, Tricia's older sister, owner of the Cookery and the Booked for Lunch café, and half owner of the Sheer Comfort Inn. Her alter ego is Nigela Ricita, the mysterious developer who has been pumping money and jobs into the village of Stoneham.

Pixie Poe, Tricia's assistant at Haven't Got a Clue

Mr. Everett, Tricia's employee at Haven't Got a Clue

Antonio Barbero, the public face of Nigela Ricita Associates (NRA); Angelica's stepson

Ginny Wilson-Barbero, Tricia's former assistant; wife of Antonio Barbero

Grace Harris-Everett, Mr. Everett's wife

Grant Baker, chief of the Stoneham Police Department

Chauncey Porter, owner of the Armchair Tourist

Mary Fairchild, owner of the By Hook or By Book crafting/bookstore

Frannie Armstrong, manages the Cookery for Angelica

Russ Smith, owner of the *Stoneham Weekly News*

Nikki Brimfield-Smith, owner of the Patisserie; wife of Russ Smith

Toni Bennett, owner of the Antiques Emporium

Jim Stark, Tricia's contractor; husband of Toni Bennett

Marshall Cambridge, owner of Vamps magazine shop

Bob Kelly, former president of the Stoneham Chamber of Commerce; Angelica's ex-lover

Fred Pillins, Pixie Poe's husband

Poisoned Pages

PROLOGUE

It had taken more than a year for this day to arrive—for justice to be served. Tricia Miles was all too familiar with that particular courtroom. She'd sat through a great deal of the two-week trial, had been the state's star witness, and with clenched fists she'd listened to the jury's verdict. That day, she sat in the front row of the crowded courtroom patiently waiting for the grand finale. The actual sentencing. She stared at her shoes, and not Bob Kelly's back, as Judge Edward Reed finally spoke. "Mr. Kelly, please stand."

Kelly and his defense team stood and faced the stern-faced judge.

"Mr. Kelly, a jury has found you guilty of the charge of the second-degree murder of Christopher R. Benson. Your behavior was brazen, deliberate, and cowardly. For this crime, the court sentences you to term of imprisonment of life without parole in the New Hampshire State Prison for Men. Do you have anything to say to the court?"

Tricia looked up, not sure what she was hoping for. An apology? Some semblance of remorse?

Kelly stared at the judge. "Not to you, sir. But—" He whirled and faced the people in the gallery behind him, zeroing in on one face, his expression twisting into a contemptuous sneer.

"It's all *your* fault, Tricia. Everything that happened was *your* fault. You're a jinx. Everything you touch is jinxed, and everyone you love is cursed. And I curse *you*. May your life be a living hell until the day you die."

Kelly turned back to the judge, who gestured for the uniformed officers to step forward. In no time, the prisoner was shackled and led from the courtroom. But as he was hauled away, he turned back to hurl one last epithet and, despite the restraints, raised his middle finger in salute.

Shaken, Tricia Miles could do nothing but stare at her black leather flats. Her sister, sitting next to her, reached over to squeeze her hand. Tricia looked up to see tears in Angelica's eyes. Were they for Tricia, Christopher—or Kelly? He'd been Angelica's lover for several years before she'd found out he had cheated on her, which was the beginning of the end of their relationship.

Tricia bit her lip as a tear cascaded down her cheek. Was she a jinx? So many in the village of Stoneham seemed to think so.

"Don't let that bully intimidate you, Trish. You did the right thing. You testified, and that beast will never be able to hurt either of us ever again."

Tricia swallowed but said nothing.

The judge had banged his gavel and the others in the courtroom had left their seats to shuffle toward the door, but Tricia and Angelica sat there, saying nothing, until they were the only ones left in the drafty room.

The press would be waiting outside the now-closed double doors leading to the hall outside, including Russ Smith from the *Stoneham Weekly News*. There'd be cameras flashing, reporters with microphones shoved in her face, and a cacophony of questions aimed at her. But just like after she'd testified, Tricia had no intention of sharing her thoughts or feelings with members of the fourth estate. She hadn't even voiced the depth of her loss, despair, and anger to her closest confidant—her sister, Angelica. If she was honest with herself, she hadn't let herself truly experience those emotions. She had grieved in private and in her own way. She didn't need anyone's permission or judgment.

And now it was over. The trial, the sentencing . . . and she was free to go on with her life. A life that would never include Christopher. Their marriage had been over for several years before his death, and though he'd initiated their parting, at the end, he'd wanted nothing more than to rekindle their feelings for each other—something Tricia couldn't see happening. But then, the future was always unknown. Would she have taken him back? She told the world—and Christopher—no, but she wasn't really sure it was a truly honest answer.

But losing Christopher had also hardened Tricia's heart, and she wasn't sure she would allow herself to love again. As she looked down at the empty ring finger on her left hand, Tricia reminded herself that the prospects in a village as small as Stoneham were few and far between.

A tap on her hand brought Tricia out of her reverie, and Angelica spoke. "Come on. We've got a party to go to."

Tricia hadn't planned for her housewarming party to coincide with Kelly's sentencing. The date had been moved up so the judge could have knee replacement surgery. Still, the timing was ironic.

Angelica gave her hand one more squeeze and then rose to her feet. "Come along." Sometimes she spoke to Tricia in the same tone she spoke to her dog, Sarge.

Dutifully Tricia followed. She wasn't in the mood for a party. She felt numb, but, as Angelica had told her earlier that day when she'd thought about canceling, "The show must go on."

And so it would.

It was time to stop letting Bob Kelly, and the misery he had inflicted, control her life.

Tricia forced a smile. "Let's go home. The drinks are on me."

Tricia and Angelica made one brief stop after leaving the Nashua courtroom, stopping at the Stoneham Rural Cemetery. Dressed all in black, Angelica waited on the path, a few yards away from the grave. Tricia had chosen to wear her blue coat, and underneath that a summer dress totally inappropriate for the cold November day—but it was a dress Christopher had admired. He would have been pleased to see her in it.

"It's over," she whispered as the brisk wind whipped her hair around her face and she bent down to place a solitary white calla lily on the grave. It was her favorite flower. Christopher had given her many bouquets of them during the happy years they'd spent together, and those were the times she chose to remember. Not the terrible sorrow that had enveloped her heart during the past fifteen months since his violent passing.

"Bob Kelly got life. He will never hurt another person, and he has the rest of his life to regret what he did to you—to us. To everyone who knew and admired you. It was a very small price for him to pay."

Tricia knew Christopher couldn't hear her words, but she needed to say them.

"I love you. I'll always remember you." And then she said the words she hadn't been able to say in more than a year, since his death.

"Good-bye."

ONE

Never had 221b Main Street, Stoneham, New Hampshire, seen so many people enter its doors. Instead of customers arriving for a book signing at Haven't Got a Clue, the village's vintage mystery bookstore, this gathering was of friends, sort-of relatives, and business associates from the local Chamber of Commerce. It was also Tricia's first stab at entertaining more than one or two people. Perhaps, she thought as another guest entered the newly refurbished living room of her loft apartment, she should have started with a more modest get-together. The space had more recently been a storeroom filled with shelves and boxes full of vintage mysteries. That stock now resided in the basement, which had also been renovated. The open-concept space was now bright, inviting, and—more importantly—felt like *home*.

"Isn't this a wonderful party?" Pixie Poe called, Tricia's newly married assistant. Pixie looked radiant in a vintage black, tight-fitting cocktail dress with a beaded bodice. Where she continually found those flirtatious frocks was a mystery to Tricia, but the style fit her to a T.

"Thanks for making the music mix CDs. They're perfect for a cocktail party."

"When it comes to entertainment, ya can't beat der Bingle, Frank, Dino, Tommy Dorsey, and the boys."

Before Tricia could reply, Angelica swooped past with a brightly polished silver tray of stemmed wineglasses filled with Chardonnay. "We've run out of red," she called as she began worming her way through the crowd.

Tricia's former assistant, and now step-niece and adopted little sister, Ginny Wilson-Barbero, had donned an apron that Angelica must have supplied and was passing around yet another silver tray with salmon cucumber rosettes. They looked adorable on the frilly paper doily–covered platter—just as Tricia had hoped they would.

As she passed by the floor-to-ceiling antique mirror that stood against the east wall of her new digs, Tricia noted she looked pretty good, too—considering she'd spent an hour or so crying her eyes out after returning from the cemetery. But now that the trial was behind her, she was determined not to think about it or Christopher's killer. When redecorating the apartment, she had allowed herself to display one framed photo of Christopher and her, taken on their honeymoon in Cancún, but that was it. She'd even stopped wearing his engagement ring on a chain around her neck. She now thought of herself as free to move on with her life, and the party was one big step in that direction.

Contractor Jim Stark and his team had finished their work on the transformation more than a month before, but Tricia had wanted to settle in—finding just the right places to set her treasures, some of which had been boxed up for years—and, more importantly, to test the recipes she'd serve at her first (and possibly only) big bash. The ones she'd fed to her pseudofamily at their weekly Sunday dinners. Nobody had complained, and, in fact, the praise had been effusive, which had given her a much-needed boost of confidence in her burgeoning culinary skills.

Tricia headed toward the dry bar she'd set up on a vintage glass-topped patio table. It had been a housewarming gift from Pixie and her groom, Fred Pillins, and it went perfectly with the eclectic furnishings she'd chosen. Although the table was laden with the best alcoholic spirits, Tricia decided she'd better keep a clear head. She plunked some ice into an old-fashioned glass, poured club soda from an opened bottle, and took a sip. *Eh.*

"Great party," Russ Smith said from behind Tricia, startling her.

"Hi, Russ. So glad you could make it." Although he certainly hadn't dressed for such a party, wearing instead his usual attire of a plaid flannel shirt and rather grungy jeans. His only concession was a tired-looking corduroy sport coat with leather patches on the elbows that he'd probably worn since college. "Is Nikki here, too?"

Russ tipped his glass, with what looked like Scotch in it, toward his wife, who was standing near one of the windows overlooking Main Street and conversing with Frannie Armstrong.

Nikki looked fabulous in the proverbial little black dress, with her hair pulled back in a chignon, looking much more sophisticated than she did when behind the counter of the village's only bakery, the Patisserie, which she owned. However, the effect was spoiled, as she looked to be bored out of her mind. In contrast, Frannie, who managed Angelica's store, the Cookery—a cookbook and sundries store—looked like a tourist who'd lost her way en route to our fiftieth state. Tricia had only ever seen Frannie wear something other than a loud aloha shirt on rare occasions. Frannie, a sturdy woman in her mid-fifties, seemed to be snagging anyone who would listen so that she could introduce her latest gentleman friend, whom she'd met via an online dating service. She found a lot of guys that way, but none of them seemed to last long. Tricia had already forgotten the poor man's name. The tall gent, with a graying beard and sparse hair, didn't seem all that enthused to be attending the party, nor being shown off like Frannie's pet dog. Tricia felt sorry for him.

"It sure feels good to be out and about—and on a weeknight," Russ said, eyeing the Scotch bottle on the table. "That's just about unheard of for us." He took a hearty slug of his drink.

"Is it tough finding a babysitter?"

"More like tough getting Nikki to leave little Russell. She feels guilty for plunking him in day care most of the week. It's not like the kid is even up this late," he lamented. Not for the first time, Tricia got the impression that Russ wasn't exactly thrilled to be a daddy.

Antonio Barbero—whom Tricia referred to as Angelica's secret stepson—passed by. It looked like he'd been enlisted to help pass out canapés as well, and he offered the mini spinach quiches around, with just about everybody taking and enjoying one. Unlike Russ, Antonio loved being a dad to his daughter, little Sofia, born the very same day as Russ's son. And though Antonio sometimes worked hellish hours, he always found time for his precious bambina. Of course, Antonio was a good ten or twelve years younger than Russ, who Tricia suspected had never contemplated marriage, let alone fatherhood, when he'd worked out his life's plan.

C'est la vie.

"Angelica said you'd made all the food," Russ said, grabbing a quiche off the tray as Antonio passed.

Tricia took a sip of her club soda. "Almost. A number of people brought goodies as well. Mary Fairchild brought some hot artichoke dip, and, of course, Nikki brought some of her marvelous mini cream puffs. A lot of people brought wine." She gestured toward the console table near the entryway, which was covered in bottles. Hmm, she ought to have mentioned that to Angelica when she'd stated they'd run out of red wine.

"Speaking of food, I'd better get back in the kitchen and make sure there's enough for everybody."

"And I'll just pour myself another drink," Russ said, but he didn't sound all that pleased about the prospect.

Tricia made her escape and found Angelica leaning against the large white-and-black-veined granite island, presumably taking a breather. Or was it her four-inch stilettos that caused her discomfort—not that she'd ever admit it? "Ange, why don't you go sit down in the living room and relax."

"Me, relax at a party? Unthinkable," she said, and picked up a cookie-crumb-littered plate from the island.

"Yes, but it's *my* party—not yours."

"Tricia, dear, you are the hostess—that doesn't mean you have to play waitress. Now, I've got everything in the kitchen under control," she said, and held out a hand to show that she'd tidied the island, which had been where Tricia had spread out some of the food, including the chafing dish that was now nearly empty of her childhood favorite Swedish meatballs.

"Yes—I also see you keep sending Ginny and Antonio out to play waitstaff."

"And they are enjoying themselves."

"Are you sure you didn't just browbeat them into helping out?"

"Of course not! Tricia, I don't think you realize it, dear, but there are a lot of people who would do anything to help you out because you're such a force for good in this town."

That wasn't true. It was Angelica who had earned that accolade in her role as founder of Nigela Ricita Associates, and anonymously, too.

In a few short years she'd helped shape the village into what it was today—a thriving success. She'd also accomplished that with her dual role as president of the Stoneham Chamber of Commerce. Tricia aspired to take her place, but she was sure she would never be able to fill her shoes. Eyeing the shiny red slingback Jimmy Choos, Tricia decided she'd much rather follow in Angelica's footsteps.

Angelica turned for the refrigerator. "Now, what else can we surprise your guests with?"

"Most of the hors d'oeuvres are probably already gone—"

"You got that right. There's just one more tray of those crab-stuffed mushrooms. Wherever did you get that wonderful recipe?"

"From your first cookbook—as you darn well know."

"Yes," Angelica said with satisfaction, "simple, but elegant. And everybody loves them."

At least those who like shellfish seemed to love them. Tricia wasn't a big fan herself, but they *did* look appetizing.

Russ entered the kitchen. "Any chance there's another bottle of soda around?"

Angelica handed Tricia the platter of rosettes and plucked the last bottle of club soda from the fridge's door. "Here you go."

"Thanks." He headed back toward the living room.

Angelica looked after him. "He's had a few tonight."

"Yes," Tricia said, and sighed. "I think he's grateful to be out of harness for a few hours. I just hope Nikki isn't going to have to drag him out of here kicking and screaming."

Behind them, someone cleared his throat. They turned to find Mr. Everett, one of Tricia's employees and an honorary family member, standing near the kitchen island.

"Mr. Everett?"

"Ms. Miles, I wanted to let you know that Grace"—his wife of four years—"and I are leaving."

"So soon?"

"We've had a wonderful time, but we pick up our little bundle of joy bright and early tomorrow morning from the Animal Rescue League. We don't want to take the risk of being late."

Tricia knew the equally elderly cat they were adopting had been waiting nearly two years to find his forever home. "I understand completely."

"Where are you parked?" Angelica asked.

"In the municipal lot."

"Let me get Antonio to walk you to your car."

"Oh, no. That won't be necessary. We don't want to bother anyone."

"It's no bother," Angelica assured him, and charged toward the living room to flag down Antonio.

"Will you be bringing pictures of Charlie into work tomorrow?"

"I wanted to speak to you about that," Mr. Everett said, sounding contrite. "I was wondering if I might have the entire morning off. I would like to make sure Charlie is well acclimated before I leave him. Grace thinks I'm being foolish, but I haven't owned a pet in a long time." He had, however, taken care of Tricia's cat, Miss Marple, for about a week the summer before. "I don't wish to neglect my pet on his first day with us."

"Of course not. Take all the time you need. Pixie and I will handle everything."

"You're very generous, Ms. Miles."

"Nonsense. I want your new family member to feel secure. I'm just so happy for the two of you. You're doing a wonderful thing adopting Charlie."

"It was a difficult decision to make. At our ages . . ."

That was why they were adopting an elderly cat—the fear of outliving a younger pet. And also the fact that taking Charlie in would give the feline the opportunity to live out the remainder of his life in a loving home.

Angelica and Antonio arrived, along with Grace's and Mr. Everett's coats.

"Dear boy, you do not need to walk us to our car," Grace exclaimed.

"It would be my pleasure. I want to hear all about your new bambino, too," Antonio said. Tricia just loved to hear his lilting Italian accent.

"I'm afraid we may bore all our friends. William has even learned to take pictures with his phone just to chronicle our boy's arrival."

Mr. Everett ducked his head, blushing in embarrassment.

"I can't wait to see them," Tricia said.

"Me, too," Angelica chimed in.

Mr. Everett slipped on his coat and buttoned it, and then he, Grace, and Antonio headed for the door, calling good-bye over their shoulders.

"Oh, dear," Tricia said. "Do you think them leaving will cause the party to break up early?"

"As we're running out of food and some drink, that wouldn't be the worst thing in the world," Angelica said.

Tricia nodded.

"Now I'll hustle that last tray of canapés out to the hungry crowd, while you check on your guests."

"Right." Tricia walked away from the island, heading for a group standing near the door. As she'd feared, several others already had donned their coats.

"There you are, Tricia," said Joyce Widman, proprietress of the Have a Heart bookstore a few doors down from Haven't Got a Clue. "Leaving so soon?"

"I've got a big sale going on tomorrow and haven't finished pricing my stock. I'll need to get to my store early in the morning. But I had a lovely time. The food was wonderful, the company even better."

"Thank you, Joyce. I'm so glad you were able to come."

"I wouldn't have missed it."

"Me, too, Tricia," said Mariana Sommers, the Chamber of Commerce's secretary, with whom Tricia hoped to work closely should she win the upcoming Chamber of Commerce election for its presidency. For months, Angelica had been quietly (for her) pushing the idea that Tricia should run for president of the Stoneham Chamber of Commerce. Now that the renovations on her home were complete, and since the campaign season was to start in three days, Tricia *had* decided to pursue the job. Oh, dear. She'd meant to make an official announcement on just that subject during the party, but had obviously waited far too long.

Tricia walked her guests down the stairs and through the front door of Haven't Got a Clue. If her visitors were going to be filtering out, perhaps she should ask Antonio to stay down there to make sure the shop was secure until the bulk of them had left.

Sure enough, by the time she made it back upstairs, four more of her guests had donned their coats and were saying their good-byes to Angelica. At this rate, the place would empty out in no time.

Tricia looked at the clock. Maybe that was good. It was nearly ten o'clock, and she, too, had to work the next morning.

Antonio entered the shop just as Joyce and Mariana exited.

"Oh, good. You're back. It's looks like we're about to have a mass exodus. Would you mind staying down in the shop for a few minutes to let everyone out?"

"Certainly."

"You're a doll." She gave him a smile and hurried toward the back of the shop and up the stairs once again. But instead of being greeted by a mob about to leave, Tricia returned to what seemed to be a ruckus going on near the windows that overlooked the street.

"Do something, do something!" Frannie frantically called.

Tricia rushed to join them, but the rubberneckers crowded at that end of the room made an effective barrier.

"Stand aside!" Angelica called as Tricia elbowed her way through the crowd. Breaking free, she saw Frannie's gentleman friend stooped, his hands at his throat, apparently choking, his face turning beet red.

Angelica was considerably shorter than him, but she came up from behind and wrapped her arms around him, one hand clasping the other at his mid-chest, and made several upward thrusts, but nothing was dislodged from his throat. Again and again she tried, with no results.

Someone shoved one of Tricia's upholstered chairs in front of the man, who fell over it, dragging Angelica along with him. "Oww!" she howled as he landed on the back of the chair, her clenched fists trapped under his bulk.

Several of the male guests moved forward to move the man to the floor.

"Does anybody know CPR?" Frannie called, still frantic.

Pixie stepped forward, but again it was Angelica who jumped into action. In a flash she was down on her knees, feeling for a pulse. "Will somebody please call nine one one?"

Several people whipped out their phones and began punching the number pads.

"Ange?" Tricia asked, feeling panicked.

Angelica didn't answer, but started chest compressions.

Except for Dean Martin in the background, wailing "Everybody Loves Somebody," the room was nearly silent as Angelica worked on the man before her, pausing every few compressions to blow air into his mouth—but it seemed that whatever he'd choked on might still be caught in his throat.

Angelica was back to chest compressions. "Can someone please turn that music off?"

Pixie darted across the room, and the music abruptly died.

Angelica continued her efforts while the wide-eyed guests worriedly stared.

The sound of thundering footsteps echoed up the stairs, and several men erupted into the room. The Stoneham Fire Department's emergency medical technicians had arrived—and not a minute too soon, for Angelica looked to be on the verge of exhaustion.

Suddenly Antonio was there to help Tricia haul Angelica to her feet as one of the EMTs questioned the crowd while the other examined the man.

"Is he going to be okay?" Ginny asked, her voice small and shaky, as one of the EMTs injected some kind of clear liquid into the man's outer thigh, but nothing seemed to happen.

Another crew had come with the ambulance, but because of the angle of the entrance to the stairs, they hadn't arrived with a gurney—but some kind of chair, instead.

"The patient is unresponsive," said one of the firefighters as his companion continued CPR. "Anaphylactic shock." He proceeded to explain how they'd treated the man, but it was obvious the shot he'd administered had no effect.

"Stand back, please," one of the newcomers asked the crowd, and everyone was herded toward the kitchen.

Angelica's brow was covered in perspiration, and she seemed to be trembling. "You'd better sit down, Ange," Tricia warned. "Antonio, can you get her some water?"

"I'll get it," Ginny volunteered, and fled to the kitchen.

Pixie wandered up to stand beside Tricia. "Damn," she cursed, and shook her head, watching the paramedics work. "Looks like you're gonna have another stiff on your hands."

Tricia turned to glare at her assistant, while somewhere across the room Frannie wept inconsolably.

TWO

"How many does this make?" asked Grant Baker, Stoneham's chief of police and Tricia's former boyfriend, staring at the sheet-covered corpse still lying on her living room floor.

Tricia glared at him but made no comment.

Baker turned to one of his officers. "Have you spoken to all the witnesses?"

"No, Chief. There were at least twenty or thirty people at the party."

"Party?" Baker whirled to face Tricia. "How come I wasn't invited?"

"Do you think you could have helped a man suffering from anaphylactic shock?"

"Maybe."

"Angelica was a hero—or rather a heroine," Ginny said emphatically. "She desperately tried to save him."

Angelica sat on one of the upholstered chairs clutching a wineglass. She'd had several since her ordeal, and Tricia had made up her mind to cut her off if she asked for another refill.

"You didn't answer my question," Baker reminded her.

"Why *would* I invite you?"

"Because I *thought* we were friends."

Their friendship, like their failed relationship, had ended several years before. And, besides, Baker now had a lady companion. Was Tricia supposed to have invited *her* as well?

Again, she made no comment.

"So what likely caused the man's death?" Baker asked the room at large.

"Obviously an allergic reaction to something he ingested," Angelica said, sounding weary.

"Who made the food?" Baker asked.

"I did," Tricia said. "Well, most of it."

Baker blinked. "You cooked?"

Tricia frowned. "Yes."

"Since when do you cook?"

"Since none of your business." She didn't like his tone; the fact that it irked her made her dislike her reciprocal timbre even more.

Baker looked back to the shrouded body. "So you poisoned the poor guy."

"I did not."

"Well, he's dead." Baker walked around the body. "What's your relationship with the deceased?"

"I had none. I never met the man until he walked through my door a couple of hours ago. He was Frannie Armstrong's date."

"Where is she?"

"In my bedroom, lying down. His death was a terrible shock."

"I'll bet," Baker grated. "So *what* killed the guy?"

"I have no idea."

"A stuffed mushroom," Angelica volunteered. "It was the last tray of them. I walked around the room offering them to everyone."

"And nobody else got sick?"

Tricia shook her head.

"What was in them?"

She shrugged. "It's a pretty standard recipe. I got it out of Angelica's first cookbook."

"A national bestseller," Angelica piped up.

Baker scowled, ignoring her. "Can you let me have it? I'll give it to the medical examiner, and he can test the stomach contents. We'll try to contact the deceased's doctor to see what his allergies may have been."

That seemed reasonable. "Do you want me to scan it right now?"

"We can just rip it from the book."

"No, you will not!"

Baker started at her tone.

"I consider it sacrilege to desecrate a book in that manner."

"Then get it to me by morning, will you?"

Tricia nodded and glanced in the direction of the body. "Will my visitor be leaving soon?"

"In good time," Baker answered, which was no answer at all.

And what about Frannie, up in Tricia's bedroom? Would she be so disconsolate that she'd want to stay the night? Tricia certainly hoped not, but neither could she kick the poor woman out.

"Are there any mushrooms left?" Baker asked Angelica.

She shook her head. "No. The dead guy—sorry, I don't know his name—took the last one."

Baker frowned, then shook his head. "Then it sounds pretty open and shut. The guy just had an allergic reaction."

Did he actually sound disappointed? A man was dead. A person who had lived a life, loved family and friends, and come into Tricia's home a stranger would be leaving in a body bag. She felt terrible about that. If only he had mentioned his food allergies, she would have been able to dissuade him from eating the mushrooms. Wasn't it the obligation of a person with severe—potentially fatal—allergies to do that?

Was she trying to talk herself out of the guilt she felt? Maybe. But she did feel terrible that a guest had eaten something fatal while in her home. Meanwhile, the police technicians went to work in the kitchen.

"What are you doing?" Tricia demanded.

"They're bagging evidence."

"But they're going through my cupboards and fridge—they're taking my staples and my serving dishes!"

"You'll get them back . . . eventually. It's just a precaution in case things aren't what they seem."

"What do you mean?" Tricia demanded.

"Just what I said. Now, I'm going upstairs to talk to Ms. Armstrong," Baker said. He knew the way. He'd been a regular visitor years before, and Tricia had shown him the space early in its renovation. For some reason, she was reluctant to have him see the final result, although she wasn't exactly sure why.

Still, she said nothing as Baker made his way through the living room and headed for the stairs to the third floor.

And then she remembered Carol Talbot's jewelry, hidden in a shoebox in the back of her closet. Carol Talbot had been murdered just five months before—and the prime suspect had been none other than Tricia's father, John. Someone had burgled her home immediately after her death. Someone had pawned her jewelry. Tricia and Angelica had found the pawn tickets and claimed the jewelry. It was their father who'd purloined the expensive rings, broach, earrings, and bracelet. They hadn't figured out how to return the jewelry to the estate without implicating John Miles, who, last they heard, was heading to Grand Cayman with their mother, once again playing snowbirds. If he thought he'd gone to a country without an extradition treaty with the US, he was sadly mistaken.

What if the ever-inquisitive Baker nosed around and found the stolen items in her closet? How was she ever going to explain having them?

"Look at the time," Ginny said, her gaze fixed on the antique clock that graced the south wall of Tricia's living room. "We promised the babysitter we'd be home by eleven, and it's almost one."

"Go home," Angelica said.

"Not until the chief says so," said the uniformed officer still standing watch over the body.

"She's already given her statement, and so has her husband," Angelica pointed out. "What's to keep them?"

The officer opened his mouth to reply, then seemed to think better of it. "Very well."

Ginny crossed the floor to give Angelica, and then Tricia, a hug. "Let us know if there's anything you need."

"Will do," Tricia said.

Antonio, too, hugged the sisters. "Call us tomorrow."

"Of course," Angelica said, and watched as her stepson and his wife donned their coats and headed for the stairs to go home.

The medical examiner returned and this time he had company.

"We're ready to remove the body now," she told the officer.

"Let's give the guys some room," Officer Henderson said, and herded those remaining into the kitchen, which was fine with Tricia; she didn't really want to watch.

"When can I go home?" Angelica asked, sounding exhausted.

"When the chief says so."

"What about Frannie?" Tricia asked.

"If she requests it, we can take her home."

"I suppose I should go with her," Angelica said.

"Are you sure?"

"She's my employee. I feel I owe it to her."

Tricia nodded.

The body had been removed by the time Baker returned with a flush-faced Frannie in tow.

"Are you okay, Frannie?" Tricia asked.

Frannie clutched a tissue in one hand, and her eyes were red from crying, but she nodded. "I just want to go home."

"I'll come with you," Angelica said.

Frannie shook her head. "No, thanks. I'll be all right, but if it's okay, I don't think I can come into work tomorrow." She glanced at the clock. "Today."

"Of course not," Angelica agreed. "And take as much time as you need."

"Please let me know if I can help in any way," Tricia said with sincerity, but Frannie's expression tightened.

"I know you didn't mean to poison Ted, but he's dead. I think you've done enough."

Frannie's frigid tone shook Tricia, but she said nothing—and neither did anyone else.

"Drive the lady home, Henderson," Baker ordered, and the officer waited for Frannie to snag her coat before the two of them left the apartment.

"You can go home, too, Angelica."

"I think I'll keep Tricia company a little while longer," she said, which hadn't been her plan only a minute before, but for which Tricia was grateful.

Baker nodded. He turned back to Tricia. "By the way, I heard you were in court today for Bob Kelly's sentencing and that he said some disparaging things about you."

"He cursed me."

"You did everything right. Because of you, that's one less bad guy who'll walk the streets of Stoneham, and I, for one, am grateful."

"Thank you, Grant." It had been a long time since she'd called him by his first name. He seemed to appreciate it.

For a moment, he rested a hand on her shoulder and gave her an encouraging smile. "I'll see myself out and make sure the doors downstairs are locked."

"Thanks again," Tricia said.

"I'm sure Harper's death *was* just an accident," he said kindly, "but I'll be in touch just the same."

She nodded. She wouldn't have expected any less. Then again, she thanked heaven he hadn't gone poking around in her bedroom.

They watched him go and didn't say a word until they heard the door downstairs close.

"Well, that was certainly an interesting evening," Angelica declared.

"How can you say that?" Tricia accused.

"I said *interesting*, I didn't say *good*—although the party really was a success until poor Ted's throat closed up like a crushed straw." She shook her head. "I've never seen anything like that, and I hope I never do again."

Tricia shuddered. "Me, too."

Angelica studied Tricia's face. "Are you okay? You're as pale as a ghost. Have you eaten anything tonight?"

Tricia shook her head. "And I don't think I can right now."

Angelica sighed. "The crime scene investigators took every scrap of food from the fridge, even the jars of pickles and olives, so there's nothing to eat anyway—unless you want to spread some of Miss

Marple's kitty pâté on a cracker. I think there's at least one unopened box of them in the cupboard."

Tricia shook her head. "Seeing them pack up my kitchen was one thing, but I was sweating bullets when Grant went up to my bedroom."

"Whatever for?"

"That little treasure trove of Carol Talbot's jewelry still sitting in the back of my closet."

Angelica cringed. "Oh, dear. I'd forgotten all about that."

"So had I. Or at least, I'd put it out of my mind. We need to find a way to return it to her estate without either of us—or Daddy—getting in trouble with the law."

"Well tonight is *not* the time for that conversation. Are you sure you don't want to go over to Booked for Lunch or my place for some eggs and toast? It's really no trouble."

"I'll pick up something from the Coffee Bean tomorrow morning. Then I guess I'll have to go to the grocery store—that is, if Pixie and/or Mr. Everett even show up for work tomorrow."

"Why wouldn't they?"

"They might be traumatized, too."

"Not much traumatizes Pixie. She once told me that in her former profession, a john or two had a cardiac arrest while they were engaged in . . . shall we say, a heart-straining situation. And Mr. Everett left the party before the poor man died. Besides, it *was* an accident—Grant even said so. If Frannie's date had terrible allergies, he should have known better than to put anything in his mouth without asking for a detailed list of the ingredients."

Hearing Angelica confirm that aloud did make Tricia feel better, but only a little bit.

Angelica yawned. "Would you like me to stay here with you tonight?"

Tricia shook her head. "No. I'm all right. I just want to go to bed—

that is, if I'll be able to get to sleep." She looked over to the front of the living room where the body had lain and wondered how long it would take—a night or two . . . or more—before she would feel comfortable sleeping in her newly refurbished home again.

And she wondered if Bob Kelly's curse had already proved effective.

THREE

It wasn't hunger that kept Tricia awake for most of the night, but dreams about a stranger lying dead in her living room. She'd awoken more than once in the midst of the dream, sweating and shaky from terror that was more disturbing than the victim's actual death. By the time morning arrived, she'd recovered her appetite and felt ravenous. And she was determined to be the first in line across the street at the Coffee Bean when it opened. The day was bright with only scattered clouds scudding across the sky, and the temperature was positively balmy for early November—already in the fifties. She hoped it meant she'd have a much better day—and evening—than the one before.

A uniformed barista, with a visor bearing the Coffee Bean logo, unlocked the door and turned the CLOSED sign to OPEN, and Tricia followed her to the counter, glad neither of the owners was in sight. She could just imagine what they'd have to say.

The barista, Emily according to her name tag, poured Tricia's large skinny latte and placed a hefty almond-glazed croissant in a cream-colored take-out bag. A year before, she would have never considered such a decadent breakfast, but as her ill-fated cocktail party had proved, life was short, and she felt she deserved some kind of compensation for having endured it.

By the time Tricia finished her makeshift breakfast, she still had nearly ninety minutes to wait until she could open Haven't Got a Clue. She rescued her copy of Angelica's *Easy-Does-It Cooking* and took it down to her basement office, where she scanned the crab stuffed mushroom recipe and e-mailed it to the chief. By then, she only had an hour to kill. She spent most of it on her treadmill. The mindless activity was about all she felt up to handling just then, though her pace was far slower than necessary to break a sweat and qualify as true aerobic activity.

Pixie arrived ten minutes early for work, laden with a big bakery box from the Shaw's grocery store in Milford. "Good morning," she called out. "And isn't it a gorgeous day? It almost feels like summer."

"Let's hope we'll have a spurt of customers—just like in the summer," Tricia said. She eyed the box. "What have you got there?"

"When I saw the cops cleaning out your fridge last night, I figured you could use some sustenance this morning." She set the box on the glass display case that also acted as a cash desk.

The thought of the police taking probable evidence reminded Tricia that Carol's jewelry still awaited its final disposition. She shook the thought away. "That was very thoughtful of you, Pixie, but I—"

Pixie held up a hand to halt Tricia's protestations. "Now, I know you only like to put healthy food into your mouth, so I bought some of the real stuff for Mr. E and me and some low-sugar, low-sodium bran muffins for you. If nothing else, it's roughage—and that's good for you."

Tricia pursed her lips, feeling guilty for having eaten the sinful pastry hours earlier. "Uh, thank you for thinking of me."

Pixie grabbed the pot from the beverage station and headed for the back of the shop to hang up her jacket and get water for the coffee. Before she could return, Mr. Everett arrived, and he didn't come empty-handed, either, as evidenced by the big brown paper bag he held.

"Good morning, Ms. Miles."

"Good morning. What are you doing here? I thought you were going to pick up Charlie this morning."

"Police Chief Baker was at our door at eight o'clock this morning. He said someone passed away at your party last night."

"Unfortunately, it's true."

"He asked us about the food."

"It seems Frannie Armstrong's friend had a bad allergic reaction."

"I'd sure say so," Pixie said, and rolled her eyes.

Yes, it sure was unfortunate for Ted whatever-his-last-name-was to die at her party, but Tricia was determined to steer the conversation away from that topic.

"But surely you would have still had time to pick up your new cat."

"We thought so, too. But then the phone rang. It was the rescue center. Something about the veterinarian paperwork not being ready. I'm on standby in case Grace calls and says we can pick him up later today after all, but it may end up being Monday."

"I'm so sorry you have to wait. I know you're eager to welcome your new family member home."

Mr. Everett nodded sadly.

"What have you got there?" Tricia asked, already knowing the answer.

"Bagels. I bought several of all our favorites because I wanted to make sure that you would be eating well and taking care of yourself after . . . after what happened last night."

Mr. Everett shrugged out of the sleeves of his jacket and shuffled off to hang it up in the back, passing Pixie along the way. She had the coffee brewing before he returned.

"Great minds think alike, huh, Mr. E?" Pixie asked, indicating the large brown paper bag he still held.

"I'm sure we can put a dent into both of your generous provisions," Tricia said, and meant it.

Pixie brought out paper plates and plastic knives, opened the container of cream cheese, then plucked an everything bagel from the bag. She passed it to Tricia, who took a poppy seed, and then Mr. Everett chose an Asiago cheese bagel.

Pixie broke the quiet. "I thought maybe you were going to announce the Chamber thing last night," she said to Tricia.

"I was going to—but that was before . . ." She didn't need to say more.

"Perhaps we should discuss your campaign strategy," Mr. Everett suggested.

"Strategy?" Tricia echoed. "I hadn't thought about it. We have a week between the time the candidates announce their intent to run and the election itself."

"Yeah, we know," Pixie said. "Mr. E and me have been doing some brainstorming and we came up with a couple of great little angles."

"Angles?" Tricia asked, wondering if she should dread the explanation.

"Yeah. We looked at an online catalog that sells all kinds of cool tchotchkes—you know, like the authors sometimes send us."

"You ordered some pens that say 'Vote for Tricia'?"

Pixie shook her head. "Too pedestrian."

"I thought it was a good idea," Mr. Everett said defensively. Had he been overruled by Pixie?

"Magnets," Pixie said. "Everybody needs them for their fridges to hang up their grocery lists, pictures of their kids and grandkids, and stuff like that." She darted around the counter and came up with a box that Tricia hadn't seen before. From the strain on Pixie's face as she lifted it, it must have been quite heavy.

"These came in just yesterday. I wanted to surprise you." Pixie opened the flaps on the box and plucked out one of the magnets, handing it to Tricia.

Tricia frowned and read the three-line text aloud, "'Tricia Miles Hasn't Got a Clue for Chamber President.'"

"Oh, no!" Pixie wailed. "That's not what it's supposed to say. It was supposed to say, 'Tricia Miles *OF* Haven't Got a Clue for Chamber President.'" Mouth agape, she grabbed the magnet from Tricia. "I proofread it at least three times. Mr. E even proofed it."

"I did," Mr. Everett agreed, nodding vigorously.

Pixie looked ready to cry.

"I—I . . ." Tricia didn't know what to say. "Perhaps they will replace the order," she said lamely.

"But it won't come in time for the election," Pixie said, her voice cracking.

"Then it's a good thing I went ahead and ordered those pens," Mr. Everett said, and it was his turn to go behind the desk and pull out a small box. He opened the flaps, took out a blue pen, and handed it to Tricia. "See, it says, 'Vote for Tricia Miles for Chamber President,' and it has a rubber tip for texting."

Tricia gave him a warm smile. "I'm very touched that both of you are pulling for me to win. Pixie, let me reimburse you for the—"

But Pixie shook her head adamantly. "No! This is my gift to you, and I'm going to make it right."

Tricia didn't know what to say, so she smiled. "Why don't we have that coffee and some breakfast. I have a feeling it's going to be a very long day." And to prove her point, the phone rang. Tricia stepped behind the cash desk and picked up the receiver on the circa nineteen thirties telephone. "Haven't Got a Clue, this is Tricia; how can I help you?"

"Tricia? It's Chief Baker."

Tricia's heart sank. What piece of bad news would he have for her now? "What's up?"

"First, thanks for that recipe. I know shellfish can sometimes be the cause of anaphylaxis. It may be what killed the guy."

It was a good explanation.

He went on. "I've already forwarded it to the ME. Which brings me to my next point; I wanted to let you know that the autopsy for Theodore Harper won't happen until at least Monday. There was a fire in Nashua last night, and—"

Hearing about yet another tragedy was more than Tricia could bear. "Oh, Grant—don't say any more."

"I thought you should know about the holdup."

"Thanks. Were you able to notify Ted's next of kin?"

"So far all we've been able to contact is the guy's ex-wife. She was quite upset. Apparently they were still on friendly terms. She said she'd try to get the number of Mr. Harper's brother and sister in Pennsylvania and get back to us."

"Ted and his ex had no children?"

"Apparently not."

Maybe that was better in the long run. Tricia felt guilty enough for possibly killing the man with a loaded mushroom—her sense of responsibility would have tripled if the man had left behind children.

"Thanks for letting me know, Grant."

"You're welcome. I wish I could be more reassuring."

Okay, why was he being so nice? Had he broken up with his girlfriend and decided he wanted to—

No, she couldn't even entertain the thought of getting back together with a man who feared commitment, so she put that idea right out of her head.

"I appreciate that. Thank you."

"I'll be in touch," he said, and ended the call.

Tricia replaced the receiver in its cradle.

Pixie was suddenly right in front of her, offering Tricia a mug of coffee and a bran muffin, with Mr. Everett right behind her holding a paper plate with a bagel slathered in cream cheese—much more food than she wanted or needed, but the looks on their faces were so earnest that she couldn't bear to let either of them down. "My word. I don't think I've seen such a fine breakfast in a long, long time." And with that, she accepted both of their gifts.

Tricia showed up at Booked for Lunch at just about two o'clock, still enjoying the unseasonably warm weather and at more or less the usual time she joined her sister for their midday meal. The café was nearly empty, and already the café's new waitress, Molly, a buxom blonde of about fifty, was filling salt and pepper shakers for the next day's opening.

"Your usual, Tricia?" she called.

"Just coffee today, Molly."

Tricia took a seat opposite Angelica at the front table that overlooked the street, not where they usually sat.

"You're not going back to your old eating habits, I hope," Angelica said, looking down her nose over the reading glasses that were perched there.

While Tricia had never had an eating disorder, for years she'd been obsessed about her caloric intake. No more. "No. Pixie and Mr. Everett both brought breakfast, and I didn't have the heart to turn either of them down; but I *am* stuffed."

"Let me guess: a poppy seed bagel and a bran muffin."

"You're positively psychic," Tricia said.

Angelica shook her head. "I just know how both of them think. It was very sweet of them to look after you today after last night's trauma."

"Yes, it was."

Angelica looked back down at the papers strewn across the table—order sheets, mostly, for both the Sheer Comfort Inn and Booked for Lunch. And yet there was another folder on the table marked PERSONAL.

Molly arrived at the table with a grilled cheese sandwich for Angelica, as well as a bowl of the soup of the day—chicken vegetable, by the look of it—and Tricia's coffee. "Thank you."

"Thanks, Molly," Angelica said, but her accompanying smile was only half-hearted.

Molly retreated to the counter to finish her condiment accounting.

"Is something up?" Tricia asked, taking in her sister's lack of *joie de vivre*.

Angelica eyed Molly and lowered her voice as she set her papers aside. "Nothing I want to discuss here. We'll talk about it tonight."

Oh-kay.

Tricia changed the subject. "I don't suppose you want to talk about Daddy's pawn ticket surprise, either."

"No."

Tricia winced. "Okay, then. I heard from Grant this morning."

Angelica raised an eyebrow, but didn't look up from her soup.

"Ted Harper's autopsy has been postponed."

"Who's that?"

"The guy who died in my apartment last night," Tricia whispered.

"Oh, Ted. Frannie is absolutely distraught."

"She came into work today?"

"She said she'd only sit at home and cry if she didn't—not that she's done much else today, but at least she wasn't alone with her morbid thoughts."

"How long had they been going out together?"

"Your party was their third date. Frannie was expecting a totally different outcome to the evening, if you know what I mean."

Tricia did.

"I feel terrible about the whole situation," Tricia said, picked up her cup, but then decided she didn't want or need any more caffeine that day. It would be difficult enough to fall asleep later that night. She didn't want to have a repeat of the dreams she'd experienced the night before—when she'd been able to sleep, that is.

Angelica took a bite of her sandwich, chewed, then swallowed. "Since I *am* eating lunch, can we refrain from further talk of autopsies?"

Tricia nodded.

"Scuttlebutt around the village is that Chauncey Porter is going to run for Chamber president," Angelica said.

"Chauncey?"

"Yes, it seems he heard you might be throwing your hat into the ring and . . . well, let's just say his reason for running isn't at all charitable."

"You mean he just doesn't want to see me win."

Angelica nodded. "That's about right."

Chauncey held a grudge—and perhaps rightly so. His former fiancée had taken her life when Tricia had discovered a deeply embarrassing episode from her past. Her death had spawned nightmares that had haunted Tricia for weeks, but worst of all, Chauncey didn't take into account the other events and people associated with the woman's death. He blamed one person: Tricia.

"What does Mary have to say about this?" Tricia asked.

"I haven't heard, but I can't think she'd approve. And maybe it will be another strike against them getting married."

"Why do you say that?"

Angelica shrugged. "One hears things."

Tricia waited, but Angelica didn't elaborate. Again, her gaze had traveled over to Molly, who may or may not have been eavesdropping. It was another topic they might discuss that evening.

"So you are definitely going to run?" Angelica asked Tricia.

"Well, it seems I have to now."

"Why's that?"

Tricia reached for her purse and dug out the pen Mr. Everett had given her earlier that day.

Angelica smiled and read the gold lettering that seemed to jump off the dark blue background, "'Vote for Tricia Miles for Chamber President.' It does have a lovely ring to it, doesn't it?"

"It does," Tricia said, and suddenly found herself looking forward to the formality of the election—and perhaps serving her community. And yet, a thread of doubt wiggled within her. If Chauncey was only running to spite her, how low was he liable to go to upset the election process?

FOUR

It was nearly three when Tricia returned to Haven't Got a Clue, which was experiencing a slow sales day. Both Pixie and Mr. Everett were reading—she standing behind the cash desk, and he sitting in one of the upholstered chairs in the nook, with Tricia's cat, Miss Marple, ensconced on his lap, purring happily.

"Still no word about Charlie?" Tricia asked Mr. Everett.

He shook his head. "Grace called. They said it would definitely be Monday."

"I'm so sorry."

Mr. Everett petted the cat on his lap, and her purring grew even louder. "I admit to being disappointed, but I shall practice being a good pet owner with Miss Marple. She doesn't seem to mind the attention."

Tricia grinned. "No, she certainly doesn't." Tricia left her employee and strode to the back of the shop to hang up her coat before returning to the front of the store and placing her purse behind the counter once again. "Anything interesting happen while I was gone?"

Pixie shook her head, not looking up from the prose before her, but reached for a sticky note. "Antonio called. He wants you to call him back."

"Anything important?"

"He didn't say, but he sounded kind of worried."

Tricia looked at the note written in Pixie's rather girlish hand. If Antonio had something serious on his mind, she wasn't about to make the call with an audience listening in. Stuffing the note into the left pocket of her slacks, Tricia headed for the back of the store. "I'm going to be working on the books downstairs for a while. Call me on my cell phone if you need me."

"Sure thing," Pixie said, never having looked up from her book.

When Tricia had first leased the building that housed her store and loft apartment, the basement was rather dank and gloomy. Since then, she'd upgraded it to act as her climate-controlled storeroom, work space, and exercise area. Although it still lacked natural light, the new system she'd had installed made the area bright and cheerful. And on that particular November afternoon, she settled at her desk in perfect comfort as she tapped the contacts list on her cell phone, choosing Antonio's work number.

"Nigela Ricita Associates. Antonio Barbero here. How may I help you?"

"Hi, Antonio; it's Tricia. Pixie said you wanted to speak with me."

"Ah, Tricia. *Grazie*—my thanks for returning my call so quickly."

"What's up?"

"Ah, it is *matrigna*—Angelica."

"Oh?" Was he about to bring up the subject Angelica hadn't wanted to talk about at lunch?

"*Sono preoccupato*—something is not right."

As Ginny had mentioned, and Tricia had noticed, Antonio seemed to lapse into Italian when he was worried or upset.

"Is this work related?" she asked, suddenly fearful her sister might have a health concern she hadn't been willing to talk about in front of the help at Booked for Lunch.

"I think so. I don't know if it's related, but ever since Michele Fowler left the Dog-Eared Page, she has seemed restless and inattentive."

Until the week before, Michele had been the manager at the village's only drinking establishment. She'd done a fantastic job getting the new business up and running, but after more than a year she was ready to move on to a new project. The pub's patrons had thrown her a big sorry-to-see-you-leave party, and Shawn, the former bartender, had moved into the managerial position. Already the new bartender, Hoshi Tanaka, seemed to be working out well, and Bev, the former waitress at Booked for Lunch, had been hired to serve the customers. She liked the work, and loved the higher tips.

"Is Angelica worried about the bar?"

"I do not think so, but I do think her worries may be business related. It's unlike her not to speak to me about problems within our company. I was wondering . . . could you talk to her?"

"As a matter of fact, at lunch she hinted that she'd like to speak to me about something later tonight."

"Ah, good."

"Now, if she swears me to secrecy—and you know how well she can keep a secret—I won't be able to talk about it to you."

"That is all right. I merely want to know if I should be worried for the business as well. She takes on far too much responsibility."

"I think that's partly why she's stepping down as Chamber president."

"She has done well for them, but I'm sure you will carry on the good work she has begun."

"I'll do my best—*if* I get elected," Tricia promised.

"Will you call me tonight to let me know if I should continue to be concerned—or encourage Angelica to call me?"

"Yes, I promise."

"*Grazie*. Until later, dear Tricia."

"Bye." She hung up the phone, staring at it thoughtfully. So, what was going on with Angelica—and should she, too, be concerned?

Late in the day, Mr. Everett made an appearance in the basement to report that a smartly dressed older couple from Boston had chosen that day to visit Stoneham and made their final stop at Haven't Got a Clue. Apparently Pixie had charmed them into trying out a number of new-to-them authors, netting enough cash from that one sale to more than cover her pay for the day.

Mr. Everett had come down to get a carton of replacement books to restock the shelves, sending them up in the dumbwaiter. Tricia accompanied him upstairs, and while he and Pixie sorted the books by author, Tricia collapsed the empty box and headed for the back of the store to put it in the big recycling bin that took wastepaper.

Tricia opened the door and stepped onto the concrete pad, where she slipped and fell, landing on her backside in quite a large pile of what could only be dog feces.

"Ooohh!" she wailed, struggling to her feet. Not only were her shoes covered in the stinky substance, but the back of her dark slacks was covered in muck. The carton, however, was unscathed. Picking it up with the only two clean fingers she possessed, Tricia deposited it in the bin. There was nothing to do but wipe her hands on the fabric covering her thighs and try to scrape off the excess gunk from her shoes before she could reenter the store. In fact, she tiptoed into the back room and stepped out of her shoes, leaving them on the floor, then shut the door behind her. She'd have to clean the handle with a disinfectant wipe, but first she needed to get upstairs, strip off her clothes, toss them into the washer, and then take a shower.

Walking gingerly, she entered the main sales floor. Pixie and Mr. Everett looked up.

"What on earth happened to you?" Pixie called, taking in Tricia's disheveled appearance.

"You don't want to know," Tricia said, and gingerly headed up the stairs to her apartment.

As she tossed her clothes into the washing machine, Tricia thought about what had just happened and what she would make of it if she were a fictional sleuth. First, the evidence. While there was an abundance of doggy doo—*brother, was there a lot of it*—the canine manufacturer had to be a small dog. Of course, Sarge, a Bichon Frise, lived right next door, but Angelica was a responsible pet owner and took care of her dog's business. Someone must have planned long and hard for this prank, because they'd had to collect an awful lot of dog poop to cause her to fall, and the day's warm temperatures and a light rain had contributed to make the pile a slippery mess. And what if it had been Mr. Everett who'd come out to the Dumpster and fallen? He could have broken a hip. As it was, Tricia's derriere ached, and she was sure she'd sport a fantastic bruise in the next day or so. What vulgar, mean-spirited person—mind—could have done such an obnoxious thing?

Twenty minutes and a shower later, Tricia returned to the shop to find two anxious-looking employees.

"I washed off the top of the landing," Pixie said, and Tricia could see the bucket and scrub brush sitting to dry near the back exit.

"And I wiped off your shoes," Mr. Everett volunteered.

"I'm sorry you had to do that," Tricia apologized.

"You'd already been through enough," Pixie said. "I also wiped down the door and its handles, so everything's nice and clean."

"Thank you so much—both of you. I don't know what I'd do without you."

"Aw, shucks," Pixie said, but Tricia could tell she was pleased by the compliment.

"Why would someone do such a terrible thing?" Mr. Everett asked.

"Spite," Tricia said, but she still couldn't think who would be mean enough to pull such a stunt.

Or could she?

Angelica had said Chauncey's reason for running for Chamber president was the opportunity to deprive Tricia of the job. Could anyone really be that petty?

Tricia was afraid she just might find out.

FIVE

For several months, the sisters had been trading off cooking at each other's loft apartments. That night it was Angelica's turn to cook, but when Tricia arrived just after six o'clock, nothing had been started, and Angelica had even forgotten to make a pitcher of martinis. Her dog, Sarge, sat at her feet, quietly whimpering. He must have been down in the dumps, as well, because he hadn't greeted Tricia at the door with his usual enthusiasm.

"Okay, what's going on?" Tricia asked as she liberated the gin and vermouth from the ad hoc liquor cabinet in Angelica's kitchen.

"Going on?" Angelica asked blankly. She'd changed out of her work clothes and wore a faded duster and pink slippers, looking small and preoccupied, so unlike her usual dynamic demeanor.

Tricia grabbed two stemmed glasses from the cupboard and filled them with cracked ice to chill them. "Yes. You were distracted at lunch, and now you've forgotten to get anything ready for dinner? Do you want to come to my place tonight?"

"I don't feel like getting dressed to go out. Besides, after last night, I'm not sure I'm up to it."

Tricia could have taken offense at that remark, but had to admit she felt relieved not to be preparing food in the space where the mushrooms had been made—and killed someone. It wasn't like they were any special kind of fungi—just the regular white mushrooms from the grocery store. Lots of people had shellfish allergies. As Chief Baker had mentioned, maybe Ted had been allergic to the crab in the stuffing.

Tricia didn't want to speculate and instead changed the subject. "I don't suppose you want to talk about Daddy's—"

"No!" Angelica said emphatically.

"Okay, then I need to mention that I had a call from Antonio this afternoon."

Angelica looked up sharply. "Oh?"

"He's concerned about you and asked if I could get you to open up about what's eating you."

"Eating me?" Angelica asked innocently.

"Yes."

Angelica shook her head. "It's nothing, really," she said, not meeting Tricia's gaze.

Tricia didn't believe her. She retrieved the jar of queen olives from the fridge, speared two each on some frill picks, then measured the liquor into the shaker. Angelica was staring into space when Tricia set the glass down before her on the kitchen island.

"What shall we drink to?"

Angelica sighed. "Kindness. It doesn't seem to be in abundance these days."

"I'll say," Tricia muttered.

They toasted and took a sip of their drinks.

Tricia also took a stool at the island. "Antonio said you've been preoccupied for the last week. He's worried."

"He's a dear boy."

"Is it the shake-up at the Dog-Eared Page that's got you concerned?"

"Not at all."

"Then will you please tell me what *is* bothering you?"

Angelica's gaze slid across the island to the folder Tricia had seen at Booked for Lunch earlier that day. She reached for it and slid it in front of her sister. "Read that."

Tricia opened the manila folder to see a creased sheet of white copy paper with a short message printed at the top.

If you don't want Nigela Ricita's identity to be revealed, be prepared to pay dearly.

Tricia's heart froze. "When did you get this?"

"It came in this morning's mail."

"Do you still have the envelope?"

"I tossed it in the trash, but it's still down in the shop."

"I could go retrieve it."

"Would you, please? And could you take Sarge out, too? I forgot to do that when I came in."

"Of course," Tricia said, but Sarge seemed to have acquired extrasensory perception and was already heading for the door.

On the way out, Tricia grabbed his leash, but didn't pick him up. She didn't know how full the little guy's bladder was, and she didn't want to end up as a urine sponge if he couldn't make it outside. She'd had enough of doggy messes for one day.

Once they returned inside, Tricia let the dog off the leash, and he scampered back up the stairs while Tricia headed for the wastebasket near the register. Even though Frannie had been in mourning for her friend, she'd still been a conscientious employee and had emptied the trash. Tricia didn't feel like Dumpster diving in the cold and dark, and she returned to the apartment and her sister.

"You didn't find it?"

"Frannie must have emptied the trash. We'll have to look for it in the Dumpster tomorrow morning."

"Damn," Angelica cursed, and took a healthy swig of her drink.

Tricia washed her hands and settled at the island once again, taking a sip of her martini before speaking. "Any suspects?"

"What do you mean?"

"Who do you think guessed your secret?"

"I have no idea. I've been extremely careful about what I say and to whom in an effort to keep it quiet."

"That's not exactly true."

"What do you mean?"

"It's pretty obvious that you have a rather close relationship with Antonio, Ginny, and Sofia."

"Really?"

"Of course. Sofia calls you Nonna—and plenty of people have heard her say it."

"She calls Grace Nonna, too—and Ginny's mother . . . when she can be bothered to come visit. There's no way on earth I'd live a thousand miles away from my grandchild."

Technically, Angelica was Sofia's step-grandmother—no blood relation at all, but the heart doesn't pay attention to those kinds of details.

"Our family dinners are rather famous as well," Tricia pointed out.

"It's not like we advertise them." Angelica frowned. "Do you think we should stop going to the Brookview?"

"Only if you've grown tired of it. Although it would probably be easier on Grace and Mr. Everett not to have to climb so many stairs to get to your apartment."

"I've asked them to tell me if it becomes a problem."

"And you know as well as I do that they would deny it even if they had to crawl up the stairs on their hands and knees to join the rest of our assembled lot."

"They do seem to enjoy our time together."

"Let's face it, none of us are close to our blood relatives, and Grace, Mr. Everett, and Antonio have no one else."

"That's what makes our group so special. Isn't it wonderful that we've all found each other, can depend on one another?"

"Yes, it is."

Angelica took another sip of her drink. "We could try having our family dinners at Booked for Lunch."

"It wouldn't be as comfortable and would be hard to seat us all in one group when it only has booths and a counter."

"Why do you have to be so logical?" Angelica complained.

Tricia shrugged. "Just part of my nature. Now, let's get back to this letter. Was there anything unusual about the envelope?"

"Only that it was addressed to me and marked *Personal*."

"Was the address handwritten?"

Angelica shook her head.

"No return address label?"

"No."

Of course not.

"I assume it's the only one you've received."

Angelica nodded. "It sounds like you don't think it'll be the last."

"I don't. And they've said you might pay dearly."

"Sounds like they mean pay *more* than just money. Do you think this person or persons is threatening any of us? I couldn't bear it if any of you got hurt because of my secret."

"What I think you should do is first thing tomorrow morning go talk to Grant Baker. He'll be able to tell you our options and open a case."

"For one thing, tomorrow is Sunday. If he's lucky, he'll have the day off. Goodness knows the poor man deserves at least *one* day off a week. This could just be a sick joke. I'll wait and see if any more letters arrive. I don't want to look foolish."

"I think you're making a mistake," Tricia admonished. "I mean, look how worried you are."

"Like you, I've read a whole lot of mysteries."

"And you know only trouble will come if you disregard the threat and try to handle the situation on your own."

"Look who's calling the kettle black. You're the one who's constantly taking on crime single-handedly."

"And I realize how dangerous it is, but you must admit I've developed some kind of skill in pulling it off."

"And it's just dumb luck that you haven't been critically injured or killed."

"Now you're getting melodramatic."

"I worry about you. *All* your friends do. You've taken some awfully foolish chances."

The conversation was getting them nowhere. Tricia polished off the rest of her drink and poured another from the pitcher. Should she tell Angelica about her drop onto doggy doo? Judging by Angelica's tense expression, the answer was no. She had enough on her mind.

"So, what have you got on hand for dinner? I'm famished."

Angelica got up to peruse the contents of the fridge. It would be slim pickings that evening, as all she had available were eggs, some veggies, and part of a loaf of Italian bread. "Omelets and toast it is!"

Tricia chopped the onions and peppers while Angelica assembled the rest of the meal. Neither the threatening letter nor the subject of the poisoning the night before entered their conversation, but all the innocuous chitchat in the world couldn't mask the heavy atmosphere in that kitchen. It felt like they were playing a waiting game, but what exactly they were waiting for, neither of them knew.

SIX

Tricia's slumber was still disturbed on the second night after Ted Harper's death on the floor below her. In fact, she found herself avoiding the living room altogether, even though her supposed ghost barometer, Miss Marple, didn't seem at all bothered that someone had died there and apparently felt no spectral vibrations. The cat still napped in her favorite chair and probably would have hung out with Tricia should she have stayed in the room, but after leaving Angelica's apartment the night before, Tricia had immediately retired to her third-floor bedroom suite. The comfortable window nook was cozy and the perfect place to read.

Except . . . she didn't do that right away. First, she dug through her closet and pulled out the plastic bag that contained Carol Talbot's jewelry, spreading it across her duvet. John Miles had liberated a pair of what looked like diamond stud earrings, a tennis bracelet, an opal broach, a gold wedding band, and a diamond engagement ring. It had cost Angelica two grand to obtain the plunder—money she had no doubt long written off to save their father from yet more jail time. But they still needed to get rid of it.

Tricia picked up the tennis bracelet and admired its sparkling diamonds, and she was pretty sure they were real, if not of tremendous value. It was probably the most valuable item in the sorry little collection. The item of least value was either the wedding band—which was engraved—or the broach. Should she just toss them in the toilet and try to flush them away? She could, but decided not to, at least not without Angelica's input. And what if the items got stuck in a pipe? It would be awkward to try to explain that to a plumber.

She gathered everything and put it back in the plastic bag, hiding it in her closet once more.

The next morning, Tricia realized she still hadn't replenished her kitchen cupboards, and she'd sent the previous day's breakfast leftovers home with Pixie, so she once again crossed the street bright and early and entered the Coffee Bean for a cup of their best Colombian brew and a much smaller muffin than Pixie had provided the day before—tastier, too.

Unfortunately, instead of a teenager behind the counter, it was one of the shop's proprietors.

"I heard there vas another tragedy at your place Friday night," Alexa Kozlov said, her slight Russian accent making the words sound just a little bit sinister. "Ve saw the coroner's vagon leave wery late."

"I guess everybody must have heard about it by now," Tricia lamented.

"Is terrible. Poor Frannie. She came in here yesterday in tears. She didn't even order her usual two glazed doughnuts and mocha double latte with extra foam."

It sounded revolting to Tricia—the doughnuts and the extra foam, that is. "Maybe she's counting her calories," Tricia offered, hoping to divert the conversation away from Ted Harper and his untimely death.

"She said it vas your cooking that killed her boyfriend."

"It was his allergies—*not* my food," Tricia asserted. And how often was she going to have to defend her culinary efforts to other villagers?

Alexa handed Tricia the bag with her muffin and the coffee to go, then rang up the sale. Tricia paid, smiled, and wished Alexa a good day before crossing the street and returning to Haven't Got a Clue. But Tricia stopped dead as she approached her store. She hadn't opened the blinds before leaving and only now saw that the front display window was covered in at least a dozen broken, runny eggs. They had to have been there since late the evening before, because they'd hardened—or were they frozen?—to the glass.

The bucket and scrub brush were going to get yet another workout, and Tricia tackled the job immediately after drinking her coffee and eating her muffin.

Sunday was Pixie's day off, and the store didn't open until noon, so Tricia still had plenty of time to kill before the first customers of the day would arrive.

It was then she remembered that she hadn't phoned Antonio the evening before. She wasn't sure what she should say. Angelica hadn't asked for her silence when it came to the threatening letter, but she decided it was up to Angelica to tell him about it. After all, he was a big part of the secret she was determined to keep quiet.

Still, she called his work number. Not surprisingly, he was unavailable. Like Chief Baker, he, too, deserved a day off. And yet Tricia had fulfilled her promise by returning the call. Of course, unless things changed, she'd be seeing him for dinner that night. Would he press her for an explanation, or would Angelica have called him and explained for herself by then? She'd just have to wait and see.

Tricia returned to the basement to attend to the paperwork that never seemed to get finished during the rest of the week. As she sat at her desk, contemplating the small stack of invoices and her checkbook, she reflected on what Alexa had said about Frannie. It bothered Tricia that Frannie was telling the world at large that she was responsible for Ted's death. Okay, technically her stuffed mushrooms *were* responsible, but only because of the man's acute allergies. Tricia hadn't killed him, and obviously no one else who'd eaten the mushrooms—and there had been at least four dozen of the baked goodies—had become ill, either.

Frannie had a right to be upset. She had liked Ted and obviously thought they were about to become more than just friends. Tricia would cut her some slack.

Her mind next wandered on the subject of what was to become of Ted Harper's remains. Would the brother and sister take care of that? Would he be buried in Pennsylvania? Would it be appropriate for her to send flowers, or might that upset his survivors?

Angelica seemed to know what was appropriate for any social situation. She'd ask her later. In the meantime, that stack of bills wasn't going to pay itself.

As Tricia could have predicted, Angelica changed the location of the weekly "family" dinner from her third-floor apartment to Booked for Lunch. Since it closed in mid-afternoon, they had the place to themselves. There wasn't room for a long table, so Tricia pulled up the small one from the front of the café and set it next to the longest booth. Getting in and out of it might be a bit of a strain, but it should be easier for Grace and Mr. Everett to navigate the ground-floor location.

Angelica unwrapped the tray of appetizers she'd made earlier in the day, setting it on the long counter. She had a prime rib of beef in one of the ovens, too, but she seemed decidedly unhappy.

"What's up?" Tricia asked, handing her a chilled glass of pinot grigio she'd recently taken a liking to.

"We should be drinking red wine with beef," Angelica muttered.

"So we'll switch later," Tricia advised.

"I love this place," Angelica said, her gaze traveling to the little window in the saloon door that separated the kitchen from the dining room, which was decorated in retro red and white that practically screamed 1955, "but it's just not the homey atmosphere I like for our dinners. And the kitchen is separated from the dining area, so I'll be in there by myself and won't get to see and talk to everybody."

"We can prop the door open or take turns keeping you company. But there're other alternatives. Since the reno, I have plenty of room, or we can go to the Brookview more often or have them cater our weekly repast," Tricia pointed out.

Angelica wandered back into the kitchen with Tricia following. "Yes, but what's a family dinner without home-cooked food?"

"What's the difference? You prepare most of the meal in the café's professional kitchen most weeks anyway, and just finish it off at home."

"Yes, but when I make a meal, I cook with love," she said, and lifted the lid on a pot of boiling potatoes, stabbing one with a fork to test to see if it was done.

Tricia really didn't see the difference, but she decided it wasn't worth arguing about.

The door to the café opened, its little bell jingling merrily. "Hello!" called a woman's voice. Grace and Mr. Everett had arrived.

Tricia hurried out of the kitchen to greet them. "Hi, Grace." She gave her a quick hug, and a welcoming nod to Mr. Everett, whose cheeks always colored at overt shows of affection.

"Let me help you with your coat," Tricia offered Grace.

"I'll get it," Mr. Everett said.

While he hung up the coats, Grace clasped Tricia's hand. "Are you all right, dear? After what happened on Saturday night . . ."

"I'm getting better," Tricia said, and proffered her glass. "This helps—a little. Can I get you a glass?"

"Just a small one. I wouldn't want to get tipsy."

Angelica ducked her head around the swinging kitchen door. "Hello, Grace—Mr. E. Glad you could make it."

"We wouldn't miss it for the world," Grace said.

"Tricia, get Grace a glass of wine," Angelica admonished.

Tricia rolled her eyes. "Always the hostess," she said of her sister, and Grace laughed.

By the time she poured the wine, Antonio, Ginny, and Sofia in her stroller had also arrived.

"Something sure smells good," Ginny said as she bent down to extricate Sofia, and then Angelica was on hand to take the baby from her.

"Don't you look pretty in your little snowsuit," she cooed.

"Nonna, Nonna!" Sofia squealed happily.

"Uh, I think she may need her diaper changed," Ginny said apologetically.

"Nonna will be glad to take care of that."

"Better you than me," Tricia muttered, just loud enough for all to hear. They all laughed. It felt *good* to laugh. Heaven only knew, after the last few days neither she nor Angelica had much to feel good about. But, unless Antonio pressed her for answers, she was determined to forget about curses, accidental deaths, and blackmail.

She hoped. But she also needed to address the situation. So, while Angelica attended to the baby, Tricia pulled Antonio aside. "I'm sorry I didn't call you last night."

"I wasn't surprised," he admitted, slipping out of his leather jacket and hanging it with the others.

"And I'm sorry I don't have anything to tell you yet."

"Then you will keep trying?"

Tricia nodded. Now she just had to hope her sister would listen to reason.

SEVEN

Pixie returned to work on Monday morning at nine fifty-five. As usual, it was Mr. Everett's day off—a day he intended to spend with his new-to-him cat, Charlie, promising to bring pictures when he returned on Tuesday.

Pixie was so excited she was practically vibrating. "I was on the phone at exactly eight o'clock this morning, chewing off the customer service agent's ear at NewHamp Promotions," she said as she unbuttoned her fashionable, yet rather lightweight, vintage raincoat—something better suited to a West rather than East Coast winter. "She managed to pull my original order and had to concede that it was *their* error—not mine—when they processed my magnets. That broad was pretty snippy, but nobody walks over Pixie Poe," she declared, and Tricia believed her.

"So are they going to replace the order?"

"Damn right. And not only that—they're going to FedEx it so that it arrives tomorrow afternoon so you can take them to the Chamber of Commerce meeting on Wednesday."

"I don't know what to say except . . . thank you, Pixie. I always know I can depend on you."

Pixie straightened to her full height—enhanced by her three-inch heels—and positively beamed. "Ah, it's nothing," but clearly she did believe it was, which amused Tricia.

Once Pixie had hung up her coat and downed her first cup of coffee, she settled down. As expected, the store was bereft of customers, and Pixie had more on her mind than finishing her latest paperback novel.

"We need to come up with a package," she told Tricia authoritatively.

"A package?"

"Yeah, you know—like the swag bags some of the authors give to their readers at signings."

"What would you put in such a bag?"

"What else? Swag—and all we can fit in there."

"Don't you think a magnet and a pen is more than enough?" Tricia asked, dreading Pixie's answer.

"Nah—you need more than that, but not necessarily stuff we'd have to order. How about a little parchment scroll tied with a ribbon."

"What do you think it should say?"

"Your platform. Ya gotta have a platform. Like, why should these schmoes vote for you? A chicken in every pot? Time and a half for overtime? Chocolate?"

As Tricia thought about it, chocolate wasn't a bad bribe. "Where would we get parchment paper?"

"The craft store up on the highway sells it by the ream."

"And chocolate?"

"There's this terrific little place just outside of Nashua called the Chocoholic, and their stuff is to *die* for."

"Let's not talk about dying," Tricia hurriedly interrupted. Ted Harper's death was still a little too fresh on her mind.

"It's just a saying," Pixie said apologetically. "Anyway, the craft store also sells little boxes that get used for weddings and showers and stuff that would be perfect for the candy. We could do something sweet, like hot-glue some little fabric ribbon rosettes to them to dress them up."

"Wouldn't something representing a book—like a sticker—be better?"

"And where are we going to find those on such short notice?" Pixie demanded. She was into this thing heart and soul.

"I guess you're right. But what would the rosette represent?"

"The fact that you'll keep the flowers on Main Street if you're elected to the board."

"Do you think that would be an issue?"

"I've heard flack that some of the Chamber members think it's a waste of moola."

"But the tourists like them. And if we keep it up, we've got a good shot at Prettiest Village in New Hampshire."

"You don't have to tell me. I'm all for it."

Tricia squinted, giving her assistant a good once-over. "Are you sure you never worked on a political campaign before?"

Pixie raised her right hand, giving the Girl Scout salute. "Never have, never will. But I read lots of decorating magazines, and not the fancy-schmancy ones with antique furniture and lotsa doodads. I'm talking *Crafting Today* and stuff like that."

Tricia shrugged. "It sounds good to me."

Pixie was practically bristling with excitement. "Okay, let's make a list of the stuff we need, and if you hold down the fort, I'll head to the craft and candy stores. Tomorrow, when Mr. E is here, the three of us can work on the swag bags. If you like, I could go to the meeting with you on Wednesday and pass out everything." Pixie was almost as bad as a child who begged to stay up late.

"Let's see how things go. But I think your ideas are truly brilliant."

Pixie grinned, her gold canine tooth flashing. She waved her index finger in the air. "And you're going to *win*."

"Let's not get ahead of ourselves. We don't even know for sure who the competition is."

"You must have heard the rumors," Pixie said. Frannie was the town gossip, and though Pixie listened to it, she wasn't one to spread it around.

"Yes, but I think I'm more qualified. I mean, I did work for the Chamber as a volunteer for almost six months."

Pixie's smile faded. "Yeah, but you're a woman. They already had one of those, and New England has its share of woman-hating curmudgeons."

"That may be, but Angelica was far more successful than her male predecessor."

"And a lot less selfish, too," Pixie amended under her breath. "But that don't mean the members will vote for the most qualified person in the room. We all know how *that* works out," Pixie alluded.

"Let's not go there," Tricia said. "Instead, let's concentrate on your brilliant campaign strategy." She grabbed a pen from the holder and a scrap piece of paper. "Now, what else do you think we need to get?"

The customers were few and far between on that brisk November morning, which gave Tricia and Pixie lots of time to research the best places to get the items they needed and for Pixie to head out to get the supplies. She made it back just in time for Tricia to head over to Booked for Lunch.

Angelica was seated in her favorite back booth, and Tricia took off her coat and joined her. "You look busy."

Angelica looked up and over the reading glasses perched on her nose. "I'm always busy," she said, and again there was a stack of papers on the table, which she quickly scooped up and put into a plain manila folder.

"That was a nice dinner last night," Tricia said. "Everyone seemed to enjoy it—even little Sofia."

Angelica sighed. "Yes, but as I suspected, I spent far too much time in the kitchen. I wonder if we should just go to the Brookview Inn and book their party room for our Sunday dinners."

"As you said; you'd lose the personal touch."

"Yes, and their menu is rather pedestrian. I mean, it's wonderful. I helped create it—but it doesn't scream *me*!" Perhaps not, but thanks to the changes she and Antonio had introduced, the inn was securely in the black, which it hadn't been under its previous ownership.

Tricia's gaze traveled to the chalkboard behind the counter, which listed the day's specials. "The menu here isn't all that spectacular, either."

"The Brookview serves three meals a day; we serve lunch," she pointed out, sounding just the teensiest bit cranky.

Tricia shrugged. "I've heard they make good meatloaf."

"You've never had it?" Angelica asked.

Tricia shook her head. "I'm not into meatloaf."

"I used to make it a lot for . . . He Who Shall Not Be Named," she said, alluding to Bob Kelly who wasn't a forbidden subject, but they tried not to mention him just the same. "He liked it with a lot of onions, which, by the way, is a very healthy vegetable."

"I'd rather have them in my soup."

"We don't usually serve French onion on a Monday, but come back on Thursday and—"

"That's okay," Tricia said.

Molly, the waitress, stopped by to take their orders. Tricia ordered a bowl of the soup that was on offer (tomato bisque) and a fruit plate, while Angelica ordered a turkey club sandwich and a cup of the same soup.

"Did you talk to Antonio?" Tricia asked, as Angelica snuck a peek at the papers in the folder.

"About what?"

Tricia leaned in closer and whispered, "About the threatening letter."

"Of course not."

"How about Chief Baker?"

"Not him, either," Angelica muttered.

"Why not?"

"I'm beginning to think it was all a prank."

"Honestly? Or are you trying to talk yourself into the idea it was some kind of a put-on?"

"I didn't get another letter, so I'm going on the assumption that the one I received the other day was someone's idea of a joke."

"Oh, Ange. Don't."

"Don't what?"

"Ignore this. Obviously someone knows what's going on with"—Tricia looked around the café to see if Molly or anyone else was listening—"you know what. They've tied you to—" And then she mouthed the words *Nigela Ricita Associates*.

Angelica pursed her lips, but said nothing.

"You need to do something about this."

"I will *not* be blackmailed."

"And if whoever sent the letter spills the secret?"

"They get nothing. I lose my anonymity, but—" She sighed. "I've decided that's not the worst thing in the world. I've treated every company I've worked with fairly"—she lowered her voice—"no matter *what* name I've done business under."

Tricia had to admit her sister was right about that. She never really did see the reason for all the secrecy surrounding Angelica's various business ventures. She always assumed Angelica liked the intrigue. She positively glowed whenever she was around Antonio, so there was no way she was ashamed of their relationship.

"What if it all comes out?" Tricia dared to ask.

"Sorry?"

"What would happen if people found out about . . ." She let the sentence trail off.

"I'm sure some would be very upset that they had to go through a middleman, so to speak, to work with the Nigela Ricita Associates."

"Management at a lot of companies is virtually unknown to the average Joe."

"That's true," Angelica agreed. "But some, maybe all, of my employees might feel that I've tried to pull one over on them."

"For instance?"

Angelica shrugged. "The staff at the Brookside Inn sometimes get crazy notions about 'the big boss' arriving on an inspection tour. They've been trying to figure out who she is for a couple of years now. Antonio says they've even gone through the reservations with a fine-tooth comb looking for repeat visitors to try to figure out who Nigela is."

"Is that ethical?"

Again she shrugged. "It's a marketing tool. Repeat customers can be one of the most important keys to a successful business. The staff has identified several customers who get extra-special treatment because of their repeat reservations—and for booking meetings and other events. It's all to the good of the inn."

"I guess," Tricia agreed, but despite Angelica's protestations, Tricia was pretty sure her sister would do everything in her power not to let the truth be known to the world at large. Angelica enjoyed being an enigma.

Molly backed through the swinging kitchen door with a big round tray filled with their lunches.

While they ate, Tricia told Angelica about Pixie's ideas for her run for Chamber president.

"You've got a crack assistant there, Trish."

Tricia plunged her spoon into her soup. "I know it. It's so cute to witness her enthusiasm. You'd think she was making a bid for the job."

"Of course, if you win, it means you'll have to give her more responsibility running Haven't Got a Clue."

"I've thought about that. I never thought of myself as a control freak, but there are some things I like done just so—and I'm the only one who can do them."

Angelica shook her head. "You have to trust your staff. Just because you do something your own way, doesn't mean it can't be done better and more efficiently by someone else. Antonio has proved that to me time and time again."

"You're right," Tricia said, and sampled the soup. "Ooh, that's good."

"Tommy makes great soups, doesn't he?" Angelica asked.

Tricia nodded and freed her saltines from their cellophane prison.

Angelica tried the soup and nodded her approval. "Although I personally love the idea, I do think you should consider how your competition could view your little swag bags."

"You mean it might look like I'm stacking the deck?"

"It's a possibility."

"I thought about it. But anyone who runs for the job has a week to campaign and do something similar. I'm getting out there with my message, along with a little chocolate. I don't see it as a negative."

"Chauncey Porter might think otherwise."

Tricia shrugged. "I can't worry about him. I just need to stay focused on winning."

Angelica smiled. "I'm pleased to hear you say that. The Chamber members would be foolish not to elect you. Have you got your campaign speech ready?"

"I haven't thought about it. I guess I could just read the text from the little scroll from our handout."

"It wouldn't hurt if you mention everyone you've ever worked with from the membership."

"Since I volunteered for six months, that's just about everybody."

Angelica nodded. "Uh-huh. People like to know their contributions have been noticed and appreciate anyone who spreads the word around."

"Duly noted," Tricia said.

"I'm only sorry I can't publicly endorse you. The fact that you're my sister, and did a phenomenal job as my unpaid assistant for nearly half a year, shouldn't be lost on the members."

Tricia hoped so.

The sisters ate the rest of their lunch in companionable conversation, but it also occurred to Tricia that while they spoke, somewhere in Nashua, Ted Harper's autopsy had either been completed or was still pending. That made talk about Nigela Ricita Associates and Tricia's run for Chamber of Commerce president seem rather frivolous. The poor man had died in her home only two days before, and here she was, planning to put together party favors and march on with her life as though nothing had happened.

They were sobering and uncomfortable thoughts that Tricia couldn't dismiss, even if she'd tried.

EIGHT

With the hands of a surgeon—wearing gloves and a medical mask—Pixie carefully divided the hundred and twenty hand-dipped chocolates (in four scrumptious flavors) and placed them in the little white boxes that Tricia had assembled. Then she wielded the glue gun with precision and added the blue rosettes to the box tops. She'd chosen that color because "pink is too girly," given that the Chamber had a 60 percent male membership. "It's a subtle point, but anything we can use to our advantage is worth the effort," Pixie had declared.

Tricia couldn't argue with that logic.

"You mentioned earlier that you'd like to go to the Chamber meeting," Tricia said.

"Yeah. Back when I was temping at the Chamber, I always hoped I'd get to go. I mean, Mariana always did, but I was always stuck back at the office."

"I'm sorry. Why didn't you mention it before now?"

Pixie shrugged, frowning. "Maybe 'cuz I ain't the most polished dame in the world."

"Oh, Pixie."

Again, Pixie shrugged. "I promise, I won't do anything to embarrass you." She looked at Tricia with puppy dog eyes; there was no way she could deny her assistant the pleasure.

"Of course you can come. I'd be proud to have you help me represent Haven't Got a Clue."

Pixie grinned, looking about ready to burst with pride.

They set the chocolates aside in a large cardboard carton wrapped in multiple layers of plastic—just in case—in the shop's coldest location near the back door to the alley, then gathered up the rest of the items for the swag bags on the beverage station. The next day, with Mr. Everett's help, they would finish the job. Tricia also called Mariana, the Chamber's secretary, to let her know that Pixie would be her guest at the Wednesday breakfast meeting. Pixie was absolutely ecstatic and, as soon as Tricia hung up the phone, started planning what she'd wear.

"Something understated yet dignified," Pixie asserted, but who knew what that meant.

Tricia called Angelica late in the afternoon to confirm their dinner plans, only to be put off.

"I'm sorry, Trish, but I've got a monstrous headache. I'm going to make myself a soft-boiled egg and toast and go to bed."

"Are you sure? I can come over and—"

"No, no! I'll be fine," Angelica said. "I just need a good night's sleep."

"Okay. But call if you need me," Tricia said.

"I will. And thanks."

And so after closing Haven't Got a Clue, Tricia retreated to her large, new kitchen for the final meal of her day and, as Angelica had suggested, had an egg for her dinner, too. The carton was about the only thing left in the fridge, and now her egg had been transformed into an omelet thanks to frozen onions and peppers, which she'd liberally sprinkled with cracked pepper. It was accompanied by one perfectly toasted piece of white bread—no butter—that she'd found in the freezer. However, there was no cocktail hour filled with discussions of her day. Yes—that's what she missed most. It occurred to Tricia that the best part of her day—what she most looked forward to—was the time she spent with her sister talking about the ins and outs of the daily tasks of being in business.

Tricia resisted the urge to call Angelica—and more than once—and she and Miss Marple retired to her bedroom suite early that evening. Still, she wasn't quite ready for bed. The whole Carol Talbot jewelry debacle kept niggling at her brain. It was obvious Angelica wasn't interested in being part of the process of returning Carol's jewelry to her estate, which meant it would be wholly Tricia's responsibility.

Retrieving the stolen goods, Tricia spread them across the top of her vanity before selecting the sparkling tennis bracelet, which she tried on. She'd learned to play the game in high school, and was actually quite good at it, but she didn't have the competitive nature—at least for sports—that it would have taken to become a champion. She removed it and examined the solitaire engagement ring, which, except for the caret size, was pretty much the same as the one Christopher had given her back on that balmy summer night on Martha's Vineyard. *Don't go there,* she warned herself and set it aside to examine the old-fashioned broach. Had it belonged to a relative? Might Carol have obtained it as a piece of estate jewelry?

Tricia returned the jewelry to the plastic bag and thought about the situation. She knew that once probate was initiated, a will became a matter of public record. It would list Carol's attorney's name and what was to be done with her earthly possessions. But did Tricia want to make it known that she was interested in the dead woman's affairs? The fact she'd been snooping around could make things awkward when the jewelry finally showed up.

No, she wasn't ready to go to the county clerk's office to obtain a copy of the document, and she couldn't ask anyone to do it for her, either. Not without arousing suspicion. Those thoughts preyed on her mind, making it difficult to concentrate on her book. Finally she just gave up and turned out the light, but it was a long time before she was able to fall asleep.

Bright and early, Tricia was up and ready for work—hours before her shop would open. That gave her plenty of time to take her walk through the village—sans Sarge, who often accompanied her—to check out some of the early holiday decorations in the other shops along Main Street. The Happy Domestic was all decked out for Christmas, with everything in its big display window a pastel pink and green. It wasn't her idea of Christmas colors, and Tricia was pleased to see that the Coffee Bean was still holding on to its fall decorations of oranges, yellows, and browns.

Entering the little coffee shop, Tricia treated herself to a banana muffin and a skinny latte—which she felt would make up for the muffin—and returned to Haven't Got a Clue. Miss Marple was already ensconced on her carpet-covered perch for the morning, snoozing. The shop seemed far too quiet, and Tricia put on some lively music. It got her revved up, and after her breakfast, she found herself working on the scrolls for the swag bags. They did look incredibly cute, and she put together a couple of bags to gauge the effect. She had wanted to use fabric ribbons to tie the bags, but Pixie thought curly ribbon would look more festive, and she was right. Tricia did like Pixie's version better.

She was about to start on the rest of the bags when Pixie arrived, pink-cheeked and raring to go. "You started without me?"

"Just the scrolls. Here's what the finished package should look like—after we get the magnets, that is. What do you think?"

Pixie positively beamed. "It's absolutely adorable. And nobody will be able to resist those chocolates."

Before Pixie had even taken off her coat, Mr. Everett arrived, all smiles. "I've brought pictures of Charlie!" he exclaimed, and had his phone out before he'd even taken off his coat. Pixie made coffee, and then the three of them sat in the reader's nook to look at the digital photos.

"My, he's a handsome boy," Tricia said, admiring the large tabby, who looked to be at least seven or eight pounds heavier than Miss Marple.

"He's a big boy, all right," Mr. Everett said, sounding as proud as a new papa.

"How old did you say he was?" Pixie asked.

"Twelve. We didn't want to get a cat who would outlive us."

"I dunno," Pixie said. "Fred's mother has had cats that lived to be twenty."

"Pixie," Tricia admonished. Mr. Everett was only in his late seventies and took good care of himself. Tricia hoped he would live to be at least a hundred.

"Charlie has had health problems. He was a very sick boy when someone turned him in to the shelter. It took months for them to nurse him back to health, but nobody wanted to take a chance on him."

"Not until you came along," Tricia said.

"And Grace. It was a mutual decision."

"Did he have a good first night with you?"

Mr. Everett's smile was positively infectious. "He slept at the end of our bed all night long and never made a peep."

"That's great."

After they'd looked at the twenty or more photos, they settled down to work on assembling the swag bags and were only interrupted by customers twice the entire morning. That would change in a few weeks when the Christmas rush began in earnest, something all the merchants on Stoneham's main drag looked forward to.

Pixie and Mr. Everett headed out to lunch together, and Tricia and a dozing Miss Marple held down the fort, until they returned and Tricia could take her own lunch break. As usual, she headed for Booked for Lunch, but when she arrived she found that Angelica hadn't yet made it in. Tricia sat down at one of the empty booths in the back, ordered her lunch, and then pulled out her cell phone to call her sister. But Angelica didn't pick up. Next, she called Antonio, but he said he hadn't heard from Angelica that day, either.

"I'm sorry we haven't had another chance to talk," she apologized.

"Has Angelica told you why she's so unhappy?"

"Yes, but she's asked me not to talk about it."

"I would not expect you to betray her confidence."

"Thank you. But that doesn't mean you shouldn't try to pin her down."

"I must walk softly," Antonio said. "She will tell me when she thinks I must know."

Tricia wasn't so sure about that.

They said good-bye and Tricia hurried through her soup and half a ham-and-Swiss-cheese sandwich before she donned her coat and headed for the Cookery.

A forlorn-looking Frannie stood behind the counter, earbuds in place, her phone sitting on the cash desk, reading a copy of *Popular Mechanics* magazine—which seemed a little odd, but then, so was Frannie. Her sad expression reminded Tricia that she hadn't heard back from Chief Baker about Ted Harper's autopsy, and she decided she would call him from her office once she returned to Haven't Got a Clue.

"Is Angelica around?"

Frannie pulled one of the buds from her ear. "Upstairs. After my lunch break, she took Sarge for a walk and then went straight back upstairs. She said she had paperwork to do."

Tricia frowned. "Thanks."

"Aren't you going to say something about Ted?" Frannie asked, sounding hurt.

"Oh, sorry. Yes. I'm . . . I'm so sorry."

Frannie shook her head. "If only I'd known about his allergies, I might have been able to help him."

"Help how?" Tricia asked.

"With homeopathic remedies. I've been reading up on it." She picked up another magazine. "You can cure just about anything with the right diet and supplements."

Tricia remembered what a nurse had once told her: that Americans had the most expensive urine in the world because they took so many vitamins and other supplements that weren't absorbed by the body. Tricia doubted a mere supplement or two could have helped Ted.

"Have you heard about any funeral arrangements?"

Frannie's eyes began to tear up. "His family is going to have him buried in Pennsylvania."

"Will you go to the service?"

"I don't know," she admitted, then snatched a tissue from the box under the counter and blew her nose loudly. "I liked him, and I'm devastated that he's dead, but I really didn't know him all that well." Her voice hardened as she looked at Tricia. "I didn't get an opportunity to know him better."

Tricia nodded meekly, but didn't know what to say on that account. "Have you spoken to them?"

Frannie nodded. "Ted's sister. She was quite upset—as you'd expect her to be."

"I'm sure she was. I would be devastated if anything happened to Angelica."

Frannie merely nodded.

"Speaking of her, I'd better go upstairs and—" Check on her? Of course that's what she meant to do, but she didn't want to give Frannie that explanation. "Speak to her," Tricia finished lamely.

As Tricia backed away from the cash desk, Frannie replaced the earbud, and her gaze returned to her magazine. Tricia hightailed it for the stairs to Angelica's apartment.

As she rounded the landing at the second floor, Sarge began to bark. "It's only me, Sarge," Tricia called. When she got to the top, she reached for the door handle and found it locked. "Ange! It's me, Tricia. Are you there?"

She received no answer. "Angelica?" she called again, more strident. Still no answer.

Fumbling with her keys, Tricia unlocked the door and burst through it. Sarge was immediately at her feet, excited as ever to see her, and she nearly tripped over him on her way to the kitchen, where she found her sister standing at one of the windows overlooking Main Street, coffee mug in hand, her back turned to the rest of the apartment.

"Ange!" Tricia called frantically. "Why didn't you answer me?"

Angelica looked up and started. "Goodness, are you trying to give me a heart attack?"

"Didn't you hear me calling you? Didn't you hear Sarge barking?"

Angelica shrugged. "I guess not. I was lost in thought."

Tricia wriggled out of the sleeves of her coat and settled it on the back of one of the island's stools.

"Why didn't you answer my call? How come you didn't show up to meet me at Booked for Lunch?"

Angelica ambled over to the island and set her cup down. "I guess I lost track of time."

"Antonio said you haven't checked in with him today, either."

"Have you been calling around town checking up on me?" Angelica asked, sounding more than a little annoyed.

"Why wouldn't I? It's not like you to pull a disappearing act."

"I've hardly disappeared," Angelica muttered.

"Well, you're certainly not acting like yourself." And then Tricia realized what was the matter. "You got another one of those blackmail letters, didn't you?"

Angelica shrugged.

"Ange?"

"So what if I did?"

"You've got to report this to Chief Baker."

"I don't need to. I've taken care of it."

"You caved in?"

"I didn't cave in," Angelica said testily. "I did the prudent thing."

"But I thought we discussed it."

"We did. But I made up my mind to just put an end to it."

"How much were you fleeced?"

"Just five grand."

"This time. You know these things always escalate. Now that you've paid, they're going to keep up the threats and demand more and more money."

"As it turns out, I *have* a lot of money, and I can spend it any way I choose."

Tricia stared at her sister. "Ange, what's come over you?"

"Nothing."

"What is it you're not telling me?" Tricia demanded.

"I've told you everything you need to know."

A wellspring of emotion seemed to bloom inside her chest, and Tricia found it hard to speak. "I thought we were done with all the secrets from the past. I thought we had moved on. I thought—"

"'Trish, drop it. Please."

"How can I? I'm worried about you—about what you're facing and how it can only get worse."

"Drop it," Angelica said, her tone deadly.

There was no point in arguing. When Angelica made up her mind, nothing could change it.

Tricia swallowed. "Okay."

Okay for *now*. But when she spoke to Baker, she *would* bring up Angelica's situation, whether her sister would want her to or not.

"I have to get back to work. Are we on for dinner tonight?"

Angelica sighed wearily. "I guess."

"My place or yours?"

"Come here. I'll pull something together."

"Are you sure?"

"Of course I'm sure," Angelica fairly snapped.

"All right. I'll see you around six," Tricia said, and headed for the door to the stairs, but paused before opening the door. "If you need me, you know where to find me," she called.

There was no answer.

Tricia stepped out onto the landing, and then pulled the door shut behind her.

Pixie and Mr. Everett were rearranging the hard-boiled suspense titles when Tricia arrived back at Haven't Got a Clue. She'd considered heading straight to the police station, but then worried that Angelica might have gone back to staring out her kitchen windows and would be able to see her walking down the sidewalk in that direction. No, she'd call. If Baker was out of the office, she'd leave a message.

Down in her office, she punched Baker's personal number into her cell phone. She'd taken him off her contacts list but still remembered the number, and she wondered why she'd committed it to memory.

"Hello, Tricia," Baker answered.

"Hi, Grant."

"I suppose you're calling about Ted Harper's autopsy."

"Well, yes . . . and maybe something else."

"Why don't we get Harper out of the way first."

"Okay."

"I probably shouldn't be telling this to you, but it'll get out eventually, and I was going to come and speak to you about it anyway."

"Go on," Tricia said cautiously.

"The medical examiner and I both spoke with Harper's private physician. He had only one known allergy."

When he didn't immediately go on, Tricia prodded, "And?"

"Sumac."

Tricia blinked. "I beg your pardon. The stuff that grows at the side of the road?"

"That's it exactly."

"How would anyone find out they were allergic to sumac?"

"Harper worked for a landscaper. He had to be very careful when clearing brush."

"Sumac is poisonous to everybody, isn't it?"

"Yes. If you touch the oil, you'll get a rash. Those with heightened sensitivity can go into anaphylactic shock by breathing in the fumes from burning plants."

"I certainly didn't put any sumac oil in my mushroom appetizers."

"The fact that nobody else became ill seems to point to another scenario."

"Such as?"

"Someone other than you put it in the hors d'oeuvre."

"Well, that's a given. Do you mean as a joke?" Tricia asked in disbelief.

"Some joke. A man is dead."

What had appeared to be a case of food poisoning now had a much more sinister connotation.

"According to the people I and my officers spoke with after your party, nobody but Frannie Armstrong even knew Ted Harper."

"So what are you saying?" Tricia asked, already anticipating his answer.

"Someone at that party tainted that one mushroom. The question is, who had access to the food?"

Tricia blew out a breath. "Just about everybody, I guess. I mean, Angelica and I were the ones who took charge of it, but Ginny and Antonio helped out by passing things around and arranging things. And don't you dare suspect any of them."

"For what it's worth, I don't."

"There was also food spread across the kitchen island, and people helped themselves."

"What concerns me is that someone at that party tainted that one mushroom, so it's not like he or she was targeting any one person. Of course, whoever did it may have wanted you to get in trouble for making someone sick."

"I can't think of anyone at the party who would have wanted to do so."

"Oh, no?"

Tricia found her patience thinning. "Who do you suspect?"

"I don't suspect anyone, but I do know that despite the fact that he attended your party, Chauncey Porter has not been your friend for some time. He blames you for the death of—"

"Tell me something I don't know. But that was two years ago. He's gotten over his loss, and he and Mary Fairchild are about to be married."

"That doesn't mean he doesn't still hold a grudge."

That was true. But Chauncey hadn't been as blatantly rude to her since he and Mary had become a couple earlier in the year, either.

"I don't know, Grant. Chauncey may not like me, but I can't see him potentially poisoning someone at my party just to get back at me. And where does one get sumac leaves at this time of year, anyway?"

"That's a good question—and I don't have an answer."

"Is the medical examiner sure it was sumac?"

"We'll have to wait for the toxicology report to make certain, but that's the line she's going after right now."

Tricia nodded—not that Baker could see her do it.

"Has anyone threatened you lately?"

"Just Bob Kelly—at his sentencing," Tricia said matter-of-factly.

"What exactly did he say?"

"I can't repeat it word for word, but he put a curse on me. That my life would be a living hell until the day I died."

"He said that?" Baker asked.

"Yes. And he may be right. Since then, someone left a large pile of doggy doo on my back steps, which I slipped in on Saturday, and yesterday someone egged my shop display window. It sounds like a teenaged prank. Has anyone reported petty vandalism?" Tricia asked.

"No. But I want you to be careful."

"You don't think Bob could be responsible, do you?"

"Not when he's behind bars, but don't forget he was a big cheese in this village for more than a decade and he had a lot of friends. You heard the character witnesses his attorney called to the stand."

She had. But their glowing words couldn't erase the testimony she and the other witnesses had given that had sent Kelly to prison, either. Tricia changed the subject.

"Frannie said Ted's family is having him buried in Pennsylvania."

"Yes. The body has been turned over to a mortuary and will be transported there tomorrow."

"I feel terrible about this entire situation."

"Which isn't surprising. But like I mentioned, you'd better think long and hard about who might have it in for you, because even if whoever put the poison in the mushroom didn't think anyone would die, he or she had to know it could make someone sick, which would make you look bad."

Again Tricia nodded. "Okay, I'll think about what you've said, and if I have any ideas, I'll get back to you on it."

"What else did you have on your mind?"

"What?"

"You said you wanted to talk to me about Harper and something else."

"Yes," Tricia admitted. "I've been told I should mind my own business—"

"And how's that going?" Baker said rather pointedly.

Tricia ignored the dig. "My sister is being blackmailed."

"What?"

"She's received letters in the mail asking for money and saying that if she didn't pay, things she'd like to remain secret will be made public."

"What does Angelica have to hide?"

"It's not up to me to betray her confidences, but rest assured it's nothing illegal, and I can't for the life of me figure out why she wants to keep it all so hush-hush. But that's her decision, not mine. I'm just concerned that even though she's paid what the blackmailer asked for—"

"And what was that?"

"Five thousand dollars—that they'll try to shake her down for more."

"Why did she pay?"

"I don't know. She doesn't want to talk to me about it."

For a long moment, neither of them spoke, and then Baker broke the quiet. "I can't do much unless she comes to the police for help."

"I realize that, but I don't know what else to do, and I trust your advice."

"Thank you, Tricia. It's nice to know you still have at least that much respect for me."

"I never stopped respecting you, Grant," she said sincerely.

"Yeah, I guess I knew that," Baker said quietly. "Look, keep an eye on the situation, and if things heat up, get Angelica to come talk to me, will you?"

"I'll certainly try. What gets me is that she seems worried about this, but doesn't seem to care if she has to keep paying through the nose to keep her secrets quiet."

"That's not good."

"No, it isn't."

"My hands are tied until she's willing to talk," Baker reiterated.

"Thanks for listening, and for telling me about Ted."

"And you watch yourself. Someone out there might be out to get you—one way or another."

His words caused a chill to ripple through her.

"Talk to you later," Baker said, and severed the connection.

Tricia punched the end call icon on her phone and set it on the desk before her. Who on earth could have it in for her? Chauncey? He'd slapped her two years before. He'd been rude to her on a number of occasions, but he'd seemed to mellow since the cruise they'd both been on the previous January, no doubt due to Mary's calming influence. The fact that he might oppose her in the Chamber of Commerce election hadn't worried her before her conversation with Baker, and if she was honest, it still wasn't a concern. Still, Tricia reached for the typed list of people who'd received an invitation to her party Friday night. As she skimmed through it, she saw the names of several people who'd also had a beef with her since she'd moved to Stoneham, however flimsy.

Nikki Brimfield-Smith had been jealous of Tricia during her courtship with Russ. Tricia and Russ had been a couple for a little over a year, and when they'd broken up, Russ hadn't taken it well. He'd even stalked Tricia for a short period of time. And then he fell in love with Nikki, although the course of their married life hadn't exactly turned out to be all roses and champagne. Nikki had wanted to be a stay-at-home mom. Russ hadn't exactly taken to fatherhood. Money was an issue, and they argued over the kinds of stories Russ covered for the *Stoneham Weekly News*. But the life they shared had nothing to do with Tricia.

Tricia and her contractor, Jim Stark, had gotten off to a shaky start, but they'd had no real friction during the months he and his team of workers and subcontractors had been transforming the building she now owned, including the space where she now sat.

David Black had made it clear that he detested Tricia, and so had Brandy Arkin, but both were out of the picture, although Black hadn't gone all that far—just the next town over—and certainly neither had attended her party.

Tricia racked her brain, but could come up with no other probable suspects. Still, somebody had poisoned that one mushroom. Which of the guests at her party could have held a big enough grudge against Tricia to cost Ted Harper his life?

NINE

The rest of the day dragged, mostly because Tricia was eager to return to Angelica's apartment and hopefully talk some sense into her sister. Or was that the wrong approach? Perhaps she should let things lie and hope that Angelica would come to her senses on her own. Then again, that wasn't likely to happen. Nobody in the world had a harder head than Angelica. There was only one person Tricia knew who might talk some sense into her—Antonio—and he had no clue what was going on.

The magnets had arrived, and they'd spent another hour putting the swag bags together, with Mr. Everett adding the last item, Pixie tying the bags, and Tricia curling the ribbon. The bags looked gorgeous.

"I think we should coordinate our outfits for the Chamber meeting tomorrow," Pixie said as she donned her coat. "I was thinking of wearing my blue suit with the white piping. It's very businesslike, and of course I'll have matching pumps and purse. What are you going to wear?"

"I haven't given it much thought," Tricia admitted. "How about my peach sweater set?"

"Oh, no," Pixie admonished. "That would clash terribly with my suit. How about your light blue sweater set, black slacks, and black flats. A nice necklace or pin would be attractive, too. I thought about wearing that nice starfish pin you got me in Bermuda. It's absolutely adorable."

Tricia smiled. "I'm glad you like it."

"And the sweater set?" Pixie prodded.

"The light blue," Tricia agreed.

"Good," Pixie practically squealed.

Mr. Everett shook his head wearily. "I'm glad I don't have to go. Wearing a suit on a weekday . . ." He shook his head.

"I think you look fine with your shirt, tie, and sweaters. In fact, everybody should wear more sweaters more often. They're so cozy," Tricia said.

"If you think so," Pixie said, sounding bored. She only wore what she called "incredibly cute" sweaters, and usually those coordinated with something else she was wearing. Tricia often wondered how big Pixie's clothes closet was, since she seldom seemed to wear an outfit more than once.

"Now, you'll be bringing the box with the goodies, right? Or do you want me to help you carry it to your car right now?" she asked.

"That's okay. I can manage it tomorrow morning."

"All right then. Good night," Pixie called.

"See you in the morning," Mr. Everett said with a wave.

Tricia waved back. "Have a great evening!"

The door closed behind them, and Tricia didn't waste any time. She secured the day's receipts, left Miss Marple an ample kitty snack, and threw on her coat before leaving her store and heading next door. The Cookery had already closed and Frannie had left for the day, so Tricia sorted through her keys and let herself in.

As she hurried up the stairs, she noticed there was no aroma—no hint of what Angelica might be preparing for their dinner—and of course Sarge was already barking a greeting. After the reception she'd received earlier that day, it was comforting to know that at least somebody would be glad to see her.

Tricia opened the door, and Sarge's barking stepped up a notch.

"Oh, hush!" Angelica called from the kitchen, and the dog instantly went silent, but that didn't stop his tail from wagging so hard Tricia thought it might fly right off.

"You're such a good boy. Into the kitchen for a biscuit," she told him.

Sarge did such an abrupt about-face that Tricia wondered if he might have hurt himself, but he went racing toward the kitchen, and she knew he'd be waiting by the counter, where Angelica kept his treats in a crystal jar. She hung up her coat and called out a cautious, "Hello."

"You know where to find me," came Angelica's voice.

Sure enough, she was at the island pouring them each a martini. Well, at least that part of their evening routine had returned. Tricia gave Sarge his biscuit, and he grabbed it and zoomed to his bed to eat it.

"I sure wouldn't want crumbs in my bed."

"That's why I never have breakfast anywhere near my bedroom," Angelica agreed. She raised her glass. "Cheers."

Tricia picked up her own and then settled on her usual stool at the island. "What kind of a day did you have?"

"Quiet," Angelica said, and sipped her drink. "I worked from home all day."

"You must have gotten a lot accomplished."

She shook her head. "Not really."

Tricia sipped her drink. She couldn't remember her sister ever sounding so depressed. She decided to introduce a new topic of conversation.

"Pixie and I are all set for the Chamber meeting tomorrow. I pretty much know what I'm going to say, and we'll see what happens after that. You *are* going to the meeting tomorrow, aren't you?"

"I *am* the Chamber president until December thirty-first, so yes, I will be there to preside over the meeting."

"Will you remain a member after your term is finished?"

"Of course." At least Angelica's tone was beginning to sound more normal. *Must be the gin,* Tricia mused.

It was time to broach a potentially explosive subject. Although, maybe she'd fudge a little first. "I spoke to Chief Baker today."

Angelica's eyes narrowed. "About?"

"Ted Harper's autopsy results."

"Oh."

Tricia nodded and sipped her drink. "It seems Ted was allergic to sumac."

"Sumac? Did they find that in his stomach contents?"

"It's too early for a toxicology report, but that's the line of inquiry they're taking."

"Sumac?" Angelica again asked. "I don't get it."

"Neither do I. Grant thinks that only one mushroom was tampered with—otherwise there would have been others who became sick."

"Nobody but Frannie knew Ted, so unless she targeted him, no one else would have had a motive. And Frannie really liked this guy. There's no way she'd have bumped him off."

"Grant thinks someone might have wanted to make trouble for me."

"Someone at the party? I can't think who."

"I've had a few altercations with a few of the people who were there," Tricia admitted.

"Such as?"

"Chauncey Porter."

"Oh, yeah—he's a given," Angelica said rather glibly.

"Nikki and Jim Stark, for another two."

"You're right. But none of those encounters were serious enough for them to come after you. And none of them are actively angry with you—right now, that is."

Tricia didn't like the implication at the end of that last sentence. Did Angelica think they might again become angry at her in the near future? She wasn't about to ask.

"Did Grant bring them up?" Angelica asked.

Tricia shook her head. "I glanced at the invitation list and they sort of sprang off the page."

"You could even add Russ to the list. He wasn't happy when the two of you broke up."

"That was ages ago, and obviously he got over me, or he wouldn't be married to Nikki today."

"And how long do you think that marriage is going to last?" Angelica asked.

She had a point. Despite speaking with Russ on at least a monthly basis for the past year, Tricia couldn't remember seeing him smile or laugh during any of their conversations. In fact, the man seemed downright depressed a good deal of the time. Was it possible he blamed Tricia for his unhappy life? She sure hoped not.

"Maybe you should let me go over the list. I do have a crackerjack memory."

"Crackerjack?" Tricia asked.

Angelica wrinkled her nose. "Okay—so I'm just a little bit hungry, although something sweet would definitely *not* go with a martini."

"I've got virtually nothing in my fridge, thanks to the police hauling just about everything away. What have you got?"

"My cupboards are pretty bare, too. But I've got some nice salty crackers. Want some?"

Tricia shrugged. "Why not?"

Angelica retrieved a brown sleeve of crackers, opened it, and scattered ten or twelve on a plate, taking one herself and offering them to her sister. Tricia took two.

"Did anything else happen today?" Angelica asked.

"I was about to ask you the same question."

"All quiet."

Was she telling the truth, or hiding some new secret? Tricia wasn't sure she wanted to know.

"I haven't mentioned it to you, but I did tell Grant that Bob Kelly's curse on Friday seems to have taken effect."

For a moment, Angelica looked confused. Tricia explained what she meant, describing the incidents from Saturday and Sunday.

"Why didn't you tell me about this sooner?"

"I didn't think you were in a position to hear it."

Angelica scowled. "I'm sorry. I *have* been preoccupied of late."

"Can you think of anyone who'd carry out that kind of mischief for Bob?"

Angelica shook her head. "We were together for over two years, and I never knew him to have any close friends."

As Tricia had suspected.

"What about those Chamber members his defense team dug up?"

"They must have owed him something," Angelica theorized.

"Well, the curse may already be lifted. I've had no more tricks since Sunday."

"Good." Angelica's stomach grumbled, and they both looked down at the empty cracker plate. Tricia hadn't even noticed that they'd polished them off. "Shall we order a pizza?"

"Only if you order lots of veggies. It's too fattening otherwise." Which was bunk. It would be just as fattening, despite the veggies.

"But of course."

They decided on toppings and Angelica made the call.

From then on, they made innocuous conversation, neither of them seeming to want to dwell on darker subjects that they apparently had no control over. Still, it felt awkward, which hadn't been the norm for quite a while.

The pizza arrived in record time, and Tricia went down to the shop's front door to retrieve it. They ate in silence, with Sarge looking at them with keen interest, his soulful eyes wide and hopeful. Tricia tossed him a piece of sausage when she was sure Angelica wasn't looking. The dog smacked his lips and looked thankful.

With not much else to say, Tricia went home earlier than usual to her beautiful and far-too-quiet apartment, thankful for the warm welcome she received from her cat. And for the first time in a long time, she felt positively lonely.

TEN

Southern New Hampshire's weather is always unpredictable in November, but on that day the meteorologist from Nashua's most popular TV station had hit the mark. The forecasted rain arrived at just about seven the next morning, making Tricia wish she had taken Pixie up on her offer to help her carry the box of campaign swag to her car. But Tricia was nothing if not resourceful. Placing the box on the shop's dolly, she covered it with a large plastic trash bag and strapped it on with a bungee cord before making her way to the municipal parking lot, then maneuvered it into her trunk without it getting wet. She would reverse the process once she got to the Brookview Inn, where the Chamber meeting was to take place in the main dining room.

Pixie had already arrived at the inn and was waiting in her car in the crowded parking lot when Tricia arrived. She got out, opened a big golf umbrella, and hurried to intercept Tricia. She looked quite elegant in a long tailored raincoat, different from the one she'd worn two days before, and her hair was pulled into a smart chignon, with modest silver stud earrings as a crowning touch.

"Looks like the joint's jammed!"

"There's a good turnout just about every month," Tricia said. "The Brookview puts on a really nice breakfast." Would Nigela Ricita Associates be so generous to the Chamber once Angelica was no longer its president? Time would tell.

Pixie held the umbrella over both them and the box, and they entered the inn through the back door. Once inside, Pixie took charge of the carton, while Tricia returned the dolly to the back of her car. By the time she entered the main dining room, Pixie was already circulating through the crowd, handing out the pretty cellophane bags and encouraging the members to "Vote for Tricia." She was grateful for the sentiment, but she wished Pixie had waited for her to arrive and let her make her own pitch. Still, she'd get to do that after the breakfast, and she certainly couldn't fault Pixie for her unbridled enthusiasm.

By the time Tricia had checked her coat and returned to the dining room, she saw that Angelica had arrived and had staked out their usual table near the front of the room.

"My, Pixie looks smart. Very professional. And she sure seems to be enjoying herself," Angelica commented.

"Yes. She kind of spoiled the surprise about my entering the race, but . . ." Tricia let the sentence trail off.

"It's not much of a surprise. I've hinted to enough people that you'd be in the running."

"Was that to *en*courage or *dis*courage others from running?"

"The latter." Angelica glanced across the room to where Chauncey and Mary sat near the coffee urns. He glared at Pixie, who seemed to be charming a number of the men with her patter. Mary's expression was indifferent as she held her cup with both hands, looking in the opposite direction.

"Do you think Mary and Chauncey are happy?" Angelica asked.

"Why do you ask?"

"Well, their relationship seemed hot and heavy up until the time they actually got engaged. Things seem to have cooled a bit. Last month I asked Mary if they'd set the date and she was rather evasive about it."

"I know she wasn't pleased by the size of her engagement ring, and the fact that Chauncey doesn't want to make a big deal about their wedding day. That may have cooled her ardor."

"Well, as someone who has trooped down the aisle four times, I could tell her to listen to her gut, but not everyone appreciates good advice."

Wasn't that the truth? And Angelica was certainly guilty of it herself if she didn't go to the police with those blackmail letters. But Tricia chose not to mention it just then.

"It looks like a good crowd," Tricia said, sizing up the gathering.

She recognized most of the merchants from Main Street. Russ Smith sat at a table with several of them, but his wife, Nikki, was not among them. That wasn't unusual. Nikki's business opened at eight, and she seldom came to Chamber meetings.

"Let's get some coffee and sit down," Angelica suggested.

By the time they had made their continental breakfast choices and returned to their table with coffee, Pixie had finished her rounds and joined them, stashing the box under the table. "What a great bunch of people," she gushed. "Everybody is so *nice*. It almost makes me wish I had my own business so I could join."

"What would you like to do?" Angelica asked.

"Open a vintage clothing store." Pixie sighed. "Unfortunately, there's no market for that in Stoneham, so I'll just have to be satisfied with the best job in the world—working for Tricia. I could do a testimonial for you if you want."

Tricia laughed. "That won't be necessary."

Pixie eyed the eats table. "I'd better go grab some grub before it's all gone. Be right back."

Tricia and Angelica sipped their coffee, but waited for Pixie to return before digging into their pastry choices.

"I didn't get a chance to see the bags you ladies made up," Angelica said.

"I've only got a few left," Pixie said, and reached under the table to retrieve one, handing it to Angelica.

"Oh, they're adorable. You do nice work, Pixie."

Pixie blushed, picked up her cheese Danish, and took a bite.

Tricia did likewise—her big indulgence for the day.

A number of people stopped by the table to offer Tricia their congratulations on her decision to run, and some serious mingling went on around the coffee urns until Angelica glanced at her watch. She usually called the meeting to order at eight thirty, and it was just about that time.

Angelica reached into her large purse and pulled out her gavel, then strode to the podium. She checked to make sure the microphone was live and then called the meeting to order.

"Before we open the floor to take names for our upcoming election, we have some unfinished business from our last meeting." Angelica donned her reading glasses and pulled out her agenda.

Tricia found it hard to concentrate on the business at hand, rather surprised at the anticipation building inside her, for the moment forgetting how much work the job of Chamber president would entail. She'd run for class secretary her senior year in high school and had been handily defeated by a popular cheerleader who had seemed more interested in making time with the football jocks and had explained to anyone who'd listen that the job would look good on her college entrance forms. Tricia hadn't sought any kind of "office" since then.

She had no one but herself to impress, and she had to admit that, should she be elected, she'd be stepping into Angelica's considerably big shoes. Then again, so would anyone else. Angelica had always been a hard act to follow.

At last, Angelica moved on to the part of the meeting Tricia had been waiting for.

"As you know, today we're seeking the names of those who wish to run for the Chamber presidency."

"You can't leave us!" hollered Joyce Widman.

Angelica smiled. "Thank you for that vote of confidence, Joyce. You're very sweet, but I must attend to my various businesses. And I'll still be a part of the Chamber and hope to work on various committees."

"Atta girl, Angelica," yelled a male voice from the peanut gallery.

Again Angelica smiled, but then sobered, looking over the assembled members. "So, those who wish to run, please raise your hands, and then you'll have a chance to share your platform."

Pixie giggled.

Tricia raised her hand, and, as expected, so did Chauncey Porter. But then she frowned as someone else in the crowd raised his hand, too.

"For the record," Angelica began, "I recognize Tricia Miles, Chauncey Porter, and Russ Smith."

Pixie's head jerked around, and she glared daggers at Russ. "What's he doing entering the race?" she demanded in a harsh whisper. "His wife already thinks he doesn't spend enough time with her and their kid. How in the world can he take on Chamber business as well?"

She was echoing Tricia's exact thoughts, but Tricia didn't acknowledge the fact.

"Well," Angelica said, sounding just a little miffed, "why don't we listen to the candidates' proposals. In fairness, we'll do it alphabetically. Tricia, would you please come to the podium?"

Tricia knew all eyes were upon her as she rose to her feet. But before she could move, Pixie thrust a copy of her platform in her hand—the same as the ones included in the swag bags they'd assembled.

Angelica moved aside as Tricia approached the lectern. A sprinkle of applause broke out among the members—a bit less than she would have expected. She unrolled the paper and held it down with one hand, intending to use it only as a guide. This speech would be pretty much off the cuff.

"Hello, everyone. As you know, I'm Tricia Miles. Thanks to the nearly six months I spent volunteering for the Chamber of Commerce while my store was out of commission last year, I had the pleasure of meeting just about all our members. My time with the Chamber not only gave me experience working with the day-to-day tasks that keep the organization running like a well-oiled machine, but it also gave me the opportunity to shadow our current president and act as a sounding board for her ideas and plans for the future.

"My wish for the Chamber is that it continue on the path that Angelica Miles has set. For one, to win the title of Prettiest Village in New Hampshire. And, of course, to win back our reputation as the safest village as well."

"And how do you plan to do that, Village Jinx?" a male voice called out.

Tricia cringed. If there was one thing she detested, it was that moniker. Still, she cleared her throat and continued.

"There are a number of ways. First and foremost, the Chamber needs to continue its close association with the Stoneham Police."

"How about some other examples?" Leona Ferguson, owner of Stoneham's Stoneware, inquired rather pointedly. Tricia and Leona had never been chums.

"Video cameras mounted along our main drag."

That suggestion was met with a number of boos and catcalls.

"Establishing a neighborhood watch. Working with the Board of Selectmen to enhance the village infrastructure with better lighting and establishing a second municipal parking lot. Encouraging our local businesses, along with the Chamber, to sponsor events like this past summer's Wine and Jazz Festival. And that's just the tip of the iceberg." Tricia cringed. How many more clichés was she liable to use if she kept talking?

"We're a great village, and the Chamber of Commerce works hard every day to make it just that much better. As your president, you can rest assured that I will make it happen. Thank you."

A smattering of applause followed her remarks, with Pixie giving her a standing ovation.

Head held high, Tricia marched back to her seat, trying to shush Pixie as she sat down once more.

Angelica stepped up to the podium once again. "Will our second candidate, Chauncey Porter, please approach the lectern?"

Chauncey rose from his chair and seemed to loom over those still seated. Tricia watched as he swaggered to the front of the room, and for a moment she thought he might actually push Angelica away from the microphone. Luckily, she stepped aside just in time.

"Most everybody knows me, but if you don't, I'm Chauncey Porter, and I run the Armchair Tourist shop on the west side of Main Street. I've been a merchant in Stoneham since the first booksellers were recruited more than a decade ago and feel that my presence has had a stabilizing effect on the village."

Tricia frowned. The Armchair Tourist had been near bankruptcy before Angelica had given Chauncey some much-needed business advice and Tricia had guaranteed a loan for him to invest in said shop, but apparently Chauncey had a short memory.

"Although some businesses in the village have done well during this difficult economy"—his being a shining example—"the Chamber wastes a lot of money on frivolous things like the flowers lining the street during the summer and hosting our meetings at the most expensive restaurant in the area."

Angelica's lips pursed at that dig—she'd been giving the Chamber a break by offering the inn's services at cost without regard to profit.

"Under my guidance, we'd also find cheaper office space. There's a warehouse at the edge of the village that's stood empty for years."

And who would refurbish the place to make it habitable? And if they couldn't find an underwriter, how much would that cost?

"Eliminating the almost daily Chamber e-mails would give us all more time to work at our businesses instead of reading silly notes. We could also cut the secretary/receptionist's weekly hours in half."

Such an austerity program had been suggested two years before. The membership hadn't had a chance to vote on it, because the man who'd proposed it had been found dead within minutes of offering his platform.

The Main Street member owners looked uncomfortable, while those located on the edge of the village—with little to no foot traffic—seemed encouraged.

"My goal," Chauncey continued, "is a leaner, meaner Chamber of Commerce. One we can all afford. Thank you."

As Tricia predicted, those without foot traffic applauded, while those on Main Street looked dumbfounded.

Angelica approached the podium once more. "Thank you, Chauncey," she said without enthusiasm. "And our last candidate is Russ Smith. Russ?"

Russ rose from his seat and walked toward the front of the room. He was dressed casually, in an open-necked, light-colored shirt and a dark blue cardigan sweater, slacks, and loafers, apparently trying to look like Mr. Rogers, of PBS fame—and much snappier than his attire at Tricia's party five days before.

Angelica stepped aside and Russ paused for a moment, looking over the crowd before he spoke.

"Hi, everybody. You know me—Russ Smith; owner of the *Stone-*

ham Weekly News. If it seems like I'm late tossing my hat in the ring, I want you to know that I put a lot of thought into what I could do as head of the Chamber. I guess you could say I'm in the middle between my two distinguished opponents. Do we need flowers on Main Street? I'd say 'yeah.' Do we need to be as extravagant? Probably not. Should we find another venue for our breakfast meetings? I'm sure our present president did her best to negotiate a great price. Lovely as it is, do we need to stay here? That would be something I'd investigate. Winning the title of Prettiest Village in New Hampshire would be nice, but I'd rather see us regain our past title of Safest Village in New Hampshire. Can it be done?" And with this he leveled his gaze directly at Tricia, as though she were personally responsible for the deaths that had occurred and had snatched the title from them. "That remains to be seen. But it's something I'd definitely speak to Police Chief Baker about.

"Are we spending too much time and money with clerical help? I'd find out, but I'm pretty sure we have a lease with Nigela Ricita Associates, and it may be some time before we can move."

"You'd better believe that," Tricia muttered. And in retrospect, perhaps Angelica had been overly generous when she'd given them such a cheap option with a five-year lease, when she probably could have charged a retail establishment at least double.

"We're a good group, full of smart people, and if I'm elected, I will listen to everyone's comments and opinions."

He'd better be ready to hear nothing but complaints, Tricia thought sourly, and suddenly wondered why she wanted the job at all. But the fact was—she did. And she didn't want to be beaten by either Russ or Chauncey.

"I'll be handing out my business cards at the door at the end of the meeting. Feel free to call me at any time during the coming week to talk about your needs as a Chamber member. Thanks."

And with a nod to Angelica, Russ sauntered back to his seat.

Angelica stepped back behind the lectern, her smile rigid. "That concludes our candidate platforms, and our meeting. There're still plenty of Danish and gallons of coffee left, and we may as well use them up. We certainly wouldn't want to waste them," she said, her tone icy.

Tricia winced. Even from a distance, she could almost feel the blistering heat of Angelica's ire.

Angelica banged the gavel against the lectern. "Meeting adjourned." She sidestepped the podium and practically stalked across the front of the room to join Tricia and Pixie, who gave Tricia a sidelong glance.

"Um . . . I think I'll head on over to Haven't Got a Clue. See you there." And she rose and hightailed it out of the dining room.

Tricia waited for her sister. "Why don't you have another cup of coffee. I know the management. I'm sure I could get you a shot of Irish whiskey to go with it."

"I may just do that," Angelica said through gritted teeth. Then, suddenly, she offered her most stunning smile and waved to someone behind Tricia, who turned to see that Russ had kept his promise and was already stationed at the door, doling out cards to those who hadn't gone to the food table to stuff several pastries into paper napkins to take with them.

Tricia turned back to face her sister. "What do you think my odds are at winning?"

"Before this morning, I would have said ninety percent. Now I'm thinking more like fifty."

"Really?"

"Unfortunately, yes. But let's not talk about it here." Angelica looked over Tricia's shoulder. "Excuse me. I need to speak to one of my constituents." She rose, and off she went.

Tricia looked down at the half-empty coffee cup at her place setting and the rest of the crumb-laden plates that littered the table. Already the waitstaff had swooped in and were clearing the tables.

Since nobody had come to speak to her about her candidacy, she reached under the table to retrieve the box that had carried her swag bags. Would the decadent candy entice votes in her favor, or would it look like just a high-priced plot to cajole the members to vote for her and her apparently extravagant ideas when following in Angelica's footsteps?

She wasn't sure she wanted to know.

ELEVEN

Much as they would have liked it, neither Tricia nor Angelica ordered an Irish coffee, and since they'd driven in separate cars, they didn't have an opportunity for a private conversation, either. Tricia would just have to wait for a powwow until they reconvened at Booked for Lunch later that afternoon.

Upon arriving back at Haven't Got a Clue, she found that Pixie had hung up her suit jacket and donned a bright pink angora sweater, which certainly looked more cheerful than Tricia felt on that gloomy morning.

"Coffee?" Pixie offered solicitously.

"I proposed something stronger to Angelica but . . . there wasn't time."

"Well, it's hot if you change your mind. What was with that crowd? And how could that Chauncey guy be so mean about Angelica's accomplishments? I read that lease agreement with Nigela Ricita Associates when I was working for the Chamber last year, and they couldn't have been nicer about it. And cheap, too."

"I know. And the same for the Brookview. That agreement will have to be renegotiated come March, and I doubt they will be as accommodating. Angelica actually negotiated a reduction from what the Chamber had been paying when—" She stumbled when it came to naming names. She wasn't about to say Angelica's predecessor's moniker aloud. "When the last contract was inked."

Pixie nodded.

Tricia swallowed before asking, "What do you think my chances of winning are?"

Pixie looked chagrined. "Not as good as they were before Russ Smith stepped up to the plate. He looks like Mr. Moderate, while you look like a spend-a-holic and Porter looks like a skinflint."

"That was my impression, too."

"Well, buck up," Pixie said encouragingly. "If it comes to it, you don't really need the hassle."

"I don't," Tricia agreed. "But . . ." She let out a frustrated breath. "I sort of wanted to show the world that . . ." She let the sentence trail off.

"That you're as good as—and successful as—your sister?"

Tricia's shoulders slumped. "Yes."

"That's pure horse-hockey. The only person who might think you aren't is you. And if anyone else does, they're jackasses. One thing I've learned over the years is the only real person you're competing against in the esteem race is yourself. Sure, Angelica has a lot of businesses, and makes a boatload of money—probably more than you—but do you really need it? Would it make you happy to work yourself into an early grave without a minute to sit back, relax, read, and pet your cat?"

When she put it that way . . . "No."

"Then ya gotta look at the situation differently. If you win, you win. If you lose, you don't win—but that don't make you a loser, either."

Pixie's simple way of looking at things made a lot of sense.

Tricia let out another breath, but this one wasn't quite so filled with frustration. "Maybe I will have another cup of coffee."

"There you go. Since we don't open for another half hour, sit back, relax, pet your cat, and maybe thank your lucky stars for all the wonderful things you got, and the terrific people in your life."

"Like you?" Tricia asked, and smiled.

"Yeah, like me. I'm a gem. No brag; just fact," Pixie said in all seriousness.

"That you are," Tricia agreed.

Just then, the door burst open and Mr. Everett entered with a smile on his lips. "Good morning, ladies. Would you like to see more pictures of Charlie?"

"Sure thing," Pixie said. "Go hang up your coat and let me get you a cup of coffee. Tricia's gonna have one, too—and she's going to pet her cat."

Suddenly Miss Marple was there at Tricia's feet, looking up at her with hopeful eyes that spelled k-i-t-t-y s-n-a-c-k. *"Yow?"*

"Yes, you may have a treat," Tricia said, and retrieved the bag of snacks she kept under the sales counter and headed for the reader's nook. Soon the four of them were assembled, with cups of coffee, a cat on Tricia's lap, and Mr. Everett's cell phone to pass around so they could admire new photos of Charlie sleeping, eating, and placidly sitting on Grace's lap. And for a few moments, winning the Chamber election didn't seem quite *that* important.

Booked for Lunch was nearly deserted, with only a couple of stragglers nursing cups of coffee at the counter, when Tricia arrived just after two that afternoon. As usual, Angelica was seated in the back corner booth, waiting for her. "There you are." She sounded much more cheerful than she had some five hours before. "How's your day going?"

Tricia slid into the booth and shrugged out of her jacket. "Slow. I'll be happy when the holidays finally arrive and business picks up."

"I'll be glad when they're over and things slow down," Angelica admitted.

Molly arrived to take their orders. "What can I get you ladies?"

"The soup of the day; a bowl, please." Angelica turned her attention to Tricia. "It's Tommy's own recipe: potato and sausage."

"It sounds rather heavy," Tricia commented.

"But appropriate, given the raw November weather," Angelica explained. "Have a bowl. It's got enough protein to get you through until dinnertime, and you won't need a sandwich."

"Potato sausage soup it is," Tricia agreed, and Molly nodded, heading for the kitchen.

"So, have you decided on what you're going to do to win the Chamber election?" Angelica asked.

"I thought my strategy was to hand out the swag bags."

"Have you got any left?"

"A few."

"Then why don't you visit some of the members who weren't at the meeting?"

"Like who?"

"Nikki Brimfield-Smith."

"Do you honestly think she'd vote for me over Russ?"

"She'd vote for anybody over Russ—that is, if she wants him to pay more attention to her and their son."

"Good point," Tricia admitted. "Who else?"

"Toni Bennett didn't make it to the meeting."

Toni owned and managed the local co-op that sold antiques and vintage items. Pixie was one of their best customers when it came to vintage clothing.

"Her husband, Jim, wasn't there, either. Hit her and maybe she'll talk to Jim. You can at least cajole her into attending next week's special election meeting to cast her vote."

"I suppose."

"And it wouldn't hurt for you to at least call every member—especially those outside the Main Street corridor. They have to believe you have their best interests at heart if they're going to vote for you over Chauncey."

"That's a good idea," Tricia agreed, but she wasn't exactly enthusiastic at the prospect. She'd made hundreds of cold calls to potential donors during her days at the nonprofit corporation back in Manhattan, but she hadn't enjoyed the task. Begging wasn't really her style.

"Any other pieces of advice?"

Angelica shook her head. "Anybody with any brains can see that gutting the Chamber would be a mistake. Your biggest competition is Russ. As a centrist, he's straddling the line. Saving money but keeping up appearances is enticing for business owners strapped for cash. And people like him a lot better than they like old crabby-butt Chauncey."

That was true.

"That said," Angelica uttered, and leaned forward, "word is that Chauncey's already got Mary calling everyone on the Chamber list."

"Really? From her expression this morning, I didn't think she liked the idea of him being Chamber president."

"Think about it. If she and he are a little iffy with their relationship, having him take on more responsibility—and being less available—might give her the perfect excuse to call off their engagement."

"Mary's not that devious."

"She could be getting desperate. I heard she may actually be quite eager to give back the ring."

"Who told you that? Frannie?"

"Who else knows everyone and everything that goes on in this village?"

Pixie was a close second, but she didn't tell tales the way Frannie did.

"Did Mary confide in her?"

"No, but they go to the same manicurist. And that's another thing, Chauncey thinks it's a waste of time—and more importantly money—for women to get their hair and nails done. What a grump. I know he was kind to her when she broke her leg, but so were a lot of other people—ourselves included—and she didn't promise to marry any of us."

"Since I'm not looking for a spouse, that's probably a good thing," Tricia said as Molly approached with two steaming bowls of soup on a tray.

"Here you go," she said, and set the bowls before them, leaving soup spoons and little packets of oyster crackers. "Eat hearty."

"Thanks," the sisters chorused.

They plunged their spoons into the soup and tasted it. Tricia swallowed, her eyes widening in delight. "Boy, is that good."

"Didn't I tell you?" Angelica practically gloated as she picked up her crackers and tore open the cellophane. "Now, it just so happens I have a list of all the Chamber members' names, addresses, and phone numbers." She picked up an envelope from beside her on the seat and handed it to Tricia. "Your assignment is to—"

"I know, I know."

"Those not at the meeting are highlighted in yellow."

"Thank you," Tricia said, not at all enthusiastic, and took another spoonful of her soup—the taste at least cheered her somewhat. "Any other orders?"

Angelica frowned. "Sell yourself. You are the best choice for Chamber president, and I'm not saying that just because you're my sister. You have greatness in you that hasn't yet been tapped. I have nothing but confidence in you."

Nice as that was to hear, Tricia loathed the idea of actively campaigning for the job. And though reluctant as she was to fight for it, she agreed with Angelica. In her heart of hearts, she felt she *was* the right person for the job.

"Now let's talk about something fun," Angelica said, before taking in another spoonful of soup. "Me!"

Tricia smiled. It felt good that the sisters were back on an even keel.

But how long would that last?

TWELVE

**Tricia parked** her car in the side parking lot, got out, and opened her umbrella, holding it and her head up high as she approached the Antiques Emporium clutching a briefcase full of swag bags—these hastily made and without the box of chocolates. Owner Toni Bennett had resurrected the old Everett's Grocery (once owned by Mr. Everett) and turned it into an antiques arcade with some thirty vendors. There was talk that she might revamp the building's basement to accommodate even more dealers. It was a pleasure to see so many of the businesses in the village prosper.

On that gloomy day, there were few customers in the store, and instead it seemed to be filled mostly with vendors updating their booths for the upcoming holiday season. Tricia bypassed the booths and headed straight for the manager's office, where she found Toni sitting behind her massive, somewhat shabby antique oak desk, staring intently at a spreadsheet plastered across her large computer screen. Tricia rapped on the doorjamb. "Hi, Toni. Have you got a minute?"

Toni looked up from her screen and smiled. "Tricia. It's always a pleasure to see you. What's up?"

Tricia was heartened by the greeting. She hadn't seen Toni since the debacle at her party the Friday before and hoped Ted Harper's untimely death would not become an item of conversation. "I noticed you weren't at the Chamber meeting this morning."

The pert brunette frowned. "I just couldn't get going. But now that I'm primed with five cups of caffeine, I feel like I could jump over the building in a single bound."

Tricia smiled. She liked Toni, who always seemed cheerful.

"Sit down," Toni offered, and Tricia took the seat in front of her desk.

"In case you weren't aware, I'm running for Chamber president."

"I'm so sorry Angelica is leaving. She's done a wonderful job."

"Yes, she has. But if I'm elected, I intend to carry on her agenda."

"I would love to change my brochure to say the Emporium is located in the prettiest village in New Hampshire," Toni hinted.

"I don't think I've ever seen your brochure."

Toni pulled open one of her drawers, retrieved a full-color trifold sheet of heavy-duty stock, and handed it to Tricia. It was very professional-looking, and she said so.

"Thanks. They're distributed throughout the state, and in Vermont, New York, and Massachusetts. Of course, we don't see as many visitors from other states in the winter, thanks to the weather, but a lot of them are on our mailing list. We send out postcards a couple of times a year that can be turned in for a discount."

"Things really seem to be hopping out there," Tricia said, and nodded toward the showroom beyond the office.

"I don't usually let the vendors restock their booths during business hours, but getting ready for the holidays takes so much longer than during the rest of the year, and things are slow this week."

"Are the rumors true that you'll be expanding in the future?"

Toni smiled. "Yes. Jim will soon start converting a good chunk of the basement to accommodate another twenty to twenty-five dealers. Of course, it won't be open until closer to summer. It's hard enough for the vendors to make their rent in the winter, but hopefully we'll have another stupendous summer that will carry them through the doldrums."

"That's great. I've got a lot of ideas on how to further market the village, and I can't wait to tell the members more about it once I'm elected."

"Such as?" Toni asked.

"More advertising. Sponsored ads online. An expanded website." Tricia reached for her briefcase. "To better let members know my platform, my assistant Pixie and I put together a small package." She retrieved one of the last of the original bundles and handed it to Toni.

"How adorable. Are those chocolates?"

"Yes, from the Chocoholic in Nashua."

"Oh, how I wish we had a decent candy shop here in Stoneham. The Coffee Bean has a small selection, but a dedicated shop could sell dozens of different-flavored fudge. Tourists *love* fudge—just like me—not to mention milk and dark chocolate bonbons," she said, and laughed. "Every holiday could be an impetus for visitors to come to Stoneham."

"It's a great idea. Maybe we can recruit such a business."

"I get the credit," Toni quipped.

"If elected, I'll make sure you do," Tricia said, smiling.

Toni laughed. "Okay, then, you've got my vote—even without the chocolates." She sobered and wrinkled her nose. "The truth is, I'm just not a fan of Chauncey Porter. He can be rather . . . terse."

"Oh?"

Toni shook her head. "At your party the other night, he spoke rather disparagingly about you—which was especially galling when he was enjoying your hospitality."

"Oh." Yes, how rude.

"I thought it was terribly tacky of him. Poor Mary Fairchild was quite embarrassed. Jim and I steered clear of Chauncey after that."

Since Toni had mentioned her chief competition, Tricia wrestled over mentioning that Russ Smith had also put in his name for Chamber president, but it didn't seem right not to let Toni know.

"Chauncey is running, but so is Russ Smith."

Toni's eyes widened. "Really? That surprises me."

"Oh?" Tricia asked, playing dumb.

"Everyone knows his wife keeps him on a tight leash. I'm surprised she'd allow it."

"I don't think I was the only one who was surprised when he raised his hand."

"Did he or Chauncey hand out campaign literature?" Toni asked.

Tricia didn't like the description, but she supposed that's exactly what she'd just presented Toni with. "No, although Russ did hand out his business cards in case anyone wanted to call and talk to him about his ideas for the Chamber."

Again, Toni opened her desk drawer, rummaged for a bit, and came up with a rather wrinkled card. "Hmm. Maybe I'll give him a call."

Tricia forced a smile. Had she just risked losing what was supposed to be a promised vote?

"I'd better let you get back to work. I still have a few more stops to make this afternoon."

Toni rose to her feet. "It was great to see you, Tricia. Let me walk you out."

Tricia gathered her umbrella, purse, and briefcase and stood, following Toni out and into the main showroom.

As they headed for the door, Tricia paused to take in a booth that was filled with some rather eclectic pieces of small furniture, most of it vintage or antique. "Oh, this is nice," she said.

Toni stopped and turned, then moved to join Tricia.

Tricia stepped inside the booth, attracted to a marble-topped dresser. On it were an antique pitcher and ewer in brown transferware. "This is pretty." She looked at the price tag. A little steep, but probably well worth the money.

"Yes. It's an antique English washstand. I got to see pictures of the wreck it was before Frannie refinished it."

Tricia straightened. "Frannie? Frannie Armstrong?"

"Yes, she's one of my newest vendors."

"I didn't know she refinished furniture."

"I guess it's something she recently took up. She sure has a gift for it. She even restored the marble. It had a few really bad stains."

"I'm so surprised. I had no idea she was into DIY."

Toni laughed. "She said she needed a second income if she was ever going to get to retire to Hawaii."

Yes, living in the fiftieth state was said to be quite expensive, since just about everything had to be shipped in. But that had been Frannie's dream ever since Tricia had first met her. She eyed the washstand. It would fill the small empty space below the west window of her living room.

She wasn't one to make impulse buys, but . . . "Do you deliver?"

"We can, but there *is* a surcharge," Toni stated.

"That's all right. Is it okay if I buy it now?"

"Of course. I'd be glad to personally ring up the sale for you."

Toni removed the price tag and walked Tricia over to the cash register. She made arrangements for the stand to be delivered to Haven't Got a Clue on Friday afternoon and handed Tricia her receipt.

"I'm so glad I stopped in today," Tricia said.

Toni laughed. "I'll bet Frannie will be ecstatic. It's her biggest sale so far."

Tricia smiled. "Okay. I'll see your deliveryman on Friday."

"And don't be a stranger. There are lots of other wonderful items here that would look perfect in your new home."

"I'll bet," Tricia said, and bade Toni good-bye.

As she walked to the parking lot, Tricia wondered why neither Frannie nor Angelica had told her about Frannie's new hobby. She'd have to ask about it the next time she was in the Cookery.

Tricia returned to her car, consulted the list Angelica had given her, and sighed. Many of the newer members had joined the Chamber but were actually located in Milford and other surrounding towns. Perhaps she'd visit those far-flung members another day. There were three other members closer at hand, and she intended to cross them off the list before the end of the workday.

She started the car and again wished she could just take on the job instead of begging for votes. But she decided that when she arrived at her next destination, she'd freshen her lipstick and put on a smile. At least running for this job, she wouldn't have to kiss any babies . . . except maybe Antonio and Ginny's daughter, Sofia. She smiled. She never minded kissing and being kissed by that sweet girl. And with that thought, Tricia drove out of the parking lot with a much happier heart.

Tricia had once vowed to never again step inside Vamps, the little pornographic literature shop just outside the Stoneham village limits. But its owner, Marshall Cambridge, who usually attended the Chamber events, was one of the names Angelica had highlighted as members who hadn't come to that day's meeting. Tricia didn't even bother bringing along her briefcase with the swag bags as she entered the shop. Thankfully, it was empty, but a buzzer sounding had alerted the owner that a live one had come through the door.

"Well, if it isn't the Village Jinx," Marshall called, and laughed, as he stepped through the beaded curtain that separated his shop from . . . she wasn't quite sure.

Tricia cringed and wished she hadn't bothered to stop in. She didn't like Marshall. She thought of him as a smarmy character, although he was actually quite good-looking—albeit rather short, compared to her ex-husband. And no doubt Marshall would be perfectly happy if the village never sported another hanging basket of flowers, or if the Chamber held its meetings in a cold and drafty warehouse.

She forced a smile. It was beginning to feel like that was the only way she could muster some semblance of pleasure at greeting and talking to some of her less favorite fellow Chamber members. "Hello, Marshall."

"I heard that instead of just finding a stiff, now you've killed someone off—and right in your own living room."

Sometimes it was just plain painful living in a small village where everybody seemed to know everything about you—and rubbed it in, too.

"I didn't kill him. The poor man died from an allergic reaction to something he ate."

That was true enough, yet she had no intention of telling Marshall that poor Ted Harper had ingested a poisonous substance that had been *added* to her mushrooms.

Tricia barreled ahead. "I noticed you weren't at the Chamber meeting this morning."

"No, I had a dentist appointment. I figured it would just be campaign propaganda and thought I could skip it, although now that I know I need a new crown, it sure would have been cheaper to go there than visit the tooth quack."

Tricia hoped he didn't use that description when sitting in the dental chair. She decided to be honest. "I considered it a lost cause asking you to vote for me, but now that I'm here I should probably just report that Chauncey Porter is in the running with an austerity platform, and Russ Smith is running with a middle-of-the-road campaign."

"And what's your shtick?"

"To carry on my sister's legacy—and pretty much do what she's doing now."

Marshall nodded. "Seems to me she's been doing a pretty good job. What's your experience?"

"I volunteered for the Chamber for about six months while my store was in limbo after the fire. I handled just about all the jobs, and boy can I carry those big gold scissors when it comes time to do a ribbon cutting."

"Sarcasm, Tricia?"

"You're not going to vote for me anyway. I wasted my time by coming here." She pivoted to leave.

"Wait," Marshall called.

Tricia turned.

Marshall pursed his lips. "I'm . . . I apologize. It was sleazy of me to call you the Village Jinx. It's gotta hurt."

That it did, although most people called her that *behind* her back. Marshall was one of the few who actually said it to her face.

"Thank you," Tricia said grudgingly.

"For what it's worth, if you're half as good as your sister, you'd be an asset to the Chamber. I've belonged to a few in my time, and the leadership at the Stoneham branch has been exemplary. Things actually get done in this village, and that's good for my business."

"Thank you. I'll pass along your kind words to my sister."

She turned once again to leave, but Marshall's voice stopped her a second time.

"Were you friends with Ted Harper?"

Tricia whirled. "No. I only met him an hour or so before he . . . before he died. Did you know him?"

"I probably shouldn't admit it, but he was a good customer of mine."

Tricia cringed. Poor Frannie. Dating a guy who was into porn.

"Don't look like that. I sell more than just girlie magazines, you know. Like me, Ted loved to read true crime."

Tricia had forgotten that in addition to selling smut, Marshall did have an extensive section dedicated to that subject. "Is there a lot of call for it?"

"I have a few regulars. They like the vintage stuff I stock. It's cheaper to buy the new magazines by subscription."

Was it worth pumping him for information on the dead man?

Why not?

"How well did you know Ted?"

"Enough that he told me a little about his life. Like he had a new lady friend and was about to get lucky."

Did the man *always* have to be so vulgar?

He must have noticed her unhappy expression, for he apologized again. Then he really surprised her. "Do you ever take a day off? Maybe we could have coffee together sometime."

"Why on earth would you want to have coffee with me?"

"Because you're pretty. Because you're smart. And you sure as hell don't seem to take crap from anybody."

Tricia thought about his offer. She didn't really like the man, but was she judging him on what he sold or on his rather abrasive personality?

"I don't take days off."

"All work and no play makes Tricia a dull girl."

"I'm a woman, not a girl."

He sized her up and smiled—not a leer. "You sure don't have to tell me that."

Tricia thought it over. If she did become Chamber president, like her sister, she would probably have to have many impromptu conversations with members and potential members—whether she liked them or not. Maybe she should start practicing now.

"Well, I do have two employees, so I can usually get away for short periods of time now and again."

"Great. I don't open on Sundays. How about then? Say, one o'clock at the Coffee Bean?"

Tricia loved their coffee, and the ambiance was perfect for everything else they sold, but with customers coming and going, it was not conducive to private conversations. "How about the Bookshelf Diner?"

"That would've been my next choice."

Tricia shrugged. "I guess so."

"Don't sound so thrilled. I wouldn't want you to have a stroke or something," he said, but there was amusement in his tone.

"All right. I'll see you there on Sunday at one."

"Great. Until then." He held out a hand, indicating the exit. Was she being dismissed?

Tricia turned and left the shop, the annoying buzzer sounding as she passed through the door.

Had she just made a very big mistake?

THIRTEEN

Angelica paused in the act of pouring the first martini into a chilled glass, looking horrified. "You made a date with whom?"

Tricia felt weary after her day of announcing her candidacy, then making personal visits and phone calls to Chamber members. She'd practically been salivating in anticipation of cocktail hour. "Marshall Cambridge, and it's not a date, it's coffee."

"Coffee can be a date," Angelica insisted. "I just don't understand what on earth you could possibly see in that smarmy little man." She handed Tricia the glass and poured another from the pitcher.

Tricia sighed. "You have coffee and meetings with people you're not especially fond of all the time."

"That's business."

"Well, this meeting sure isn't going to be for pleasure. He called me the Village Jinx—right to my face."

"And you still agreed to go out with him?"

"I'm not going out with him. And if it will make you feel better, I'll pay for my own coffee."

"You don't have to get *crazy*," Angelica declared, and took her first sip of gin and vermouth. "I'm just very surprised."

"No more surprised than me. He said I was pretty—and smart—probably to soften me up."

"Well, at least he noticed you've got a brain. I wouldn't have given him that much credit."

Tricia shrugged and took a hearty gulp of her martini. After the day she'd had, she deserved it.

"There must have been another reason why you said yes."

"Maybe it was because he told me a little about Ted Harper. He might even know more."

"What could he possibly know about poor dead Ted?"

"That he was a lover of true crime. Apparently he bought a lot of it from Marshall."

"Much too gory for my taste," Angelica remarked.

"Mine, too."

"So you intend to pump him for more information?"

"Not really. As Grant suggested, someone was probably trying to make trouble for me, not targeting Ted."

"If you say so."

"I do."

"And you're going to the Bookshelf Diner? Why aren't you coming to Booked for Lunch?"

"So you and Molly can hang on our every word? Forget that. I figured we'd have a little more anonymity at the diner. Besides, I haven't been there in ages."

"You might be going there more often once the Chamber's contract with the Brookview ends."

"Is that a threat?"

"Not necessarily. But you'll be negotiating with the catering manager, not me."

"And you wouldn't put in a good word?"

"An awful lot of Chamber members seemed perfectly happy to change venues. I may just let them do it."

"Out of spite?" Tricia asked.

"Out of economic necessity." Angelica took another sip of her drink, and then turned to poke around in her cupboard. "I got some jam samples from a possible new distributor. Want to try them on crackers?"

"Why not? What are the flavors?"

"Sweet—like peach and apricot—and laced with jalapeños."

"I once had red pepper jelly. Something like that?"

"Exactly." Angelica dumped out the rest of the crackers from the sleeve she'd opened the night before, and then scrounged a couple of spreaders. Tricia opened the jar of peach jalapeño jam and spread a thin layer on one of the crackers, then sampled it. "Oh, my, that's good."

Angelica slathered a thicker layer on her cracker and practically devoured it. "Oh, that one's a keeper." They sampled the other jar of jelly, and Angelica decided she'd stock both in the Cookery.

"So who's this new distributor?" Tricia asked.

"Someone in Milford, actually. She used to make tiny batches for her family, but was encouraged to start making it commercially. She now makes it in a licensed kitchen, and voilà!"

"How did you hear about her?"

"She dropped the jars off at the store. I really would like to encourage more entrepreneurs. You should, too, when you become Chamber president."

"As a matter of fact, Toni mentioned that Stoneham needs a candy shop. She said tourists love fudge."

"You could look into it for the village. I mean, all you have to do is make a few calls. It would show the members you're interested in keeping the Chamber strong."

"I could," Tricia said rather half-heartedly. "And speaking of entrepreneurs, how long has Frannie been in the furniture business?"

"What?" Obviously Angelica knew nothing of her employee's new business venture.

"She has a booth at the Antiques Emporium. I bought one of her pieces this afternoon. A charming English washstand. It's going to go perfectly in my living room."

"When does she have time to run a business? She works for me six days a week."

"She told Toni she needs the money to retire to Hawaii."

"Well, I knew that. But she hasn't talked about it so much lately." Angelica scowled. "Do you think she deserves a raise?"

"That's up to you. I know what you pay her, and it's more than fair."

"I do have June working on Sundays, but Frannie insisted she wanted to work on Saturdays—probably for the extra money."

"Don't worry about it. If Frannie had a complaint, I'm sure she'd voice it. She's never been shy about that sort of thing in the past."

Angelica sighed. "I guess you're right. When do I get to see this washstand?"

"Rats. I should have taken a picture of it. It'll be delivered on Friday afternoon."

"Then I guess I'll plan on having dinner with you on Friday night."

"Can do. If I let Pixie close the shop, I can make something a little more elaborate than grilled cheese sandwiches and canned tomato soup."

"Yes. She should get used to doing that, since you'll be busy with Chamber business on a regular basis come January."

"If I win."

"I'm pretty confident."

Pretty? Before the meeting that day, she'd been absolutely sure.

Tricia spread a thin layer of jelly on another cracker and wondered if once she went home for the evening, she should start researching the candy business.

Tricia entered Haven't Got a Clue the next morning with a sheaf of papers filled with raw data on the profitability of candy making. She still had more research to do that day—especially finding potential vendors—and wondered how she should present it to the Chamber members if she went through with the plan. Probably after the election was over. That way they would be able to see that she truly did have the village's—and the Chamber's—best interests at heart, and it wouldn't look like a grandstand play.

And if she didn't win?

She didn't want to think about it.

Pixie arrived ten minutes early with a smile on her face and singing "With a Song in My Heart" off-key. She'd never win a karaoke contest.

"Mailman's on his way," Pixie said as she shrugged out of the sleeves of her faux fur coat. "He was at the Patisserie when I passed. Looked like he was buying one of those giant sugar cookies with the colored jimmies. Made me want to stop and get something, but I decided I didn't need to pack on any more pounds, what with the holidays coming up and everything. I'll get the coffee going," she said, and snagged the pot on her way to hang up her coat.

"Good morning to you, too!" Tricia called cheerfully.

A minute later, Pixie stood in front of the beverage center, tipping coffee into the grounds basket.

"Do you think Stoneham needs a candy store?" Tricia asked.

"Candy? I'm trying *not* to think about cookies, and you bring up candy?"

"For the tourists."

"Tourists do like fudge—and saltwater taffy, but I think that goes over better at seaside towns." She hit the on switch, and the machine started to gurgle.

"I was talking to Toni Bennett yesterday, and she suggested the next Chamber president should recruit a candy shop," Tricia said.

"I'll bet Mr. E would be their best customer. He'd probably buy Grace a couple-pound box or two every week. He's such a sweetheart—and he has a sweet tooth, but not like mine." Pixie grinned broadly, showing off her gold canine.

Tricia couldn't help herself and laughed.

Just then, the shop door opened, the bell rang, and the mailman entered. "Mail call!"

"Hi, Randy. I hope you brought more than bills," Pixie said.

"Don't kill the messenger," he said, and handed her the small stack of envelopes.

The two of them said the same thing just about every day—and every day it made Tricia cringe. She was sure they never considered it a veiled reference to her being known as the Village Jinx.

"See you tomorrow," he called, and headed out the door.

Pixie brought out the sugar, nondairy creamer, napkins, and paper cups for the customers, and their own china mugs, setting them on the counter. "So you're going to find us a candy store?"

"I was thinking about it. And by the way, did you know Frannie Armstrong had a booth over at the Antiques Emporium?"

"Oh, sure. We talked about it for a long time last summer back at the Wine and Jazz Festival. She asked me if I'd look for small pieces of crappy furniture when I go on my tag sale runs. We even went out together a few times to look. So she's finally got enough stock to get going, huh?"

"Apparently. I bought a piece yesterday. It'll be delivered tomorrow afternoon."

"Oooh, can't wait to see it."

"What do you suppose made her choose furniture?"

Pixie shrugged. "I guess her mom and dad did it for a hobby, and that's where she learned the ropes. When I first got out of stir, I thought about working for a tailor, but they pay ditz, so I was glad I learned other, more lucrative skills."

"You've certainly been an asset to me."

"Aw, thanks, Tricia." She poured coffee for the two of them. "So, where are you and Ginny going for lunch today?"

"Oh, dear. I forgot it was Thursday. We'll probably just go to Booked for Lunch."

"Ha-ha! You don't have to pay when you go there."

"I usually do when Ginny's my guest." Tricia didn't want to sound like a freeloader, so maybe they should patronize the Bookshelf Diner. But Booked for Lunch was so convenient—just doors away from where both women worked.

The shop door opened once again, and Mr. Everett entered.

"Good morning," both Tricia and Pixie called. Mr. Everett offered a wan smile.

"I'll hang up my coat and be with you in a few moments."

They watched him trudge to the back of the shop.

"No spring in his step today. I wonder what's wrong," Pixie said.

"I'm sure we'll find out."

Mr. Everett returned to the front of the shop, looking hangdog.

"Is everything okay?" Tricia asked.

Mr. Everett shrugged. "Charlie didn't seem to want to eat this morning."

"Sometimes Miss Marple gets that way, too. She used to love canned tuna, and now she often turns up her nose at it."

"I hope you're right, Ms. Miles."

"How about a nice cup of coffee?" Pixie offered. "The world seems better when you've had a fresh cup of joe."

Mr. Everett's smile was tentative. "Thank you, Pixie. I'd like that."

Once Pixie had poured another cup, the three of them took their coffee and retired to the reader's nook. As though sensing the old man needed comforting, Miss Marple joined them and settled on Mr. Everett's lap.

"Now, what seems to be the trouble with Charlie?" Tricia asked.

Mr. Everett shook his head, absently petting the store's mascot. "He's drinking a lot of water, but he played with Grace for a bit this morning, batting at the feather wand. Perhaps I'm just overly worried about him because of his age."

"I expect that's it," Tricia said, not quite sure she believed it.

"He is a wonderful boy, and he seems to have settled right in. I can't believe we waited so long to have a pet."

"I'm glad he's bringing you so much pleasure." Now to hope he wouldn't bring the old man unwanted pain.

Pixie and Mr. Everett took their lunch break early, which allowed Tricia to meet with Ginny at Booked for Lunch at just after one. Ginny was usually late, but seldom took more than half an hour for her noon meal, so Tricia knew she'd be back to her store in good time.

"Hi," Ginny called, sounding cheerful. She whipped off her little white beret and shrugged out of her scarf and jacket, tossing them on the bench seat before sitting down across from Tricia. "Boy, it got cold fast this year. And where did the time go? Next thing you know, we'll be toasting with champagne and singing 'Auld Lang Syne.'"

"We'll be so busy at the shop—at least on weekends—that the rest of the year will just whiz by."

"Yeah, and you'll be twice as busy come January when you take over as Chamber president."

"If I win," Tricia said demurely.

"You're a shoo-in," Ginny said, and picked up the menu, not that either of them needed it. They usually ordered the same couple of items. "Everybody I've talked to is voting for you. And thanks for the chocolate in the swag bags. I was selfish and didn't share one piece of it."

"You weren't at the meeting. How did you get one?"

"That doll Pixie gave Antonio two and asked him to bring one to me. You know, we really need a candy store in Stoneham."

"That's what Toni Bennett over at the Antiques Emporium said."

"Too bad one couldn't open before Christmas. When in doubt, a box of chocolates will always be a welcome gift—at least to me!"

Molly arrived at their table. She knew Ginny didn't have a lot of time to spare. "What'll you ladies have?"

"I'll go for the soup of the day and the half chicken salad sandwich," Ginny said.

"What is the soup?" Tricia asked.

"Chicken rice."

Tricia wrinkled her nose. Not that she didn't like chicken rice soup, because every soup Tommy made was good, but she just wasn't in the mood for it that day. "How about a BLT?"

"With chips?" Molly asked skeptically.

"Of course." Tricia knew Ginny would help her eat them.

"Be right back," Molly said, and gathered their menus.

"Whoa—Tricia ordered chips, that's a big surprise, but not as big as you dating Marshall Cambridge."

"Who told you that?" Tricia said, looking around to make sure no one was listening in on their conversation.

"Angelica. She told me you have a lunch date on Sunday."

"Coffee," Tricia stressed. "It's just coffee."

"Coffee can be a date. But I'm a little surprised you're going with Marshall." She shuddered. "Ick—he sells porn."

"That isn't all he sells."

"I wouldn't know. I'll probably never darken his door."

Did Ginny think less of Tricia because she *had* entered Vamps?

Tricia decided to change the subject. "So, what big project are you working on today?"

"Next summer's jazz festival. We almost broke even this year, and believe it or not my employer"—she mimicked the way Antonio spoke of his stepmother and boss—"was ecstatic. I learned so much—and a lot of it was what *not* to do next year—that I know we'll make a profit, which is fabulous. Sometimes it takes three or four years to just break even."

If anybody could do it, it was Ginny.

"I hear Frannie's got a new hobby," she said, and looked toward the back of the café, no doubt hoping her order would arrive quickly. Sometimes Tricia felt like these weekly lunches were stolen time.

"Yes. I bought an antique washstand. It's whitewashed with a marble top."

"Sounds cute. You could make it your dry bar."

"I hadn't thought about that." After Ted Harper's death, Tricia had half decided she'd never entertain again.

Molly arrived with their lunches and bade them to "eat hearty."

Ginny picked up her sandwich and immediately took a bite. "Tommy makes the best chicken salad. He puts little slivered almonds in it. To die for!" she said, and took another bite.

Tricia ate one of her chips and tried to decide how she'd approach her sandwich, which was much taller than she'd anticipated. "What else is new?"

"We've got a prankster here in the village."

"Tell me about it. Someone left a big pile of doggy doo on my back step, and my store's been egged. Not vicious damage, but difficult to clean in freezing temps. What have you experienced?"

"My windshield was egged, too. And someone—and I'll bet it was a teenaged boy; they can be so obnoxious—stuffed a russet potato up the tailpipe of my car. We had to have it towed to the shop when it wouldn't start. I was late to pick up Sofia at day care—it was a real pain in the butt. I'm only grateful it wasn't an expensive repair."

"When did this happen?"

"Yesterday afternoon."

"And the eggs?"

"That was Monday."

"Did you report it to Grant Baker?"

"Not personally. I called the station and was told they couldn't spare the manpower to investigate and that I should come in person to file a report."

"Will you?"

Ginny shrugged. "I don't know when I'll have the time. There was no real harm done either time. It was more aggravating than anything else."

Yes, it was.

"I wonder who else has been hit?"

Ginny shrugged. "Funny enough, I looked around the parking lot but didn't see any other cars that were egged."

Tricia frowned. It seemed odd that she, Angelica, and Ginny had been targeted. Or was she just being paranoid?

She hoped so.

FOURTEEN

Tricia returned to Haven't Got a Clue just before two o'clock and found a stranger standing at the cash desk with a couple of nasty-looking cartons sitting on the glass case. Pixie stood behind the counter while Mr. Everett looked on. It wasn't often that someone stopped in and tried to sell a box of moldy old paperbacks from a dank basement.

"Here's the owner now," Pixie said as Tricia unbuttoned her coat.

The older man, who wore a black Greek fisherman's cap, turned. "This lady here said you're the buyer, and that only you could decide whether to take my stuff or not."

"That's right," Tricia said. When (and if) she took on the Chamber presidency, she'd have to give Pixie more authority. Maybe now would be a good test. "Let me take off my coat and we'll have a look."

By the time Tricia returned to the front of the store, Pixie had donned a pair of reading glasses and had emptied the boxes. She stepped back. "It's all yours, Tricia."

"Why don't you take a look first?"

Pixie nodded. Her expression was impassive, but Tricia could tell by the look in her brown eyes that they might just have a treasure trove in front of them. Pixie inspected each book, looking at the copyright dates and edition numbers, inspecting the spines and dust covers. She looked up at Tricia, who nodded for her to continue. She watched as Pixie went through every book and sorted them into three piles, just as Tricia would have done: For sure, maybe, and no way!

Pixie removed her glasses. "I need to speak with my colleague for a moment," she said dispassionately.

"Sure," the guy said.

Tricia and Pixie retreated to the back of the store, with Pixie keeping her back to the customer.

"Oh my God," she nearly squealed, but in a hushed tone. "I could kill to own some of those books."

"Well, we don't want that," Tricia said.

"A figure of speech," Pixie whispered.

"From what I saw, I agree with you. What do you think a fair price would be?"

Pixie looked pensive. "Considering our overhead—and I'm only guessing, because I'm not sure what you're paying for utilities—I think fifty would be a fair price. We should lowball, maybe thirty-five, to keep him interested, and then make our best offer."

"That sounds reasonable. Why don't you do the negotiating."

"Really?"

"Yes. If I get the job at the Chamber, you might have to do more of this in the future."

Pixie's eyes widened, and she looked about ready to jump for joy. But then she took a breath and composed herself. "Okay."

She turned and headed for the front of the store, as confident as a supermodel on a catwalk. A bemused Tricia followed.

Pixie resumed her place behind the sales counter. "I'm afraid we wouldn't be interested in these books. They've been stored in adverse conditions." She placed the no-way pile of books back in the first box. "We might be able to find customers for these." She indicated the other two piles of books. "What are you asking for them?"

The man stood a little straighter. "Make an offer."

Pixie shook her head. "I wouldn't want to insult you. Please, tell us what you think they're worth."

"I think they're worth a couple hundred bucks."

"Oh, well. Then I'm afraid we won't be able to do business." She began to pack the books back into the second box.

"Wait a minute. What do you think they're worth?"

Pixie shrugged. "Thirty-five?"

"Now you are insulting me. They're worth at least a hundred."

Pixie shook her head and continued to repack the boxes.

"Okay, seventy-five."

Another book went into the second box.

"Sixty?"

Pixie placed the last book into the box and pushed it forward. "Thank you for thinking of us. Maybe we can do business some other time."

"Fifty, and that's my final offer," the man said, sounding just a teensy bit angry.

Pixie gazed at the box for a few long moments, looking bored, then she sighed and glanced in Tricia's direction. "What do you think?"

Tricia pretended to mull over the offer, then finally nodded.

"Very well. We'll probably take a beating, but fifty it is." She began to unpack the box once more. "Ms. Miles, would you be so kind as to get the checkbook so we can pay this gentleman?"

"I'd like cash."

Pixie stopped unpacking. "We don't usually deal in cash."

"Cash or nothing," the man said.

"Perhaps you could write out a receipt," Tricia suggested.

Again Pixie sighed. "Very well."

She ought to get an Academy Award for her performance.

She bent down and retrieved a receipt book. She wrote out the transaction and asked the man to sign. He did, but whether he used his own name they didn't know or really care. Then Pixie opened the register and took out the cash, counting it into the man's palm.

"There you go. Thank you for visiting us today."

The man stowed the money in his wallet, took his leftovers, and bade them good-bye. The bell over the door jingled as he left the store. Once he was out of earshot, Pixie did squeal and actually jumped!

"Holy smoke! Did you see those books?"

Tricia laughed, while Mr. Everett looked subdued.

"Who were you channeling?" Tricia asked.

"I don't know—just some dame I heard on TV. Did I do okay?"

"You did great, and you got us a great buy on those books."

"I was sure I was going to give myself away."

"Will we be offering these titles in the store or online?" Mr. Everett asked.

"Online. Would you like to put them in the inventory and write out the descriptions?" Tricia asked.

Mr. Everett nodded. "I'd be happy to do so, Ms. Miles."

"Let me carry the box to the dumbwaiter for you," Pixie said.

"And mess up your pretty sweater? No. I'll do it," Tricia said. The box really was cruddy. "And you've more than earned your pay for the week."

Pixie positively beamed.

"Why don't we transfer the books to a nicer box," Mr. Everett suggested. "Then we can discard this moldy one."

"Good idea. I think there's one in the back of the shop."

"I'll get it." Mr. Everett took off and returned moments later with a clean box, and he and Pixie repacked the books. "I'll put this in the recycle bin."

"Thank you, Mr. Everett."

He started for the back of the shop, and Tricia hefted the new box, following him to the back of the store and setting it in the dumbwaiter. She sent it down to the basement and was about to head back to the front of the store when Mr. Everett reentered through the back door.

"Uh, Ms. Miles. There's something outside I think you should see," he said gravely.

More doggy doo?

Mr. Everett held the door open for Tricia. She looked around before stepping outside. What was it she was supposed to see?

She turned back to Mr. Everett—and then understood what he'd meant. In big purple letters, sloppily spray-painted on the back of her tidy brick building was the word *JINX*.

Finding her building tagged had put a damper on the rest of the afternoon. Tricia dutifully reported the damage to not only the police but her insurance company. Was she covered? They weren't sure. They'd get back to her. Meanwhile, Pixie hit the Internet and found a company that specialized in graffiti removal. They'd just have to wait to see if insurance would pay for it or not.

But as Tricia entered the Cookery later that evening and headed for the stairs to Angelica's apartment, she was determined not to start happy hour with the bad news first. Pixie deserved her success story to be told in a cheerful tone.

"You should have seen her in action," Tricia told her sister as Angelica poured their drinks.

"I always knew she had it in her. And to think you were reluctant to hire her."

"That was before I knew her. I can't say I've ever regretted hiring her—and I was just so proud of her today."

"You did take a chance hiring an ex-con, but it paid off."

"I knew she wasn't a thief when I hired her." No, she'd been a lady of the evening, but according to her parole officer, Pixie had never been accused of stealing. "I swear, she was walking on air for the rest of the afternoon. It was so fun to see someone that happy." Tricia sighed. "I wish I could say the same of Mr. Everett."

"Oh?"

Tricia nodded. "Charlie wouldn't eat this morning. Poor Mr. Everett worried about him all day. He called Grace several times, and she reported that Charlie was sleeping under their dining room table for most of the day."

"Poor kitty. Do you think there's anything wrong with him?"

"I don't know. Sometimes Miss Marple has an off day where she does nothing but sleep."

"I thought that's all cats did every day," Angelica said, and took another sip of her drink.

Tricia managed a weak laugh. "You're right. But I wouldn't be surprised if Mr. Everett comes in late after taking Charlie to the vet."

"Better safe than sorry," Angelica agreed. "Did anything else happen today?"

"I had my weekly lunch with Ginny."

"How is my dear girl?"

"Like you haven't spoken to her at least once today?"

"Um, I may have. Strictly about work."

"Uh-huh. Anyway, did you know her car had been egged, and that someone stuck a spud up her tailpipe?"

Angelica sobered. "No, I didn't."

"And today, after Pixie's triumph, Mr. Everett discovered that someone had tagged the back of my building."

"What did it say, or was it just gibberish?" Angelica asked, as though dreading the answer.

"What else? 'Jinx.'"

Angelica winced. "How bad is it?"

"I'd say the person wasn't all that tall—and not very good at street art."

"Did you report it?"

"Yes. To the Stoneham police and my insurance company."

"And?"

"Neither seemed all that interested."

Angelica reached for a cracker and a piece of cheese that she'd set out as an appetizer. "I don't like this."

"Neither do I, but you must admit, so far this vandalism has been rather benign."

"Yes, but who knows when it could escalate?"

"Like the demands of your blackmailer?"

"Don't go there," Angelica warned.

Tricia sipped her drink.

"Why do you think Antonio or Ginny didn't tell me about these incidents?"

"Probably because they know you're preoccupied about something and they don't want to worry you."

Angelica looked thoughtful. "I wonder if I ought to hire a security firm to watch out for all of us."

"That would take a lot of money."

"I've got a lot of money, and I want my family to be safe."

"Why don't I talk to Grant first?"

"Did you speak to him today?"

"No. Just one of his officers. He probably doesn't even know about it. I'm sure he's got other, bigger problems than a report of graffiti."

"Would you call him tonight?"

Tricia shook her head. "Tomorrow morning will be good enough."

"Let me know what he says."

"I will."

Tricia reached for a cracker and then decided against it. She really wasn't very hungry. With so much on her mind, she wondered how long it would be before her appetite returned.

FIFTEEN

After a restless night, Tricia got up early, made a pot of coffee, and practically paced the floor until eight o'clock, when she called Chief Baker's office only to be told that he was attending a meeting out of town and wouldn't be back until at least ten. She hung up the phone and left a message on his personal phone and hoped he'd check it sooner rather than later.

Feeling antsy, Tricia made another pot, and drank nearly all of it before she went downstairs to Haven't Got a Clue to begin her workday. Miss Marple accompanied her but immediately sought out her perch behind the cash desk to take a well-deserved nap. So much for having company.

Tricia started yet another pot of coffee for Pixie, Mr. Everett, and whatever customers arrived that day, and figured she had at least one thing to look forward to: the delivery of her antique washstand. It would be such a pretty addition to her living room. Perhaps on Sunday morning, when she had a few hours to kill before the shop opened, she'd go through the box of bric-a-brac she hadn't yet found new homes for and decide what should grace the stand.

It was pleasant to have something else to think about besides blackmailers and pranksters.

Pixie arrived, a minute late and breathless. "Sorry," she called, and practically flew to the back of the shop to hang up her coat. "I popped a button on my blouse and couldn't find the right color thread to fix it." That seemed hard to believe, since Pixie had once told her she had several thousand reels of thread. Then again, maybe that was why she couldn't find the right shade of orange to match the vintage top that went with a matching skirt. The color was a bright spot on an otherwise gloomy day.

Pixie arrived at the front of the shop and headed for the coffeemaker. "Can I pour you a cup?"

"No, thanks. I've already had more than my usual caffeine allotment for the day."

"So soon?"

Tricia nodded.

"Anything on tap for the day?" Pixie asked as she fixed her coffee.

"Just my furniture delivery this afternoon."

"I thought we might want to start planning our Christmas decorations. Or do you want to just do what we did last year?"—and by the tone of her voice it was obvious that Pixie wanted to do something entirely different.

"Sure; but let's wait until Mr. Everett comes in."

"Oh, he won't care. He's a man," Pixie said, as if that explained everything.

She was probably right.

The shop door opened and Randy the mailman once again sang out, "Mail call!"

"I hope you brought more than just bills," Pixie answered as he handed her the small bundle.

"Don't kill the messenger," he said, and laughed. "See you tomorrow."

"Bye." Pixie handed the mail to Tricia, then she and her cup headed for the shelves on the north wall, which were in need of straightening.

Tricia sighed and went through the envelopes. Bills, credit card offers, and several publisher catalogs. On the bottom of the stack was a copy of the latest edition of the *Stoneham Weekly News*. Tricia seldom read it. Usually she glanced at the top story before tossing it into the recycle box. That day her mouth dropped as she read the headline out loud.

"'Death Visits Bookseller Again'? *'Death Visits Bookseller Again'*?" she repeated even louder.

Pixie turned. "What?"

But her breath caught in her throat and Tricia couldn't seem to speak.

Pixie made it across the shop in three big steps and snatched the paper out of Tricia's hands. "Let me read it first and see if it's fit for your eyes."

Tricia stood there, her mouth open, as Pixie's eyes shifted from left to right while she took in the article. "Oh, dear. Oh, dear."

Tricia slapped her palms against her cheeks. "You'd better read it out loud."

"Only if you sit down," Pixie cautioned. "I don't want you having a stroke or something and keeling over."

"Is it that bad?"

"It's pretty bad," Pixie admitted.

Feeling rather shaky, Tricia made her way to the reader's nook and practically fell into the first chair. Pixie took one opposite. She cleared her throat and began to read.

"'There's a reason some people call Tricia Miles, owner of the Haven't Got a Clue bookstore, the village jinx. She has a penchant for finding dead bodies.'"

"Oh, no!" Tricia wailed.

"'In this most recent case, however, the body in question died in her own home after eating food Miles prepared in her own kitchen.'" Pixie wrinkled her nose. "He could have at least called you Ms. Miles, and he should have left out that second *own*."

"This is no time to play critic," Tricia admonished.

Pixie started reading again. "'In this instance, the body was a guest at a dinner party Miles threw to celebrate the ostentatious remodel of her home.'" Again Pixie stopped. "For one, it wasn't a dinner party—sloppy reporting right there, because he was actually *at* the party—and two, what's so ostentatious about your apartment? I think your new digs are positively gorgeous."

Tricia groaned. "I don't think I want to hear any more."

"Want me to just read the highlights?"

No! She didn't, but Tricia supposed she had better listen. Maybe there were grounds for a libel lawsuit. "Okay," she said as she fell limply against the back of the upholstered chair.

"Let's see . . . Uh, suspected food poisoning . . . waiting for autopsy toxicological reports . . . Uh, then he kinda lists all the stiffs you've been acquainted with. Want me to read them to you?"

"No, thank you. Unfortunately, I clearly remember them all." Tricia let out a long breath. "Why? Why would Russ do this?"

"To shitcan your chances of winning the election, what else?"

"But the paper goes to bed on Mondays."

"Well, he knew you were going to run for the job. I mean, that's what a bunch of people were talking about at the party, right? He was there lapping it all up. He'd probably already decided he was going to make a bid for it himself. What better way to smear your opponent than with the power of the press?"

What indeed?

"What are you going to do about it?"

"I don't know." Confront him with the evidence. Yeah, that's what she'd do. But first she needed to calm down.

"What did Russ say about Ted Harper?"

Pixie consulted the paper once more. "Uh . . . that you claimed you hadn't met the guy before the party."

"Claimed? I never saw the man before in my life. I didn't invite him. He was Frannie's date!"

"It doesn't mention that fact. Makes it sound kind of sneaky or something, huh?"

Sneaky? Maybe. Or that Harper might have been a party crasher who hadn't been asked to leave? Tricia wouldn't know until she read the article herself, and she wasn't in a hurry to do so.

"Anything else?"

"Uh, just that before you moved here, Stoneham used to be the safest village in New Hampshire. Uh, it kinda hints that you're responsible for the extended crime wave."

Tricia felt like weeping.

And then the phone rang.

Tricia sat bolt upright and the two of them stared at it.

It rang again.

Pixie got up from her seat and hurried over to the cash desk where the vintage black telephone resided. "Haven't Got a Clue; this is Pixie. How can I—" She went silent. "Yes. Yes!" she said, piqued. "No, you can't speak to her. You should be ashamed of yourself. Good-bye!" She slammed the receiver down on the cradle.

"Who was that?" Tricia asked with dread.

"Um—nobody!" Pixie said, her voice high and squeaky.

The phone rang again.

They both stared at it.

It rang again. And again.

Finally, Pixie picked up the receiver. "Haven't Got a Clue; this is Pixie. How—"

Tricia watched as a plethora of emotions twisted Pixie's features, anger the most apparent one.

"I'm hanging up on you, you mean-mouthed jerk!" Again she slammed the phone down.

The phone immediately rang again.

And again.

"Um, maybe we should switch it over to the answering machine," Pixie suggested.

"Sounds like a good idea," Tricia said, and sank farther back in the chair. She let Pixie take care of it.

Hunching over, Tricia covered her face with her hands, willing herself not to cry and trying to find the intestinal fortitude to make herself read the hack job Russ had done on her.

It took the better part of an hour before Tricia felt she could speak coherently to Russ—she cringed at even the thought of his name, and her cheeks burned with outrage when she thought back to a time when she had actually trusted the jerk. Yes, he'd proved himself to be a jerk on too many occasions. Why had she ever deigned to speak to him after he'd shown his true colors after first dumping her, then stalking her three years before?

It was close to eleven before Tricia marched across Main Street and headed north for the *Stoneham Weekly News*. Yanking open the heavy glass door, she entered.

"Hi, Tricia," called Patty, the paper's receptionist and classified ad-taker, her voice sounding just a tad shaky.

Tricia didn't answer and barreled toward the closed office door.

"You can't go in there! Russ is—"

But nothing was going to stop her. Tricia yanked open the door and stomped into the tiny office.

Russ was immediately on his feet and stepped behind his office chair as though to shield himself from a physical attack. "Hello, Tricia. What brings you here?"

Tricia slapped the by-now wrinkled copy of the paper's current issue onto his desk so hard it made him jump and his half-filled coffee cup tremble.

"What's the meaning of this? Are you trying to smear me so you can win the Chamber presidency?"

Russ gave a feeble laugh. "All's fair in love and politics."

Tricia's glare was icy.

"You wrote this hack job before you announced your candidacy—but you'd already planned to announce your bid to run, right?"

"I was undecided until . . . until the actual meeting."

Tricia didn't believe him for one minute.

"Why would you do this to me? We *were* friends."

"We *used* to be lovers," he reminded her.

"That was a long time ago."

"I haven't forgotten those days."

"And I've done my best to put them out of my mind," she asserted.

Russ took his seat once more, and leaned back, looking more than just a little smug. "Our lives would have been very different if you had taken me back. At least *my* life would be different."

"You dumped me when you thought you would get that job at the *Philadelphia Inquirer*."

"A lapse of judgment, I'll admit."

"And I didn't force you into a relationship with Nikki," Tricia pointed out.

"No, but it was a blatant example of a rebound relationship, and we all know how successful those are."

Should she fight fire with fire? Say that *she* was on the rebound after her divorce from Christopher and that's how she ended up with him? But that wasn't true.

"You're a grown-up. You made your choices—and now you have to live with them. Don't blame me for what you now see as a big mistake. Take your lumps like a man."

Russ bent lower, his eyes narrowed. "She'd bleed me dry. You don't know how nasty she can be."

Tricia had always enjoyed Nikki's company before she became involved with Russ. It was after she started going out with him that she'd undergone a profound personality change. Suspicious; sometimes a shrew. Maybe divorce would be the best thing for both of them. But that didn't concern her.

"You've done your best to ruin my reputation in Stoneham."

He shrugged. "Only with the locals. Chances are it won't hurt your business. Maybe it will even prove beneficial. After all, you make your living promoting murder."

Revulsion roiled through her, and Tricia had to hold herself back from reaching down to slap the arrogant expression from his face.

Russ leaned back in his chair, resting his elbows on the armrests and folding his hands, as self-satisfied as a spider spinning its web for a juicy kill. "Just for the record, I don't even want the damn Chamber presidency. I just want to see you squirm to get it."

Tricia's stomach turned. "What on earth did I ever see in the likes of you?" And with that, she turned, stepped out of the office, and slammed the door behind her. With her head held high, she stalked past Patty and out the door.

* * *

Tricia spent the rest of the morning holed up in her basement office, letting Pixie and Mr. Everett handle the customers—and anyone else who entered the store. Humiliation pressed down on her like a physical weight; she didn't want to face anyone. But Pixie called down to her when the truck pulled up from the Antiques Emporium and the men unloaded the washstand, much earlier than Tricia had anticipated.

"Wow, that's a beauty," Pixie said in admiration, and brushed her hand across the pristine marble.

"Very attractive," Mr. Everett agreed.

"Where do you want this, ma'am?" one of the guys asked.

Tricia directed the men up the stairs to her apartment and oversaw the installation, and then tipped them generously. They made no mention of the article, but they didn't seem to want to look her straight in the eyes, either.

After they left, Tricia stayed upstairs, just puttering around. She tried several vases, a pile of books, and some crystal candy dishes on the washstand, but didn't like any of the vignettes and put most of the items back in a box.

She should go back down to her store. She should go back down to the basement office to check online for the status of the sundries she'd ordered for the holiday season. She *needed* to go to the grocery store if she was to feed Angelica that evening, and she was nearly out of cat food, so that was a major consideration as well. Instead, she wondered what the reach of the *Stoneham Weekly News* was. Did the citizens in Milford, the next town over, get copies of it, or did they have their own weekly rag? If she wore a scarf and sunglasses, could she appear in the produce section incognito, or would she look like a Russian spy from a bad Cold War movie?

Maybe she'd just ask Pixie to go to the store and let Mr. Everett handle the customers in her shop below. Considering the circumstances, Tricia knew her assistant wouldn't hesitate to help out. But that was the coward's way out—and she was not a coward.

She was going to have to face the aftermath of Russ's betrayal by holding her head high and swallowing her embarrassment.

But nobody said she had to enjoy it.

SIXTEEN

That afternoon, Tricia arrived at Booked for Lunch ready to dump her tale of woe on her sister, but when she sat down at the table in the back booth opposite her, she noticed Angelica's red-rimmed eyes.

"What's the matter?" she asked, wondering if her sister was just as upset as she was over the hatchet job Russ had done in his article, because she was more than ready to commiserate.

Instead, Angelica reached down beside her and picked up a trifold piece of plain white paper. Tricia quickly read the typed page.

Thanks for making your latest payment. I'll be expecting the same amount, in cash, every week for the foreseeable future. You wouldn't want everyone to know all your sordid little secrets, would you?

Under that were instructions on where to send the money, and the threat that contacting the authorities could end up with the death of a loved one.

A very *young* loved one.

Naturally, the note was unsigned.

Tricia placed the paper on the table. "Ange, you've *got* to talk to Chief Baker about this."

Angelica leaned forward and whispered harshly, "And risk my granddaughter's life? Never!"

Tricia sighed. "Then if you aren't willing to do that, you're going to have to come out with your secrets—only, don't do it in the *Stoneham Weekly News*," she added bitterly.

"What makes you think that coming clean will stop this monster from hurting Sofia?" she hissed.

"Because I have faith in law enforcement."

"This is Stoneham we're talking about. We're not dealing with *real*, big-city cops."

"I think you've underestimated Grant Baker. He was a top-notch detective with the sheriff's department before he—"

"He worked for a clown, and you know it. Wendy Adams couldn't find her badge pinned on her own shirt. Anybody would look good standing next to her."

"That's an elected position. Grant was well trained, and—" Tricia stopped. It felt odd to be singing his praises, but she really did believe he was good at his job. Methodical. He had to be for his investigations to stick when it came time for the assailant to be prosecuted. He'd done his job well when it came to collecting the evidence to convict Bob Kelly for murder. But then, with so many eyewitnesses, his job had been much easier.

The last thing Tricia wanted to think about was Bob Kelly . . . but his last words to her had haunted her—that her life should be a living hell until the day she died. Well, despite the ups and downs of the previous week, her life was *not* a living hell. But . . . it had been aggravating and frustrating, and it felt as though his curse had rubbed off on her sister, too. Still, it was a prophecy that seemed to be more based in reality than Tricia would prefer, and had started the very day of the sentencing, with Ted Harper's death, and then the vandalism that seemed to plague her place of business. And then there were the pranks against Ginny, and Angelica being blackmailed. It certainly seemed as though Kelly had some kind of uncanny power of prognostication.

Molly appeared before the sisters. "Made up your minds?"

Tricia looked up at the woman, whose crow's feet hinted at years of smiles. "What's the soup of the day?"

"It's Friday," Molly said with a laugh. "Good old New England clam chowder. We've got a nice fish sandwich to go with it, too."

"Tricia will never be able to eat that much," Angelica said offhandedly.

"Sounds good, though. How about we share the sandwich and both get the soup."

"Fine with me," Angelica agreed.

Molly nodded and headed for the kitchen to put in their orders.

"It's my turn to cook tonight," Tricia said. "Do you want anything special?"

Angelica shook her head. "I don't know if I'll even be able to eat lunch today—or anything else."

"I'm going to the grocery store right after I leave here. Can I get you anything?"

Angelica shook her head. "I've been raiding the café's kitchen for days. I really need to go to the store, too."

"Why don't we go together?" Tricia suggested, but again Angelica shook her head.

"I don't have time today. I might go tomorrow—Sunday at the latest."

"I called Grant this morning to report the graffiti and left a voice mail. Maybe I'll drop over at the police station when I return."

"He's sure taking his time to get back to you—or is that old bat of a receptionist at the station not passing along the message?"

It wasn't like Angelica to make disparaging remarks about people. She really must be depressed. Tricia ignored the snipe. "I called his personal cell phone."

"Maybe he just doesn't want to talk to an old girlfriend," Angelica suggested.

"Maybe. Or maybe he's out investigating a more important crime."

"Like what?"

"Who knows. I didn't read the Police Beat in the latest issue of the *Stoneham Weekly News*." No, she'd been too upset to read anything other than the front page story, and it wasn't likely she'd ever read the rag again.

Molly returned with two cups of soup and some packets of oyster crackers. "Bon appétit."

The sisters ate their lunches in silence, which felt awkward and just plain *wrong*, and Tricia hoped the last meal of the day wouldn't be a repeat performance.

Tricia did not go to the grocery store in disguise, and nobody seemed to even notice her presence, which was a huge relief. She figured since Angelica was down in the dumps that she should get something decadent for their dinner—but since she hadn't done any preplanning, she settled for a roasted chicken. She snagged a can of cranberry sauce, a couple of russet potatoes, and a package of frozen peas, along with an apple tart, figuring they would have a sort of makeshift

Thanksgiving dinner from a beginning cook—and she definitely still considered herself a beginner when it came to food prep.

Now that she was cooking on a somewhat regular schedule, Tricia found grocery shopping took a lot longer, but it was something she could enjoy. She had always been good about reading nutrition labels, but tried to stay away from processed food as much as possible. And now she cringed when she saw how much food was laced with corn syrup. She hadn't eaten a carton of yogurt in months.

It was nearly four when she arrived back at Haven't Got a Clue with her little metal shopping cart in tow. She'd always cringed to see her grandmother tote such a device, but found walking several blocks with her arms loaded down with bags to be a terrific bore, as well as a pain in the biceps.

Once she had unloaded her groceries, she left the shop in Pixie's and Mr. Everett's care once more and hoofed it over to the Stoneham police station. This time, she found Chief Baker in, although his receptionist, Polly, still gave her a hard time about seeing him. While standing right outside his office, she called him on his cell phone and this time got through. "Can we talk?" she practically begged.

"Come on over," he said.

"I'm already here. Polly won't let me see you."

The intercom buzzed. "Polly, Tricia has my permission to enter my office."

Polly sniffed and curled her lip, then turned away, and Tricia opened the door, letting herself in.

"What is with that woman?"

"She doesn't like you," Baker said.

"No kidding. What did I ever do to her?"

"Nothing. But she holds a grudge for you breaking my heart."

"I did not break your heart."

"She doesn't know that."

"Well, perhaps you could mention it to her at some point," Tricia said, taking a seat in front of his rather cluttered desk.

"What's up?" Baker asked.

"I left a message for you this morning."

"And I've been busy. You're not the only citizen in Stoneham with a problem, you know."

"Tell me about it. Ginny Barbero has had her windshield egged and a potato shoved up her car's tailpipe, and Angelica's being blackmailed. We're thinking about hiring private security, since the local cop shop doesn't seem very interested in the vandalism that appears to be running rampant in the village," she said rather hotly.

"I wouldn't call three or four incidents rampant."

"More like five or six. And how many would it take for you and your force to take the problem seriously? We're never going to get back our former title of Safest Village in New Hampshire at this rate."

"Well, that's a given," he said flatly.

Tricia sighed and shook her head. "Did your office tell you about the graffiti on the back of my building?"

"I heard. I saw the picture. It's not gang related."

"I could have told you that. And how much malicious mischief do we have to put up with before somebody cares? Does one of us have to get hurt?"

"I can't do anything about Angelica's problems until she makes a formal complaint. As far as I know, Ginny hasn't filed any official reports with our department. It's hearsay as far as we're concerned. Will your insurance company pay to have the graffiti removed?"

"I think so. But it won't happen anytime soon if my experience waiting for a check to come after the fire in my shop is a prime example."

Baker just looked at her, his face impassive.

"Well?" she demanded.

"Well, what?"

"Should we hire private security?"

He shrugged. "If it makes you feel better. But they can't be everywhere—protecting you and the outside of your building."

"Angelica's more worried about the threats to her—" She couldn't say "granddaughter." Baker didn't know about Angelica's connection with Antonio and his family. She assumed most people thought the friendship was based on Tricia's connection with Ginny as her former employee. "Threats to her extended circle of friends," she finally amended.

"Until she makes a complaint, there's nothing I can do. And you should encourage her to make that complaint, and the sooner the better."

"I've tried. She's just—"

"Stubborn," he supplied. "I know; it's a Miles trait."

That it was.

Tricia stood. "Well, thanks for your time—if nothing else."

"You're welcome."

"Let me know if you ever hear from the state lab about Ted Harper's toxicology reports."

"That could be months. It's only been a week."

Was that all? In some ways it seemed like a lifetime ago that Tricia had held her little cocktail party and the poor man had suffocated.

"Have a nice Thanksgiving. And Christmas. And New Year's, and probably Easter, too," she said with more than a little sarcasm.

"Aw, c'mon, Tricia. Don't be like that."

She turned to leave. "All right, then have a good weekend. I probably won't."

"Oh, no? I heard you've got a date on Sunday."

Tricia whirled around. "A date?"

"With Marshall Cambridge."

"It's for coffee. And how did you find out about it?"

"Everybody's talking about it," he said enigmatically.

Tricia let out a harsh breath. *Everybody who?* "Good-bye, Grant."

"Good-bye, Tricia."

Baker let Tricia see herself out.

SEVENTEEN

Not surprisingly, Angelica called that evening just as Tricia was peeling the potatoes to say that she was canceling their dinner date. "I just don't feel up to company tonight."

"Do you want me to bring something over for you?" Tricia asked.

"No. I have a lot of thinking to do, and I need some alone time to do it." She sounded sad and utterly defeated.

"Call me if you need me."

"Thank you. I will."

She wouldn't.

As Tricia hung up the phone, she thought about the little cooked bird sitting in her fridge that would never be warm again. Oh well, she liked chicken salad, and she was sure Miss Marple would enjoy a chopped chicken snack.

After a light and lonely dinner, Tricia went up to her new sleep suite and went to bed with a good book, reading far into the night.

The phone rang at 7:05 Saturday morning. Tricia opened one eye and reflected that calls that came that early never contained happy news, and she was filled with dread as she reached for the landline next to her bed.

"Hello?"

"Oh, Trish, why didn't you tell me?" Angelica demanded, sounding terribly upset.

Tricia allowed herself to relax, if only a little. "So you finally got a chance to see the latest issue of the village rag?"

"Yes. Frannie gave me the mail last night at closing, but I didn't bother to go through it until just now. Why didn't you tell me at lunch yesterday or when I spoke to you last night?"

"You're dealing with enough. I wasn't about to dump any more crap on you."

"Have you thought about consulting a lawyer over this?"

"Why bother? What Russ wrote is all pretty much true."

"Yes, but it was his intent. It was vicious. I know he's been worried about his newspaper's bottom line; well, I'm going to make a definite dent in it by yanking all my advertising from that nasty fish wrapper. I'll make sure he regrets his decision to smear the Miles family name."

"Ange—"

"I've made up my mind."

"Okay," Tricia said in defeat. "But please, don't make a scene about it. He could make it worse for all of us."

Angelica said nothing for a long moment, and then, "You may be right about that. I'll think about this for a while. But at the very least, I will not buy another ad from that terrible tabloid."

Tricia wondered if she should tell her sister what Russ said about his marriage, or that he'd admitted his jumping into the Chamber race as a revenge tactic. Now didn't seem the time.

Tricia sat up in bed, and Miss Marple got up, too, coming over to rub her head on Tricia's shoulder, reminding her that it was breakfast time.

"Did you read the other story?" Angelica asked.

Uh-oh. "What other story?"

"About Bob's trial."

"No. I was so angry, I could barely see straight to read the one on me. What did it say?"

"Russ's second hack job. He made it sound like Bob was some kind of victim, and barely mentioned Christopher's death. He also pointed out that it was *you* who testified against him and who was responsible for him getting life without parole."

"I wasn't the only one who witnessed his terrible crime."

"He forgot to mention that."

Tricia sighed. "I threw away my copy of the paper. I don't think I want to read that article."

"That's probably best," Angelica said. "I have a second reason for calling."

What else could go wrong? "Oh?"

"Yes. It seems that your vandal has decided to spread the misery around."

"How?"

"By breaking *all* the lights on the buildings along the alley."

"All of them?"

"From what I could see. It's a good thing I was holding Sarge when I stepped outside, or else he would have sliced his little paws to ribbons on the broken glass."

"That's terrible. But maybe if all the business owners that back up to the alley complain to the police, they might finally do something."

"What did Grant say when you spoke to him yesterday?"

"That there was no crime wave. I got the impression he thought I was overreacting."

"And you defended him to me," Angelica said flatly.

Tricia didn't want to argue about it. "I still think reporting these incidents to the proper authorities is the right thing to do."

"Hmmph."

"Are we on for lunch and dinner tonight, or have you got more thinking to do?"

"I'm available," Angelica conceded.

"Did you come to any conclusions during your alone time last night?"

"No."

Too bad.

"I have a lot to accomplish this morning, so I'd better get started," Angelica said.

"Me, too. See you at Booked for Lunch around two."

"Bye."

Tricia put the receiver back in its cradle. Miss Marple reminded her that breakfast still hadn't happened, so Tricia threw off the covers and got out of bed, willing, if not eager, to start the day.

By the time Tricia fed her cat and herself, showered, dressed, and gave her e-mails a passing glance, it was almost nine thirty, which didn't give her as much time as she would have liked to get the shop ready for the day. First on the list was to clean up after the latest episode of vandalism.

As Angelica had reported, there was glass scattered all over the concrete pad that led to the stairs down to the Dumpsters behind Haven't Got a Clue. If the light had been broken in the summer, Tricia could have climbed a ladder herself and changed the bulb, but she wasn't sure she wanted to do it on a cold November morning. Still, it would only take a minute to sweep up the mess. Since Angelica—and all the other business owners—would need to have their lightbulbs replaced, too, maybe they could hire someone to do the job in one fell swoop.

The dusting of snow that had fallen overnight had mostly melted when Tricia returned to the step with a dustpan and brush to sweep up the mess. She thought she'd have better luck getting all the glass if she took a position several steps below where most of the glass had landed, but she hadn't counted on slipping on black ice. She went down hard, smashing her right forearm onto the cold concrete step, the hunks of glass instantly embedding in the flesh on her forearm.

She let out a yelp of pain and said a very naughty word—or maybe four—before she stopped seeing stars and reached to grab her arm, chagrined to find it gushing blood at an alarming rate and ruining the sleeve of her pretty pink sweater.

She'd dropped the brush and dustpan when she'd fallen, but left them behind as she crawled up two stairs until she could stand, and then stepped up to her feet and backed into Haven't Got a Clue.

The washroom was just inside the back door, which she used her foot to close, and she staggered inside. She sat on the toilet seat while blood dripped down her fingers, and she made a grab for the paper toweling, pulling out ten or more sheets, meaning to stanch the blood, but when she tried to wrap it around the wound, she ended up pushing the glass even farther into the deep cuts and howled in pain.

"What's going on?" came a voice from the front of the store—Pixie!

"Help!" Tricia called, but found that her voice had no volume.

"Tricia?" Pixie called.

"In the washroom."

In seconds Pixie appeared before the opened door. "Oh my God! What have you done to yourself?"

"I fell . . . outside . . . on glass . . . and got cut."

Pixie shrugged out of her coat, tossing it on the floor. "Let me look at it."

Tricia was grateful to relinquish her arm to her assistant, because the truth was her stomach was roiling and she felt light-headed enough to faint.

Tricia watched through squinted eyes as Pixie plucked the largest pieces of glass from her soggy-with-blood sleeve and then gently peeled back the sweater to assess the damage. "Oh, Tricia. This is bleeding too much. It's not an artery, or you'd probably already be dead, but we need to stop the bleeding, and paper towels ain't gonna do it."

Tricia had already figured that out.

Somehow Pixie managed to remain incredibly calm. "I'm going to pick out some more of the glass so we can wrap that up and get you to Urgent Care. I want you to hang on to the wall with that other hand and brace yourself, because this is liable to hurt."

"It already hurts," Tricia managed, her voice sounding strangled.

"It's gonna hurt more," Pixie promised.

Tricia did as she was told and closed her eyes, wincing as Pixie pulled the worst of the glass from her arm.

"You did good," Pixie asserted. "Let's get the long-sleeved sweater off and wrap it around the wound, and then I'll run up to your bathroom and get some towels. Do you have old ones that you don't care about ruining?"

"Any towel you can find is fine," Tricia said, feeling her muscles quiver.

"Okay. Just sit here and *don't move*," Pixie commanded.

Tricia had no intention of disobeying her.

Pixie ran for the stairs, and it seemed like half of forever before she reappeared with a stack of towels and washcloths.

Tricia began to shiver, and yet a rivulet of perspiration ran from her temple down her left cheek.

"We're going to make us a pressure bandage," Pixie asserted, and wadded several washcloths before pressing them into the wound, which sent another wave of agony up Tricia's arm. "You're going to hold this while I wrap the big towel around it. There you go, and then we're going to walk to the reader's nook and you're going to sit there until I bring the car around."

"Shouldn't we call an ambulance?" Tricia asked weakly.

"It's a bad cut—but it's not life-threatening," Pixie asserted.

"How do you know?"

"Didn't I ever tell you? I worked on a volunteer ambulance crew for a while—community service. I got a lot of great training, but I also had a weakness for my old way of life and kind of fell back into it, if you know what I mean. Then I ended up back in stir. You don't want to go to the ER with this, because you'll end up sitting there for three or four hours—if not longer—when you can be in and out in an hour or less at Urgent Care."

"Okay, I trust you on this."

"Good. Now, let's get you to the nook. I'll bring my car around, but you sit tight until I come back in and walk you out. I don't want you keeling over on the floor—because if you do, then we *will* have to call an ambulance."

"Okay."

Pixie helped Tricia to her feet and guided her to the reader's nook, then went back to get her coat from the floor. Grabbing her purse, she headed out the door, hollering, "Stay right there!"

Tricia had no desire to move. And she held her arm up, feeling her pulse pounding through the afflicted appendage.

This was not how she'd envisioned starting her workday.

And the question was, now that she'd gotten hurt, would Baker finally take this mini crime wave seriously?

EIGHTEEN

Pixie had been right. They were in and out of Urgent Care in just over an hour, and nobody seemed to notice that Haven't Got a Clue opened just over an hour late.

It had taken fifteen stitches—and a tetanus booster—before Tricia had been outfitted with a sling and advised to take it easy and "don't get that arm wet!" Pixie had wrapped her own sweater around Tricia's shoulders, but she only had to walk from the shop to the car, then from the car to the medical building, then back again, so she never really had a chance to feel the cold. Once they returned to the bookstore, Pixie had insisted Tricia sit in the reader's nook while she made cocoa for both of them.

"Too bad we haven't got a shot of something stronger to put in it," she muttered.

"Whiskey in cocoa?" Tricia asked, holding her arm up so that it didn't throb quite so much.

"I was thinking more like crème de menthe."

"What are we going to do about lunch?" Tricia asked. "I don't think I can woman the register by myself—at least not today."

"We could call Mr. Everett. I'm sure he wouldn't mind coming in for a couple of hours."

"I hate to do that on his day off."

"I could call in a take-out order from Booked for Lunch."

"You wouldn't mind?"

"Not a bit."

"And it will be my treat."

Pixie grinned. "If you say so." She brought their cocoa over to the nook and sat down. "There you go. Do you need help?"

"I've got it," Tricia assured her, and picked the cup up with her left hand. "I don't know what I would have done if you hadn't arrived so early. And why was that?"

"I don't know. Fred is working overtime today and I felt antsy. I figured I'd come in and maybe get a couple of minutes' reading in before the crowds descended." She laughed. "They're not here yet, but they will be next week."

She was right. The Chamber had arranged for tour buses to bring in people to spend the holidays in Stoneham for the five weekends before Christmas.

Tricia sipped her cocoa. It was warm and she felt herself begin to relax. "I've been wondering; the night Ted Harper died, Angelica sprang into action to try to save him. If you've had so much training, why didn't you help?" She hoped that didn't come out sounding like a criticism. She hadn't meant it that way, and quickly tried to reassure Pixie of that fact.

She shook her head. "I saw she had everything under control. Well, not under control, but that she was capable of handling the situation."

"Did you realize it was anaphylaxis and not a question of choking?"

"Not right away, but when he didn't respond I kinda figured that might be the problem."

Tricia stared into the bubbles around the rim of her mug, frowning.

"Angelica did what she could," Pixie reiterated. "It just wasn't ever going to be good enough for the poor guy."

Tricia nodded, feeling bad all over again.

The door opened and a customer entered. Pixie was immediately on her feet, greeting the woman and taking a position behind the register. Tricia drank her cocoa, feeling rather useless, and incredibly tired. Why had she read until after two the night before? It wasn't like she didn't know the outcome of John Dickson Carr's *The Hollow Man*, which she'd read at least five times before.

Another customer entered, and Tricia smiled as the man walked past her, staring at her bandaged arm and bloodstained sweater. She really ought to go upstairs and change, but it could wait a few more minutes.

She finished her cocoa and set the mug on the big square coffee table, then sat back in her chair. Her arm was getting sore from being held upright, and she laid it across her chest, her fingers grabbing hold of a handful of sweater. She closed her eyes for just a few seconds, and the next thing she knew, someone was shaking her.

"It's lunchtime," Pixie said. "Angelica will be waiting for you over at Booked for Lunch."

"It can't be," Tricia said, and went to rub her eyes with her right hand, and her arm began to throb again. She'd almost forgotten about her little accident. She glanced at the clock across the way and realized she must have been asleep for more than two hours.

"Why didn't you wake me?"

"I didn't have the heart. Don't worry. You weren't snoring and you didn't have your mouth open or anything—else I woulda woken you."

"But what about the customers?"

"Nobody noticed," Pixie blatantly lied, waving a hand in dismissal. "I figured you'd want to change before you crossed the street. Do you need help?"

"I think I can manage," Tricia said, and awkwardly rose from the chair. She took a deep breath before walking across the shop. She was not going to coddle herself—however, she wished she had a banister on the left side of her stairwell. At least she could hold on during her trip back down.

Tricia was glad Pixie had awakened her almost half an hour before she had to meet Angelica, for it took her an awfully long time to get her sweater off and a clean one on. She wasn't sure the bloodied one would ever come clean—and since it had lost its long-sleeved mate, it probably wasn't worth keeping—so she tossed it in the wastebasket.

Once downstairs, Tricia had to decide what coat to wear. She'd have it on for only a minute or two going and returning, and decided the hell with it, and crossed the street wearing just her peach sweater set and the not-so-stylish sling.

She entered Booked for Lunch and headed for the back table, where Angelica sat with an empty coffee cup before her.

"What on earth happened to you?" she demanded, and practically rocketed out of the booth, instantly at Tricia's side.

She shrugged. "It's only a flesh wound."

"What?"

"Let's sit down and I'll tell you all about it."

Angelica stood by, looking anxious, as Tricia eased herself into her side of the booth. Once again she raised her arm in the air, resting her elbow on the table.

"Do you need anything?" Angelica asked, her voice sounding shaky.

"Maybe just some soup—and a roll and butter. Comfort food."

"Molly!" Angelica called, and the waitress looked up from behind the counter, where she'd been warming up her customers' coffee, then scurried around it and hurried to their table.

"Oh my goodness! What happened to you?" Molly asked, concerned.

"It's too long a story," Tricia said wearily. "What's the soup today?"

"Broccoli and cheese."

Tricia wrinkled her nose. "Maybe not."

"You can have anything you want—Tommy can *make* you anything you want—and then you must tell me what happened," Angelica insisted.

Tricia ordered the chicken pot pie and mashed potatoes—and that roll and butter—and then told Angelica the whole story.

"Thank goodness Pixie arrived when she did and knew just what to do. But why didn't you call me?"

"There wasn't time, and then when we got back to the store, I fell asleep in the reader's nook, although Pixie assured me I didn't have my mouth open or snore," she said with chagrin.

"Thank heaven for small favors." Angelica shook her head. "I knew I should have walked next door and swept up the glass on your step, too. I feel terrible. But I was in a hurry and had to—"

"I wouldn't have expected you to do that, so don't give it a second thought."

"Well, I'm going to call Grant Baker and give him a piece of my mind."

"And I'm going to let you; otherwise it would just sound like sour grapes—or something like that—on my part."

Molly arrived with their lunches, setting the plates on the table. "I had Tommy cut up the pastry crust so you could handle it better."

"That was very thoughtful of you, Molly. Thank you."

"Let me know if you need anything," she said sincerely.

"Thanks." Tricia picked up her fork with her left hand and stabbed a piece of chicken. It was almost as good as Angelica's.

"What are you going to do now that you're one-handed? You should come and stay with me," Angelica said.

"I can manage," Tricia said, but then wondered if she'd be able to pull the tab from the top of a cat food can. But then it was her forearm that was injured, not her fingers. She was sure she'd get used to her limited mobility in a day or so and learn to compensate. Besides, she didn't want to sleep on Angelica's couch when she had a perfectly fine bed of her own. "But maybe you could come and make supper at my place tonight? I've got nearly a whole roasted chicken sitting in the fridge."

"Of course. I'm sure I can whip up something for us."

"Thanks."

They ate in silence for several minutes, and again it felt odd and awkward, and Tricia had no doubt it would continue to do so until something else happened. Something not good. Something that might shatter all their worlds. Her own—and especially Angelica's.

Pixie was an absolute doll. She took care of all the end-of-day tasks, cleaned the beverage station, and closed out the register. "Can I do anything else before I leave?" she asked sincerely.

Tricia shook her head. "You've done more than I could have hoped. Thank you. I don't know how I would have made it through the day without you."

Pixie's cheeks colored, but she was obviously pleased to hear such praise. "I can come in tomorrow if you need me."

"Definitely not. You need to spend the day with Fred. Besides, Mr. Everett will be here, and I'm sure we'll make out fine. And hopefully I'll be as good as new by midweek."

Pixie looked skeptical, but nodded anyway. "Okay. Then I'll see you on Monday."

"Yes. And thank you again for everything."

Pixie waved and headed for the door. Tricia locked it behind her, set the lights to low, and headed for her apartment. If she wasn't going to be able to make dinner for her sister, the least she could do was make a pitcher of martinis. Easier said than done, however, and she was glad she started ten minutes before Angelica's anticipated arrival. And she vowed that, for the foreseeable future, she would not tighten the bottles quite so hard.

"Hello!" came Angelica's voice from the stairwell, sounding more cheerful than she had at lunch. Seconds later she entered the apartment.

"Just in time," Tricia said, and poured the first drink left-handed, slopping a little onto the counter.

"Well, that's no good," Angelica said. "Now I'll just have to lick up the excess."

"Don't be disgusting," Tricia chided, but couldn't help the smile that tugged at the corners of her mouth.

Angelica removed her jacket, tossing it on one of the kitchen island stools, and accepted the martini glass. Tricia poured another and they toasted.

"Do show me this magnificent washstand you purchased," Angelica said, and looked around the room until she saw it. "Oh, my—that is pretty." The sisters crossed from the kitchen to the living room windows that overlooked Main Street. "And you said Frannie refinished this?"

Tricia nodded.

"She certainly did a beautiful job of restoration. She may have missed her calling."

"What do you mean?"

"I don't know if there's any money in that kind of work, but she obviously has a talent for it."

"You're not unhappy with her work at the Cookery, are you?"

Angelica sighed. "No. But she seems to have lost her passion for it lately."

"Was she ever passionate about retail—or cooking, for that matter?"

"No. And she does a good job—just not . . . inspiring."

"I know what you mean. Pixie is passionate about vintage mysteries. She's great with the customers, and she was almost a certified EMT, for which I am extremely grateful," she said, brandishing her sore arm.

Angelica ran her hand over the washstand's cool tiles. "What are you going to do with it?"

Tricia shrugged. "Ginny suggested using it as a dry bar."

"That's a great idea."

"Maybe. But I'm awfully fond of that little table Pixie and Fred gave me as a housewarming gift."

"Well, you don't have to decide today what to put on it." She looked down at the furniture in question. "This vase is far too small."

"Yeah. I'll have to dig through some of my stuff to find the perfect accent piece or pieces. Or maybe I'll do as Toni suggested and go back to the Antiques Emporium to find the perfect solution." She looked down at her injured arm. "Although it probably won't be anytime soon." She glanced at the bandage poking out from beneath her three-quarter-length sweater sleeve and shuddered. It was time to think of something different. "Do you want to get started on dinner?"

"Not yet. I need to sit for a while." Angelica took the nearest chair—the one Ted Harper had fallen on during Angelica's rescue attempt. She didn't seem to notice. "What a day." She eyed her martini, then took a healthy swig.

"Did you ever call Chief Baker to give him a piece of your mind?" Tricia asked, taking the matching chair.

"Er, yes," Angelica said, sounding sheepish. "After I said my piece about your accident, he asked me about being blackmailed."

"And you said?" Tricia asked cautiously.

"'What blackmail?'"

"Oh, Ange."

"Well, there's no way I'm going to risk my family."

"You need to report it."

"Well, that's not going to happen anytime soon. Now, can we talk about something else?"

Tricia sighed. "How about dinner tomorrow?"

Angelica nodded. "I was thinking about serving it at Booked for Lunch, but it just wouldn't be practical—and now that you're a southpaw, it would be even harder. Could we have it here? I can take care of all the prep—in fact, I'll get it started at the café and then bring it over."

"Of course we can meet here. It'll give me a chance to try out my new dining room table. There's a reason I bought all those extra leaves for it."

"Thanks. Can I bring Sarge?"

Tricia's gaze traveled to her newly refinished floors and thought about Sarge's claws and how he liked to race around to fetch a ball. "You know he and Miss Marple don't get along."

Angelica sighed. "Yes. All right, but that means I'll have to miss the little guy two nights in a row."

"He'll be all right," Tricia said, feeling like her floors had just dodged a bullet. Her stomach growled. If Angelica wanted to delay the dinner hour, she'd need to buy her stomach some time. "I've got some cheese and crackers. Would you like some?"

"Sure."

"Only you'll have to cut the cheese—and that was not a rude joke. I've got a slab of Vermont cheddar in the fridge."

"It really should breathe for a while."

"I don't want to wait," Tricia said.

Angelica shrugged. "Very well."

The sisters got up from their chairs and headed back to the kitchen, where Angelica found the cheese while Tricia took the box of crackers from her pantry. "So, are you excited about tomorrow?" Angelica asked.

"Tomorrow?"

"Your big date with Marshall Cambridge."

"Gosh, I'd completely forgotten about it. And it's coffee—not a date."

"Whatever. What are you going to wear?"

"A sweater set and slacks—like always."

"You could glam up just a bit."

"I thought you didn't like him. Why would you want me to glam up?"

"If nothing else, to keep in practice. You never know when a *real* date might come along."

Tricia shrugged. She wanted to talk about this so-called date as much as Angelica wanted to talk about her blackmailer: in other words, not at all.

The whole pornographic thing really bothered her. She liked to think of herself as a feminist, even if the term was deemed either old-fashioned or detrimental. But, honestly, she'd read articles that showed different sides of the story. First, that sexual exploitation was demeaning—that it objectified women, that most of it was downright disgusting. And yet some women found it exhilarating—liberating, even. Those were the women who controlled their destinies and reaped the financial rewards of such a life/business. However, those women were few and far between.

Tricia had to look at this coffee meeting with Marshall—which sounded so much more clinical than a date—as a make-nice-with-the-constituents affair.

There was one thing that really worried her, however: what if she actually liked the guy?

NINETEEN

When Mr. Everett arrived the next morning, he was quite upset to find Tricia's arm in a sling. "You should have called me," he insisted.

"Pixie took care of everything. She was an angel."

"Then at least you were in good hands." Mr. Everett's words were positive, but his demeanor was anything but.

"Is something wrong?" Tricia asked.

Mr. Everett shook his head. "No. We're just worried about Charlie."

"Why?"

Mr. Everett shrugged. "Grace thinks he's failing to thrive."

Tricia had only heard that term applied to sick babies. Charlie was an elderly cat.

"We're going to call the vet first thing tomorrow," Mr. Everett added. "Just to make sure."

"It's a wise precaution," Tricia agreed.

Mr. Everett nodded.

"Are you having second thoughts about adopting Charlie?" she asked.

Mr. Everett's brow furrowed. "Maybe."

He said no more, just staring at his feet, and Tricia had to fight the urge to hug him. That just wasn't his style.

The shop door opened and a woman entered. Mr. Everett perked right up, probably ecstatic to have his attention diverted. "Hello. Welcome to Haven't Got a Clue. My name is William. Feel free to look around, and don't hesitate to ask for help if you need it."

The woman nodded and moved to peruse one of the shelves.

Tricia spoke to Mr. Everett. "I've got an appointment at one. Would you mind if I left for a while this afternoon?"

"Not at all. I can take care of the shop." He looked toward the cat perch behind the cash desk. "And Miss Marple."

The first hour of business that day at Haven't Got a Clue wasn't exactly busy, but the two customers who visited were pleasant and obviously avid readers, as evidenced by the bulging bags Tricia packed while Mr. Everett expertly rang up the sales.

At five to one, Tricia headed for the back of the store to retrieve the cloak she'd dug out of the back of her closet. She figured it would be easier to wear than a coat with sleeves—at least until she lost the bulky bandage on her right arm.

"My, you look smart," Mr. Everett said.

For a moment, Tricia wasn't sure what he meant.

"The cloak. It reminds me of Mr. Conan Doyle's most famous creation."

Tricia laughed. "Sherlock Holmes?"

"Perhaps you just need a deerstalker cap and a magnifying glass to complete the outfit," Mr. Everett suggested.

It was so rare when Mr. Everett cracked a joke that Tricia set off for her rendezvous with the porn master in a much better state of mind.

Summer Sundays at the Bookshelf Diner were always crowded. Sundays in November . . . not so much. Tricia entered the restaurant and looked around, seeing no sign of Marshall Cambridge. Well, she was a few minutes early. The sign at the front of the restaurant said SEAT YOURSELF, and Tricia found an empty booth about midway down the left side of the main aisle and sat down, pulling off the cloak and settling it across her lap. From past experience, she knew when the door opened there'd likely be a blast of arctic air.

It was an unfamiliar waitress who stopped by her table. "What can I get you, ma'am?"

Ma'am! That term always sounded like it should be applied to someone in her late eighties.

"I'm meeting someone, but we're only going to have coffee, so I guess you could bring it to me now."

The waitress frowned. Good tips weren't made on such skimpy orders. Without a word, she turned and headed toward the big steel urns behind the counter.

Actually, since she hadn't had a bite to eat since her toast and jam breakfast some six hours before, Tricia *was* in the mood for lunch. Why shouldn't she order soup or a sandwich? She'd told Angelica she'd ask for separate checks anyway.

The waitress returned with a coffeepot and poured, dumping several containers of creamer on the table. "Get you anything else?" she asked without hope.

"I think I'm going to go ahead and order lunch. Could I please have a menu?"

"Sure thing." She certainly brightened in anticipation of a bigger order.

The diner's door opened and, sure enough, a bone-chilling breeze whooshed through the diner, and in came Marshall wearing jeans, a brown leather bomber jacket, and a black knit cap. Outside of his dark and gloomy store, he actually looked rather nice, something Tricia hadn't noticed when at Chamber meetings. He looked around, caught sight of Tricia, and moseyed on down the aisle, slipping into the opposite side of the booth.

"Cold enough for you?" he asked.

Oh, dear. Was this going to be a tedious conversation?

"Yes," Tricia answered flatly.

"For me, too. I like summer better, although in my business, the seasons don't seem to make much difference."

"Why? Do people buy porn year-round?"

He shook his head, seeming not to take offense at her rather impertinent question. "Nah, I'm not dependent on the tourist trade like most of the shops and stores around here. My customers are pretty much local—and there're a lot of them."

Tricia blinked. "Really?"

"Sure. Why do you think I relocated here? I did my homework."

Tricia wasn't sure she wanted to know what that homework entailed. And he didn't seem all that aware, as he hadn't seemed to notice her sling.

The waitress dropped by with a couple of menus and filled Marshall's cup.

"Thanks."

"I'll give you a few minutes."

"Don't hurry," Marshall said.

The waitress departed, and he leaned back in the booth.

Marshall rested his arms on the table and folded his hands. "So, what's with the sling? Did you break your arm since Wednesday?"

"No, I fell on some broken glass behind my store and ended up with fifteen stitches."

He winced. "Sounds painful."

"It was—is," she amended.

He nodded, and for a few long moments they sat in awkward silence. Marshall broke the quiet. "Boy, the *Stoneham Weekly News* sure did a hack job on you last week."

Tricia slapped her palm to her forehead, suddenly wanting to cry. "Please, let's not talk about that."

"Why not?"

"Because it's embarrassing."

"Well, yeah, but one of the reasons I wanted to meet with you was to talk about your experiences with all these murders."

"Why would you want to do that?"

"I thought I made that clear on Wednesday. I read true crime. You attract it. You must have tons of fascinating stories. I was kind of hoping to pick your brain."

Tricia had never thought of her experiences in quite that light. "Well, I guess so."

"I did some research on the local murders that have occurred in the past six years. It is quite a coincidence that they happened after you arrived, and I don't think most people really believe you're a jinx."

Oh yeah? Should she tell him about the graffiti spray-painted across the back of her building? "You seem to call me that every time we meet."

"I was just having fun with you."

"Well, I don't find it funny."

"Oh, come on. When you get all pissed off like that, your forehead wrinkles. It's not all that attractive."

"You're the last person I'd like to be attractive for."

He seemed hurt by her reply. "Why'd you say that? I'm a great guy."

"Great as in your opinion of yourself?" she countered.

He raised his hands in submission. "Okay, let's start over. Hi, Tricia. It's good to see you. I've been looking forward to it for days."

Tricia studied his face. He seemed to be sincere. "Hello, Marshall." She didn't elaborate, since she *hadn't* been looking forward to their meeting.

"I'm sorry if I embarrassed you. I thought you might want to talk about your experiences to a neutral third party."

"Or do you just want to hear the salacious details?"

"Maybe a part of me does, but I also think the village hasn't given you enough credit for what you've done. Your sister, too."

Her eyes narrowed. "And what have you heard?"

"That you both have hired ex-cons. You gave that old man who works for you a second chance. Some people say he'd be dead if you hadn't given him a job. But now look at him. He's got a wife and a job, and you've practically adopted him. From what I've heard, he seems to be very happy."

Had he been gossiping with Frannie Armstrong?

"Mr. Everett is very special to me—and to my sister."

"Why do you call him by his surname?"

"Because he's an old-fashioned gentleman, and he calls me—and my sister—Ms. Miles."

Marshall shrugged. "Whatever."

"What else have you learned while poking around in my private life?" Tricia accused.

"That you had to testify against the bastard who killed your ex. That had to be hard."

"It was much harder to watch him die," she asserted, "but yes, it was very difficult."

"And that wasn't the first time you've had to testify in criminal—murder—trials, was it?"

She shook her head. "No."

"I also heard that you and Russ Smith used to go out. Was there a bad ending to the relationship? Is that why he trashed you in the last issue of his little birdcage liner?"

"You're asking some very personal questions," Tricia said.

Marshall shrugged. "I guess I'm just interested in what makes people tick."

"And what makes *you* tick?" Tricia asked.

"Well, for one thing, I don't actually read porn."

Tricia blinked. "Then why on earth do you sell it?"

"I gotta make a living, and the stuff sells—despite all the crap available for free on the Internet. If it stops selling, I'll figure out something else to do."

"What have you done previously?" Tricia asked, not the least bit interested in his answer.

"Waiter, used car salesman, college professor."

"College professor?" Tricia asked a little too loudly.

Marshall nodded.

Okay, now *she* was becoming just a little interested in the man. "What did you teach?"

"Criminal justice. As I said; I've always been interested in crime, but I never wanted to actually work in the field. I figured teaching might be satisfying."

"But it wasn't?"

He shook his head. "Kids today come to class totally unprepared. Some of them actually want to learn, but the emphasis on testing from K through high school means they don't learn how to think critically. And they don't read. Too boring."

Tricia sighed. That was true enough. And too often schools seemed to use reading as a punishment, forcing kids to read stuff they had no interest in. When she was a child, her mother would punish her by *not* letting her read.

"And I'm also betting that since you work with books, you don't get to read as much as you'd like."

"I make time every day, but you're right. Since I opened the store, I don't get nearly enough time to read, despite the fact that I have two employees." She smiled. "When it's slow, I let them read on the job. I think that's why they're so happy working for me."

"I'll bet you pay them well, too. You seem like that kind of a person."

Tricia didn't acknowledge the compliment. "Do you always work alone?"

Marshall nodded. "I close on Sundays—not for religious reasons, but just because a guy's gotta have at least one day off a week. And it also keeps the straitlaced from beating up on me too much."

"The two times I've been in your store, you've always come into the sales floor from the back."

"That's where I live. It was a bear to get the zoning board to agree to it, but eventually they saw it my way."

"I haven't seen any customers. What do you do back there to kill time?"

"Read. Watch TV. Do the laundry—just what every other single person does."

"Have you ever been married?" Tricia asked, finding the guy was beginning to grow on her.

"Now who's asking personal questions?" Marshall asked, but there was a smile on his lips.

Tricia felt a blush warm her cheeks.

"Yeah, I've been married."

"And?" Tricia prompted.

"The first time, we were too young. The second time, she died."

"Oh, I'm so sorry."

He shrugged. "I'd probably still be teaching if April was alive."

"Do you mind my asking—?" But she didn't finish the question.

"She jogged. Was going to live forever because she believed in healthy living. A car clipped her—hit-and-run. I got worried after a few hours and went looking for her. I found her in a gully."

"That must have been terrible for you."

"Yeah, it was, but I don't like to dwell on it. Like I said, I'd probably still be teaching—and unhappy as hell. At least this way I got to try some different things until I found something that worked. What's the story with you and your ex?"

Tricia sighed. "Midlife crisis. He up and moved to the Colorado mountains—until he realized how lonely he was and came back east to try and win me back."

"It didn't take?"

"No. I loved him, but I didn't want to be married to him anymore. It turns out . . . I don't mind being single. It didn't happen overnight, of course, but I'm not as lonely as I thought I'd be. And my sister and I have gathered around us some very special people. They make us feel like a family."

"I've heard about your famous Sunday dinners."

"What?"

"It's a small village. People talk."

The waitress arrived. "Having lunch?"

Tricia looked to Marshall to answer.

"I wouldn't mind."

"Me, neither," Tricia said. "What's the soup of the day?"

"New England clam chowder."

"It was a given," Marshall quipped.

"I'll have a bowl," Tricia said.

"Me, too. And a turkey club sandwich."

The waitress gathered up their menus. "You got it. And I'll be 'round to warm up your coffee."

"Thanks," Tricia said.

After she'd left, Marshall leaned both elbows on the table and gazed into Tricia's eyes. "So, shall we keep trading life stories?"

"I guess."

Tricia hated to admit it, but she was beginning to like Marshall Cambridge.

TWENTY

For the rest of the afternoon, Tricia found herself smiling, and it wasn't just the cheerful Irish music that was playing on the shop's sound system. Even Mr. Everett noticed.

"I'm so glad to see you so happy this afternoon, Ms. Miles."

"After the last few days, I'm happy to feel a little happier."

"Better days are always ahead, I say. And we have dinner to look forward to tonight, and right upstairs."

"Yes, we do."

"It's my favorite time of the week," he admitted. "I'm grateful to be able to share such happy times with you and your sister, Antonio, Ginny, and the baby. I never would have had the opportunity to be a grandpa without you."

Tricia smiled, remembering what Marshall had told her earlier. She felt just as lucky at finding Mr. Everett and Grace—her surrogate parents.

"Do you know what we'll be having?" Mr. Everett asked.

She shook her head. "Angelica likes to surprise me—and I'm almost always surprised."

"She's a wonderful cook," he agreed. He glanced at the clock on the wall. "My goodness, is that the time?"

Yes, closing. And during the dull days before the holiday season shopping jumped into high gear, it was sometimes the best part of the day.

"Are you going home to pick up Grace for dinner?"

"Yes."

"Then why don't you go now, and I'll see you back here in a little while."

"But you still need to close."

"It'll only take a few minutes, and my arm isn't feeling too badly, then I'll be heading upstairs to get things ready."

"Very well." Mr. Everett retrieved his coat, hat, and muffler from the back of the shop and headed out the door.

"See you soon," Tricia called, and waved. Then she turned for the beverage station to dump the last of the dregs and wash the pot.

She was just heading back to the front of the shop when the door opened and Antonio stepped inside. He stamped his feet from the cold, and his chapped cheeks told her that he had walked some distance.

"Don't tell me you hoofed it here all the way from your house."

"I did," Antonio agreed, rubbing his hands to warm them.

"But that's at least three miles."

"Exercise is good," he replied. "And I had a lot of thinking to do."

Uh-oh. That sounded rather ominous.

"The coffee's gone, but I could make you some instant cocoa to help warm you up," she offered.

Antonio shook his head. "I wouldn't want to spoil my dinner." He looked at her sling. "Angelica called to tell us of your accident. Is there anything I can do to help?"

"I'm good," she assured him. "I take it Ginny will be driving here with the baby?"

He nodded. "Yes. Can we sit?" he asked, and indicated the comfortable chairs in the reader's nook.

"Of course."

They sat down facing each other across the expanse of the large square coffee table covered with magazines that needed straightening.

"You look like a man with a lot on his mind," Tricia said, and again Antonio nodded.

"It is Angelica, of course," he said, his voice soft. The way he said her name was almost lyrical, thanks to his Italian accent. "I know we have spoken of this before—but it still concerns me. Something is very wrong and she will not tell me what it is. This past week, I've sometimes thought she might be avoiding me. And her eyes have been red and swollen. She tells you everything. Is she all right?"

Tricia couldn't help but laugh. "Everything? Hardly."

"Is she ill?" he demanded.

Tricia shook her head vehemently. "No, nothing like that."

"But you *do* know what is bothering her."

Tricia sighed, and it was her turn to nod.

His dark eyes were earnest. "Can you please tell me?"

"She's asked me not to."

"And do you think that is the wisest course?"

Tricia shook her head. "If I tell you, you would immediately go to her and demand answers. She'd feel betrayed."

"Could your relationship weather such a betrayal?"

Tricia found it hard to meet his gaze. "I'm afraid it might not. I was without my sister for decades. I don't want to be without her ever again. And yet . . . I don't think she's making wise decisions. She thinks it's—" Tricia was about to say *in your best interest*, but stopped herself. "She thinks she's doing the right thing."

"And you don't?"

"No."

Antonio nodded and looked thoughtful for several long seconds. "Is she being blackmailed?" he said at last.

Tricia looked up, startled by the question.

"As I suspected," Antonio said softly, taking her expression as assent.

"What do you mean?"

"I have known her most of my life. After all this time, I can read her quite well. What I don't know is *why* she would be blackmailed."

"I think it's silly. I don't know why she cares so much."

"Please tell me."

Tricia felt torn. But honestly, if Sofia was in danger, her father—both parents—should be made aware of the threat. "Someone has discovered that Angelica is Nigela Ricita and has vowed to hurt your daughter if she doesn't pay to keep her secret quiet."

Antonio frowned in confusion. "But that is absurd."

"I know. She says that the other merchants might feel betrayed that she wasn't up front about her companies. She thinks they may be angry that she owns so many of the village's more successful businesses—that somehow she has an edge over them."

"She has done nothing but bring jobs and prosperity to Stoneham. How can anyone object to that?"

"You know as well as I do that people make assumptions, and once they do, often they can't be talked out of them."

"The *polizia* should be called."

"I know. I've tried to talk her into it, but she won't listen."

"She will listen to me. And we will take steps to protect Sofia, even if we must leave the village to do that."

"Oh, no! She couldn't bear to be apart from the three of you."

"Then what do you suggest?"

"I don't know."

"How much has she paid?"

"Five thousand. And now the blackmailer is demanding she pay more on a weekly basis. She's got a lot of money, but nobody can pay forever."

"She should never have made one payment. She should have immediately gone to the *polizia*," he said testily.

"She wanted to keep your family safe. And for that, you can't be angry."

Antonio let out a long breath. "I suppose you're right."

"What will you do now?" Tricia asked.

"I must speak to Ginny before I can do anything. We will make a decision together. But I want you to know that I will not allow her to be upset with you. You have been a good sister, and you only have her—and our—best interests at heart."

Just like Angelica. But if that was so, why did Tricia feel so guilty?

The atmosphere at the weekly family dinner was tense, and everybody seemed to sense there was something amiss, as evidenced by the awkward silences, rigid smiles, and a serious lack of appetite on everyone's part despite the wonderful meal Angelica had prepared. Sofia's golden laugh as she chased Miss Marple around the apartment was the only highlight of the evening.

The gathering ended earlier than usual. Angelica waved away offers of help to clean up, and the guests all departed. Then she, impeded by Tricia, rinsed the dishes, loaded the dishwasher, and washed the pots. Once that was accomplished, Angelica poured another two glasses of wine and the sisters sat by the window that overlooked Main Street, watching snowflakes whirl outside.

"That was a wonderful roast," Tricia said.

"We'll be eating leftovers for days," Angelica lamented. "Do you like hash?"

"I bet I would if you made it," Tricia said, and offered her sister a smile.

That evening, Angelica seemed incapable of a reciprocal expression. Tricia's guilt rose as she thought about her conversation with Antonio, but she was determined not to talk about it.

Angelica sipped her wine, her gaze focused outside the window, staring at the cloudy sky above, when she looked up sharply. "With everything that went on today, I completely forgot to ask you about your date with Marshall Cambridge."

"It was *not* a date. It was lunch."

"Lunch? I thought you said you were going to have coffee only."

"It was after one. I was hungry. A girl's gotta eat, you know."

"So what kind of a pig is he?"

"Ange, it's not like you to say things like that."

"You like him?" Angelica accused, sounding incredulous.

"Much to my surprise, yes."

"Why?"

"Because, like you—I originally judged him by what he sells."

"I'd say that was pretty good criteria."

"I admit, I don't approve of porn. It's distasteful; it demeans women. But the more we talked, the more I kind of liked him."

Angelica looked skeptical.

"He isn't even into porn; he likes to read true crime, which he also sells. He actually wanted to pump me for information on my experiences with local deaths."

"Including Ted Harper?"

Tricia shook her head. "We barely spoke about him. And after a while, we just talked. And ate lunch," she added as an afterthought. "Maybe he's a little odd, but I think in spite of what he sells, he may have a modicum of decency." Tricia changed the subject. "Have you heard from your blackmailer again?"

Angelica's expression soured. "Of course not. It's Sunday. Those letters come through the US mail."

Antonio might call or show up at any time, and Tricia needed to try one more time to get her sister to face the inevitable. "You know, Grant could probably get a DNA sample from the envelopes."

"Yeah, and in six months or a year he'd finally hear from the backed-up state criminal lab. I know how these things really go. And besides, a damp cloth will seal an envelope just as well as a wet tongue."

"You're making excuses."

"Did you hear Sofia laugh this evening? Did you really listen? The idea of never hearing her laugh again would kill me. And if it was my fault she was hurt or killed—I'd kill myself."

"Oh, Ange. Don't even talk like that."

"I mean it." From the fire in her eyes, Tricia believed her.

"You should talk to Antonio about this."

"Absolutely not. And don't you, either," Angelica commanded.

Tricia didn't promise, because she'd already done the deed.

Angelica drained her glass and stood. "I need to get home and feed my dog." She retrieved her coat, dipping into the pocket to capture her keys. "I have meetings in the morning, but I'll be back well before lunchtime and see you at the café at the usual time, right?"

"Okay."

Tricia stood and, on impulse, pulled her sister into a hug. "It's got to get better," she said in what she hoped was a reassuring tone.

Angelica sighed. "I sure hope you're right."

* * *

Tricia followed Angelica downstairs, locked Haven't Got a Clue, and set the security system, then ventured back up to her apartment, where she found Miss Marple patiently waiting behind the door.

"Did Sofia terrorize you tonight?" she asked as she bent down to pet her cat. Miss Marple rubbed her head against Tricia's legs, purring happily.

"I suppose you'd like a kitty snack as a reward."

"*Yow!*" the cat answered enthusiastically. She didn't have a huge vocabulary, but Miss Marple sure knew that term.

"Just a small one. I don't want to spoil your dinner," Tricia said, and led the way to the kitchen. She opened the cupboard door, picked up the package, and then shook a few of the little pillow-shaped morsels into the waiting bowl. Miss Marple dug in, and Tricia sniffed the bag and shuddered, unable to see the appeal. She put the package away and wandered back into the living room, restless. About then she needed a comfort read. She paused in front of the temperature-and-light-controlled cabinet where her most valuable vintage mysteries were stored. Of course, she had duplicates of the tomes that she could actually handle and read, but sometimes she just wanted to take them out, flip through the fragile pages, and sniff the binding. There was nothing like the smell of a good book.

But instead she wandered around the apartment, ending up by the windows that overlooked the street where the snow still swirled.

Miss Marple hopped onto the top of the washstand beside her. "*Yow!*"

"You know better than to jump up there."

Miss Marple sashayed across the marble top, her tail flicking back and forth.

"Get down right now," Tricia ordered, but the cat was obstinate.

Tricia sighed. Her cat was seldom bad. Of course, she had no idea if Miss Marple stomped across the counters and breakfast bar when Tricia wasn't nearby to scold her, but she seldom had to reprimand her furry companion.

"Please get down now!" she said more firmly.

Miss Marple sat down and said, "*Yow!*"—and rather defiantly, at that.

"Now!" Tricia said again.

Miss Marple stood and batted at a pen that someone had put on the table. Plop! It landed on the newly sanded hardwood floor.

"You're being very naughty," Tricia told the cat.

Miss Marple pawed at the tiny crystal bud vase at the back of the stand, and that was when Tricia turned. "No you don't," she said, and made a dive to catch the glass before it could shatter on the floor.

"You're a bad kitty," Tricia admonished, and she got down on hands and knees, crawling forward to retrieve the pen when she looked up and saw it—whatever *it* was. Something that looked like a small black disc that had been attached to the washstand's back apron. "What the—?" she said, leaning in closer to examine the little round plastic object. Whatever it was, it didn't belong there. She was about to reach for it to pluck it off when she thought better of it. Instead, she sat back on her heels and stared at the object.

It didn't look like a camera. Some kind of recording device? Yes—she could believe that. But who would want to be listening in on her conversations?

She'd bought the washstand at the Antiques Emporium. Any number of people at the shop could have known she'd purchased the table. There'd been a number of vendors present stocking their booths when she'd purchased it. Could Toni have put it there? Or what if Russ or Chauncey had put it there? What would they hope to gain by recording her? Did either of them want the job of Chamber presidency that much that they'd stoop to eavesdropping on her to try and get something they could use against her? Neither of them had been in her apartment since the table had been delivered, but could they have paid one of the deliverymen to attach it either before it was delivered or before the men left her home?

Tricia swallowed, her body tensing with irritation that bordered on rage.

"*Yow!*" Miss Marple said, in what sounded like satisfaction, which was absurd. The cat couldn't possibly have known the recording device was there. And now that Tricia knew about it, she wondered what she should do. Her first impulse was to yank it off and stomp on the offending thing, but that wouldn't tell her who had placed it on the washstand in the first place.

"*Yow,*" Miss Marple said, and began to purr.

"You think you're so cute," Tricia said, and Miss Marple closed her eyes briefly and seemed to nod.

Tricia got to her feet and removed the cat from the washstand. "Come along, miss. You're going to get what you deserve."

Tricia took her cat into the kitchen and opened the cupboard, taking out the package of kitty snacks. This time she shook a generous amount into Miss Marple's empty bowl, and the cat descended on them like she hadn't eaten in a week, instead of just five minutes before. Tricia stood over her, watching, and thinking about her next move. Maybe she should take a picture of the offending article. Yes, she'd do that and then get on the computer to see if she could find the nasty little bug.

Retrieving her phone, she did just that, then sat down at her laptop and began her computer search.

Most of the recording devices displayed online were bigger and bulkier than the little snooper attached to the washstand, and Tricia was getting frustrated with her choice of keyword searches when she found it: the Whisper Ear 3200. Whoever had planted it had spent nearly two hundred dollars on the sound-activated device with a thirty-two-hour battery life. That "life" only passed by when the recorder was activated—which meant it could be viable for weeks, if not months. Her apartment was silent for most of the day and night. And the device could be controlled via a cell phone with a radius of almost a thousand yards. Did that mean someone had to be within that distance to listen to the device, or just to control it?

Tricia sat back and noticed that Miss Marple had joined her, sitting quietly at her feet. She was about to commend the cat for her detective work, but then thought better of it. Someone was listening to her every move—her every sound—making her feel self-conscious.

Okay, now that she knew she was being recorded, what should she do about it? Tell Chief Baker? That was an option. It was blatantly illegal to surreptitiously record someone—and whoever was doing it obviously didn't care about legalities.

Tricia sat up straighter and entered a new query into the browser's search field: *how to tell if you're being bugged.*

Almost immediately the computer presented her with a website with advice on how to tell if there were spying devices in your home. As she read down the page, one of the questions made a shiver run down her spine: *Are you the victim of a stalker?*

Tricia wasn't currently—at least that she knew of—but she *had* been stalked in the past, and by none other than Russ Smith.

He'd made no bones about the fact that he blamed her for the current unhappy state of his life. Could he really be petty enough to stalk her again?

Anything was possible. She hadn't thought him capable of menacing her three years before, and yet he'd done it. She'd trusted him—until he proved untrustworthy. After he'd fallen for and married Nikki, she'd let her guard down. While she wouldn't call them friends, she did think of him as an acquaintance she could trust. Obviously, that trust had been given far too freely.

Now the question was, what was she going to do about the situation?

TWENTY-ONE

Tricia suffered yet another troubled night of sleep. Not so her cat, who comfortably snoozed at the bottom of her bed. With orders not to get her arm wet, she did her best to give herself a sponge bath. Even after a couple of cups of coffee, Tricia still felt groggy when she left her apartment to descend the stairs to the bookshop below, with Miss Marple following in her wake.

She was early, and decided to get the coffee going before Pixie or Mr. Everett arrived. And she still didn't know what she wanted to do about her discovery of the listening device under the washstand the evening before.

Truly, she had one real option: report it to Chief Baker. But she wasn't sure she wanted to do that just yet. First, she wanted to talk it over with her sister. Angelica was respected and well-liked by a majority of the Chamber members. However, the fact that there was support for Chauncey's bid to take her job meant that a minority of members—and Tricia hoped it was just that—had not been pleased with Angelica's contributions to the association. More fool them.

But the plain fact was that Angelica was being blackmailed. Might she, too, be bugged?

On impulse, Tricia retrieved her cell phone from her slacks pocket and tapped Angelica's name under her contacts list.

"Morning, Tricia," Angelica said, more cheerful than she'd sounded the day before. "You're calling early." And obviously she hadn't spoken to Antonio; otherwise Tricia was sure her sister's greeting would have been anything but warm.

"Hi, Ange. I wanted to catch you before you took off for your meetings. I was wondering if we could break our routine and have lunch at the Brookview today."

"Oh? Do you have something special to celebrate?"

"Not exactly."

"What's this all about?" Angelica asked, sounding intrigued.

"It's a surprise." Boy, was it.

"I like surprises . . . most of the time," Angelica said cautiously.

Yeah, and this was a doozy.

"Okay. Only, I've got that meeting in Nashua with my fellow Chamber presidents. It's my last one, and I can't miss it. It won't end until at least eleven thirty. But I can meet you at the inn by one."

"Great. I'll ask Mr. Everett and Pixie to switch lunchtimes with me. I'm sure they'll be accommodating."

"Fine."

"By the way, I called around and found someone to replace all the bulbs that were broken over the weekend—or at least they'll knock on each business owner's door to ask permission before they do. I told them not to bother you—just to do it and send the invoice to me. He'll show up sometime today."

"Thanks for taking care of it." Yes, one less thing to worry about.

"I'll see you later at the inn. Toodles."

Tricia hit the end-call icon and stared at her screen for a few moments, making the decision to postpone her chat with Baker—at least until she spoke with her sister. Of course, the Brookview was also treacherous territory, for Antonio's office opened onto the main lobby. Still, it wasn't likely to be bugged.

Next, Tricia went back to her computer and did a quick search to find out about jamming devices. Yes! They were available. No, they weren't cheap. But she could get one in Nashua that very morning. In fact, maybe she'd get two of them—one for her and one for Angelica's home—just in case.

With that decided, she pulled out her phone once more and scrolled through her contacts until she found the number for the Brookview's front desk, but just before she tapped the call button, she decided perhaps it would be prudent to check out her store for listening devices. Since that would take longer than contacting the hotel, she decided to make her call. Two minutes later, she was crawling on her hands and knees as she looked for a camera or listening device. She found none, but that could simply mean she'd missed finding it—or them.

She had just finished her search when the shop door opened and Pixie breezed inside. "Good morning!"

"I sure hope so," Tricia said, and looked at the clock. "I've got to run an errand. Are you okay with taking care of the store this morning? And I'm afraid I'm going to have to ask you and Mr. Everett to again accommodate me for a different lunchtime today, as well."

"Not a problem," Pixie said, donning her Haven't Got a Clue apron and tying it around her waist. "After all, once you're Chamber president, we'll both be taking on more responsibility."

Tricia smiled. "Thank you. But let me remind you, it isn't a done deal."

Pixie positively grinned. "Yet!"

Driving with one arm impaired was a challenge, and even more so since snow flurries chased Tricia to and from Nashua, but she picked up the scramblers and another device and made it back to Haven't Got a Clue in time for Mr. Everett to take his lunch. Pixie had no problem waiting a few extra minutes for her own lunch hour, and Tricia left in plenty of time to get to the inn by one.

The Brookview was all decked out for Thanksgiving, with pretty orange-and-gold-leafed garlands coiling around the massive columns on the big front porch.

A staff member escorted Tricia to the private dining room, and she ordered a couple of martinis before taking off her cloak to wait for Angelica. The wait wasn't long—less than five minutes—before her sister arrived. During that time, Tricia had crawled around the room, looking under tables and chairs until she was satisfied that she and Angelica would have complete privacy.

"What a hair-raising ride over here," Angelica said, taking off her hat, coat, and scarf and hanging them up by the door. "My meeting let out early because of the weather, but it took me over an hour to drive here."

Tricia looked out the window; still no measurable snow in the village. "It must have been a localized storm," she said, hoping Stoneham would be spared an accumulation.

Angelica sat down on the upholstered love seat and patted the cushion for Tricia to join her. "Now, what's this surprise you've cooked up?"

"It's not a happy one, I'm afraid." She withdrew her phone and pulled up the little photo she'd taken of the listening device, tapping it to make it fill the screen. She handed the device to Angelica.

"What on earth is *that*?"

"The Whisper Ear thirty-two hundred."

"And that is?"

"A bug."

Angelica scrutinized the photo, frowning. "It hasn't got legs."

"It's a listening device," Tricia clarified. "I found it last night under the washstand I just bought."

Angelica's frown deepened. "You're kidding."

Tricia shook her head.

"Who'd want to listen to you?" She seemed to realize her mistake and rephrased the question. "I mean, *why* would someone want to listen to you?"

"I have a few ideas, and that's why I wanted to speak to you about it in private. Although I did a search this morning, I'm not so sure my store, or yours for that matter, isn't also being bugged."

"Do you think Booked for Lunch is vulnerable, too?"

"It's not a secret that you and I eat there almost every day at closing. And we usually sit at the same table in the back, too."

Angelica nodded, looking uneasy. "I never thought I'd have to worry about that kind of thing."

"Me, neither. And let's not forget, you're being blackmailed, and I've got two contentious opponents in the Chamber race."

Angelica blanched. "How did you ever find the *bug*?"

Tricia explained about Miss Marple's naughty behavior.

"You owe your cat a dozen bags of snacks. Who's on the top of your suspect list?"

"Russ, of course. Then again, he's so cheap, I wonder if he would cough up a couple hundred bucks to pay for such a device—at least without Nikki knowing it."

Angelica shook her head. "He might consider it a business deduction."

Tricia hadn't thought of that. "Of course, Chauncey and I aren't exactly pals, either. He'd love to defeat me and take your place as head of the Chamber, so I wouldn't put it past him, either."

"And now you've got me wanting to check out my own home and businesses."

"It's the prudent thing to do."

A knock sounded, and a waiter with a white shirt, black tie, and black slacks entered with a tray. He set cocktail napkins on the coffee table and settled their glasses on top. "Are you ladies ready to order?"

"I wish I could say no, but I have other things to do this afternoon," Angelica lamented.

"Me, too," Tricia agreed.

"I'll have the quiche of the day," Angelica said.

"Make that two."

"Very good. I'll be back soon with your lunches."

They watched him go, and when the door closed behind him, Angelica picked up her glass and spoke once more. "Are you going to Chief Baker with this?"

Tricia shrugged. "I know I should. But part of me wants to turn the tables on whoever has violated my home."

"You mean by planting some false information and seeing who spills the beans?"

Tricia nodded. She, too, picked up her glass and took a sip. Damn fine. "I ran an errand to Nashua this morning and bought a couple of jammers. If you don't want to be overheard, all you have to do is turn it on." She reached for her purse beside the love seat and brought out one of the devices, handing it to Angelica. "I'll show you how it works."

Once Angelica understood how to use the device, she picked up her glass again. "You don't suspect Pixie—and certainly not Mr. Everett—do you?"

"Of course not. I trust them both implicitly."

"And I trust my employees, too," Angelica agreed. "Everyone I work with is exemplary."

Tricia nodded.

"I've been thinking about lapses Antonio or I might have made that might have given a clue about our relationship to someone within the Nigela Ricita umbrella of companies. We're very discreet." She chewed her bottom lip. "I wonder if I should have Antonio check *his* office for bugs, but then how would I explain the situation?"

"You could tell him the truth."

She shook her head. "That's not an option." Angelica looked thoughtful. "It occurs to me that while we've taken safety measures here at the inn, my company isn't centralized. We have no one person dedicated to taking care of all our security needs. It's something I never gave a thought to—until now."

"Are you sure you don't want to talk to Chief Baker about all this?"

Angelica shook her head.

"He could set up a sting."

"No."

"How about if *I* went to him to set up a sting? Maybe we'd end up killing two birds with one stone."

Angelica studied her glass, took a sip, and looked thoughtful. "I guess I would be okay with that. But you wouldn't emphasize my difficulties, right?"

"No." This was one promise Tricia felt she could keep. "Not until you say so."

Angelica nodded. "This could be dangerous for you."

"I have every confidence in the Stoneham Police Department."

Now if she just believed it.

TWENTY-TWO

The sisters agreed to have dinner at Angelica's that evening, but not before Tricia did a sweep of the place for yet another bug.

Before she left the inn, Tricia stayed behind in the Brookview's private dining room and called the Stoneham Police Department. As usual, Baker's receptionist gave her a hard time about speaking with the village's top cop, but Tricia stressed that it was a matter of great importance, and Polly reluctantly transferred the call.

"Hello, Tricia," Baker said wearily. "There's nothing new on Ted Harper's murder case."

"That's not why I'm calling. Do you have time to see me this afternoon—in fact, right away?"

"What for?"

"My home is being bugged, and I know that's illegal."

"It certainly is," Baker said, sounding a lot more interested than he had just seconds before.

"Then you'll see me?"

"Come right over to my office."

"I'm not sure I want to be seen walking into the police station. Someone could be watching my every move. If we want to catch this guy, we need to be discreet."

"That sounds reasonable. But start from the beginning so I know where we stand."

Now that she'd already told her story once, the second telling went much faster and smoother, and she felt confident she'd made the right decision in talking to him.

"Can we run a sting?"

"I need to give this some thought. And I want to see this bugging device for myself."

"Of course. But it'll look suspicious if you just show up at my store unannounced."

"Well, I certainly have no social reason to be there these days."

"You could say you want to talk to me about Ted's poisoning. You don't have to actually say anything you haven't already told me."

"If we're being listened to, I'd say even less."

"Good idea."

"Is there any other reason, besides running for the Chamber presidency, why someone would want to bug you?"

"No." That was the truth. She would not say another word about Angelica's difficulties.

"Okay. Why don't I show up half an hour from now?"

"Good. It'll give me a chance to get back to the store and play it cool."

"Where are you now?"

"The Brookview. Angelica and I had lunch here."

It wasn't at all suspicious, and Baker didn't inquire about the change of location from their usual midday meal haunt.

"All right. I'll see you in thirty minutes," Baker said, and hung up.

Tricia stuffed her cell phone back in her purse, donned her cloak, hat, and scarf, and left the room to pay the bill at the inn's front reception desk.

The snowflakes had finally made it to Stoneham, and a light coating covered the streets. Tricia made it back to Haven't Got a Clue with nearly twenty minutes to spare. It bode well that a couple of customers browsed the bookshelves as Mr. Everett dusted the baseboard, and Pixie flitted around the store, straightening books on the shelves, tidying the cash desk, and organizing the magazines on the coffee table. The atmosphere was electric with the anticipation of a sale, giving Tricia an excuse for appearing just a little bit jittery.

Baker arrived right on time, looked around the shop, and then called out, "Tricia, have you got a minute to speak to me?"

"Chief Baker, good to see you. Of course."

"How's the arm?"

"Getting better all the time."

"That's good. Is there any chance we can speak in private?" he asked.

"Sure. Right this way." And Tricia led him through the store to the back and up the stairs to her loft apartment, while Mr. Everett joined Pixie to help with the impending sale. Miss Marple tagged along, probably hoping to squeeze in an extra kitty snack.

Tricia unlocked the door to her apartment, and Baker and the cat followed her through. Tricia pointed to the washstand and mouthed, *It's under there.*

Baker nodded, but didn't move.

"So, what did you have to tell me, Grant?"

"Just that Ted Harper's death was ruled accidental." It hadn't been; at least not yet. "They buried him last week."

Which Tricia already knew. "It's so sad."

Baker slipped out of his shoes and crept slowly across the new floor. Tricia was glad the refinished floorboards no longer squeaked.

"Will I ever get my serving dishes the lab team took last Friday night?"

"Oh, yeah, I'll make sure of it." Baker got down on his knees, withdrew a pen-sized LED flashlight, and shone it under the table. He stared at the listening device, and Tricia figured she ought to say something to avert suspicion.

"It was dark the night of the party. You didn't get a chance to see my new balcony."

Baker got up and walked across the living room again. "I don't suppose you had an opportunity to use it before it got cold out."

"No. Would you like to see it?"

"Sure."

Tricia grabbed the cashmere throw from the couch and wrapped it around her shoulders, then unlocked the sliding glass doors that led to her tiny patio, which was really only big enough to hold two people, her small gas grill, a couple of chairs, and a bistro table.

"Nice," Baker said, as she closed the door behind them.

"Well, what do you think?"

"You've got a bug all right."

"What do we do about it?"

"I'm going to have to think about this for a day or so. Do you feel comfortable about leaving it there for a few days?"

Tricia nodded. "At least I know how it got there. If someone had breached my security alarm and gotten inside my apartment—I'd be a lot more nervous. And I've got the jammer, in case I need to talk and not be heard. But the election is on Wednesday. That doesn't give us a lot of time to figure this out."

"Even if you lost, someone may want to keep listening—just to be a voyeur."

"At least it's in my living room and not my bedroom."

"Oh? Were you planning on entertaining up there?" Barker asked, with just a hint of judgment in his voice.

"No, not that it's any of your business."

"How did your date with Marshall Cambridge go yesterday?"

"My, word certainly gets around," Tricia said sourly.

"He doesn't seem like your type," Baker muttered.

"And what *is* my type?"

"Not *him*."

"Because he sells pornography?"

"For one."

"And for another?"

"He's got an arrest record."

Tricia's eyes widened, and for a moment she just stood there, the snow gently settling on the throw and catching in her hair. "How—how do you know?"

"I do my due diligence whenever we get new people in the village."

"Isn't that a little like Big Brother watching?"

Baker shrugged. "Just part of my job."

Had he looked up Marshall's record before or *after* he'd learned of Tricia's lunch date with the man? Why did Baker continue to hold a grudge? He'd moved on—he'd been dating someone for months. Why did he always throw verbal zingers her way when it came to her love life—or lack thereof?

"Are you going to tell me what he was arrested for?"

Baker shook his head. That had to mean it was a minor offense. Surely if Marshall had been a killer or otherwise violent, Baker would have felt compelled to warn her. Now he was just being petty.

She decided not to press the issue.

"It's going to seem suspicious to my listener if we stay out here much longer," she said, and reached for the door handle, pulling it open. Baker followed her back inside, and she locked the sliding glass door. Miss Marple was nowhere in sight, and Tricia figured she must have wandered up to the bedroom—or found a comfy place to settle by the nearest heat vent.

"I need to get back to the station," Baker said.

"I'll walk you out," Tricia said, but took a moment to toss the throw back on the couch once again.

Baker preceded her down the stairs, and Tricia locked her apartment once more. It wasn't something she usually did during the day, but since finding the bug, she felt just a little nervous about leaving her home vulnerable.

The shop was once again devoid of customers, and Pixie and Mr. Everett had gone back to reading.

"I'll keep in touch," Baker said, and headed out the door.

"Thanks. And bye," Tricia called as the door banged shut behind him.

Pixie looked up from her paperback. "What was that all about?"

Tricia shrugged. "Nothing much. He told me about Ted Harper being buried."

"And that's a secret?"

Again Tricia shrugged.

Pixie closed her book. "I've been thinking what else we could do to make sure you get elected as Chamber president on Wednesday."

"What have you come up with?"

"Well, there's the sympathy angle."

"Sympathy?" Tricia asked.

Pixie lifted her right arm.

"No!" Tricia said emphatically.

Pixie frowned. "We could make a slideshow video and send it to all the Chamber members by e-mail."

"What would it say?"

Pixie shrugged. "Basically repeat your platform, but add pretty pictures and catchy music."

"How could we find someone to make such a thing on such short notice?"

"You're lookin' at her."

"You can do that?"

"Sure, there's lots of software on the computer—it costs a bit by subscription, but if we only bought a month, it wouldn't even cost a C note."

"Really?"

"Sure. I know a few websites where we can get royalty-free pictures and put the whole thing together. They even have cool music. And you know what, as long as we have the service for a month—we could make a few more videos for the store's website. You know, pushing what we sell, and especially for the holidays."

"You've got me intrigued."

Pixie grinned, and her gold canine tooth flashed.

"When could you do it?" Tricia asked.

"How about now? If you'll authorize the charge on your credit card, I could have something ready before the end of the workday."

"Really?"

"Sure."

"Where did you learn about all this?"

"From talking to Mindy Weaver from Milford Travel at the Chamber meeting last Wednesday. She's made a couple for the agency, and they look pretty good for an amateur. And if I do say so myself, I think I'm a little bit more creative than her—I've learned a lot about graphics from doing scrapbooks."

"I didn't know you were into that."

"Oh, sure. You should see the one I made for my bridal shower."

"Oh, I wish you'd shown it to me before this." Especially since Tricia had paid for the shower and hadn't been able to attend most of it.

"I'll bring it in tomorrow."

"I'd like that."

"So would I," Mr. Everett said.

Pixie's smile could've melted a glacier.

TWENTY-THREE

Pixie retreated to the main computer in the basement and commenced working on the video, using free photos from the Internet and those Tricia had stored in a folder on her desktop from shots taken during author events at Haven't Got a Clue. There was even one from the grand opening of the Antiques Emporium that showed her and Toni Bennett cutting a big wide ribbon with an oversized pair of gold scissors. Russ had taken a similar photo for the *Stoneham Weekly News* that was even better, but Tricia didn't want to get into a copyright issue with him, and the grab shot one of Toni's vendors had taken with Tricia's phone would work just fine.

Pixie clicked the produce button and they had what could very well be the video's final cut. They decided to sleep on it and in the morning determine if any changes were necessary, but Tricia uploaded it on an unlinked page on the store's website so that she could show it to Angelica later.

The phone rang, and Pixie answered it. "Haven't Got a Clue—

we're about to close, but how may I help you?" She listened. "Oh, sure. She's right here."

Was it Baker getting back to Tricia about her bugging situation?

"Hello?"

"Tricia? It's Marshall."

"Oh. Uh, hello."

"What are you doing tonight for dinner?" he asked, and Tricia turned to find Pixie and Mr. Everett trying to look innocent of any form of eavesdropping.

"I'm sorry. I've already made plans." Did he think she'd been sitting by the phone just waiting for him to call?

"That's too bad. How about tomorrow?"

"Uh, yes. I suppose. Where and when?"

"I can pick you up—or are you worried about making it home unscathed?"

She wasn't sure if she was annoyed by the question. "No. But I am rather rusty at this."

"So am I. Gives us something else to discuss over drinks, huh?"

"Maybe."

"How's six forty-five, and I'll pick you up outside your store?"

"Okay."

"Right. See you then."

"Bye."

Tricia hung up the phone.

"Somebody's got a date," Pixie sang.

"It's just dinner. Food. Sustenance is required to support life."

"Uh-huh," Pixie said, not believing a word.

"Was that Mr. Cambridge?" Mr. Everett asked. She hadn't told him who she'd had lunch with the day before, but it seemed the entire village already knew.

"Yes."

Mr. Everett didn't look happy—rather like a concerned parent or grandparent—but he said nothing. Pixie, on the other hand, looked elated. Before she'd met her husband, Fred, she'd gone for bad boys, and to the village at large, Marshall had just that reputation.

Tricia glanced at the clock. One minute to six. "Time to close."

"I'll get our stuff," Pixie said, and headed to the back of the store at a fast clip, returning with their coats, scarves, and hats. They donned them quickly and headed for the door. "Good night!"

Tricia waved good-bye to her employees and locked up, giving Miss Marple a snack before leaving for Angelica's and dinner.

She made it up the long flight of stairs to Angelica's third-floor apartment to the accompaniment of Sarge's excited barking from within.

"Yes, yes! It's good to see you, too," Tricia said as she walked through the door. Much as she loved Miss Marple, there was something about a dog's greeting that never ceased to make her smile. "Biscuit!" she called, and Sarge went flying off in the direction of the kitchen while Tricia hung up her cloak and removed the bug finder from her slacks pocket.

"Hello!" Angelica called.

Tricia entered the kitchen just as her sister was pouring their first martinis. "Just what I need."

But Sarge was not to be ignored and continued to bark.

"Hush!" Angelica commanded, and the dog went silent. Tricia tossed him a dog biscuit, and he happily retreated to his kitchen bed to eat it.

"I brought some deviled eggs back from Booked for Lunch. I thought they'd be a nice appetizer," Angelica said.

"Yeah," Tricia said, noncommittally.

"Don't sound so bored—I made these myself. They've got a wonderful little kick."

"Did you add gin?"

"No. Just wait."

"Speaking of waiting," Tricia said, and brandished the bug finder, then held a finger up to her lips to warn her sister from saying anything she might not want overheard. Angelica nodded.

"Let me get those eggs out."

Tricia nodded and switched on the device. She took a step forward, and the little gadget let out a squeal. She quickly turned it off and bent down. Sure enough, under the lip of the granite counter was another one of the little round listening devices.

Angelica's lighthearted smile immediately evaporated.

"Do you mind if I borrow your bathroom?"

"Sure; go ahead," Angelica said.

Tricia signaled that she was going to do a circuit around the apartment to look for more of the offensive little contraptions. The living room was clear, as was the bathroom, but she found two of the little buggers in Angelica's bedroom: one under the nightstand where her telephone resided, and another on the underside of the bed frame. *How tacky!*

Tricia made a show of flushing the toilet and then running the sink, in case Angelica's listener had tuned in.

Upon returning to the kitchen, she removed a sheet of paper from the pad that was stuck to the fridge via a magnet and wrote a quick message.

Three bugs in all. Two in the bedroom. Night table and bed.

Angelica's mouth opened in horror, but Tricia silently hushed her again.

We'd better be very careful what we say. Grant said not to disturb them. He'll get back to me soon—she hoped—*with instructions on what to do.*

Angelica nodded, but didn't look mollified.

"Where's that drink?" Tricia said, and Angelica handed it to her.

She took a sip and had an idea. "Why don't we go sit in the living room and relax a bit before supper." She pointed to the kitchen's bug and then the jammer.

Angelica nodded in understanding. "Sounds heavenly. You take your drink, and I'll bring the rest of the stuff."

But before Tricia left the kitchen, she switched on the jammer. Still, neither of them spoke until they were far from the kitchen island.

Angelica set the small platter of egg halves on the coffee table and sat down on the couch, while Tricia took the adjacent chair. "Having a bug sure curtails spontaneous conversation," she complained.

"I agree, but better safe than sorry."

"Do you think you'll hear from Chief Baker tomorrow about those nasty little contraptions?"

"I hope so."

"What do you think having three of them in my apartment means?" Angelica asked. "It kind of blows your theory about you being the target."

"Not necessarily. Just about everybody knows I spend more evenings here with you than at my own place. And it's you who's been telling anyone who'll listen that I was your heir apparent to the job of Chamber presidency."

Angelica nodded and reached for a deviled egg. "But why my bedroom?"

Tricia shrugged. "Have any strangers been up here lately?"

Angelica looked thoughtful and took a bite of her egg, then moaned in ecstasy. "God, that's good." She shook her head. "I don't think so. Just our little family. Although . . . come to think of it, I did have someone in to look at the fridge."

"A repairman?"

"One of the guys from the Brookview. Antonio sent him. I thought the back might be clogged with dog hair, but he said I should consider getting either a new gasket for the freezer or a whole new fridge. He thought the gasket was the better solution. I have had a few things freeze on me." She ate the rest of her egg.

"What do you think?"

Angelica chewed and swallowed. "A gasket would be easier than hauling this monster down the stairs and another one up. I'll save that for when I do my remodel in the spring."

"Do you think he could have planted a bug?"

Angelica looked uncomfortable. "I did let him use my john."

"We should ask Antonio about him."

"Will do," Angelica agreed.

"Anyone else?"

"Jim Stark and one of his helpers, about a week ago—just before your party. That's when I asked him for a quote for my proposed remodel. He and the other guy traipsed through the whole apartment, and down in my storeroom. Do you think he's a possibility?"

"Jim and I haven't always gotten along, but he seems okay. Did you recognize his helper?"

"Why would I?" Angelica asked.

"Maybe he was the one who planted the bug." Tricia reached for one of the eggs and took a bite—immediately surprised by the sharp tang of horseradish. She coughed. "Wow!"

"I did warn you they had a kick," Angelica said, and took another. When she finished it, she picked up her glass and took a sip before speaking once again. "All this talk of bugs and conspiracy is freaking me out. Let's drop it."

"Agreed."

"Did anything else happen today?"

"Pixie made a video as a last-ditch campaign promotion."

"Really?"

"Here, I'll show it to you."

Tricia pulled out her phone, tapped the appropriate icons, and handed it to Angelica, who watched, enraptured. "It's wonderful!" she cried, delighted. "The production values aren't spectacular, but for your purposes, I think it's just darling."

Tricia smiled. "Pixie thought we should sleep on it in case we wanted to make any changes before sending it out in an e-mail blast to the Chamber members tomorrow, but I think it's perfect as is."

"Pixie is certainly surprising me with all her creativity and experience. I'm beginning to think she's too good to be just a salesclerk."

"Don't you dare think about poaching her from me."

"If I could find the appropriate place for her in Nigela Ricita Associates, would you really deny her the opportunity of advancement?"

Tricia's shoulders slumped. "Not when you put it that way. But that would be two people you've grabbed from my store."

"Can I help it if you excel at nurturing talent that fits in with my business plans?"

"What kind of a job would you offer her?"

"I have no idea. But I'm sure I could find something better for her to do than sell old books."

"Would you do the same for Frannie?"

Angelica's enthusiasm waned. "Mmm . . . probably not."

"Why? I thought that you were very happy with her work."

"I was—I mean, I am. But she doesn't show a lot of initiative. She doesn't have that *spark* of someone who really cares about her job."

"After four years behind a register, she's probably bored out of her mind."

"You're right. I should try to think of other things for her to do . . . it's just other women to whom I've given a chance have been proactive about their jobs. Ginny is my star, but even Bev has stepped up her game now that she's moved to the Dog-Eared Page. She's like a new person, and she told me she loves going into work every night."

"Couldn't you find a clerical job for Frannie?"

"I'm not sure she'd want to go back to that kind of work."

"Why don't you ask?"

"Maybe I will." Angelica polished off her martini. "Is anything else new?"

Tricia sighed, wondering if she should admit she'd made another date with Marshall. But then, Angelica would have to know that she was unavailable for dinner the next night anyway. "Yes. I'm having dinner with Marshall tomorrow night, so I won't be available."

"Oh. Okay."

"Okay?" Tricia asked.

"I figured you two would probably go out again."

"Yes, but—I thought you'd try to talk me out of it."

"Do you want me to?"

"No?"

"Then what's the problem?"

Tricia had no answer.

"Where are you going?"

"I didn't ask."

"Then let's hope it'll be a nice surprise."

Angelica got up and headed for the kitchen. Tricia followed. "We'd better not—" And she pointed to the counter and the bug.

Angelica nodded.

"What's on the menu tonight?" Tricia asked, and tripped the switch on the jammer, turning it off.

"Pork medallions with a balsamic honey glaze; another fabulous recipe from my first cookbook," she said in the vicinity of the bug. What was she doing—making a commercial for their listener?

"Sounds heavenly."

"But first I need another drink," Angelica said, and glared at the edge of the island where the bug lurked below.

"Me, too."

"You pour, and I'll start dinner," Angelica said.

Tricia did just that. But the fact that someone, somewhere nearby, was tuning in to their every word was inhibiting.

She hoped Chief Baker would have something to tell them in the morning that would be the start of the end of being surveilled by an unfriendly entity.

TWENTY-FOUR

For the first time in what seemed like ages, Tricia had a good night's sleep. Her arm didn't hurt as badly, and the video going out and the dinner with Marshall were things she had to look forward to. She treated herself to a big bowl of oatmeal, laced with raisins and walnuts, and instead of coffee, made a mug of tea and enjoyed it when she went to the basement to fire up the computer for the day. After going through her e-mail and reading the day's headlines on the Internet, she prepared the promotional e-mail to go out to the Chamber members later that morning.

Miss Marple seemed eager to go to the shop and start her hard labor of sleeping soundly for most of the day, so they headed back up the stairs to the shop a little early, which gave Tricia plenty of time to get the beverage station up and running. She even had time to sneak over to the Patisserie to get a treat for Pixie and Mr. Everett.

Donning her cloak, Tricia locked the store and briskly walked four doors down to the bakery. There seemed to be a lull, as there were no customers inside and no one stood behind the counter. "Hello!"

"Be there in a minute," came Nikki's voice from the back room.

Tricia examined the refrigerated glass cases filled with decadent sweets, breads, and savories, making the decision of what to get all that much harder. Mr. Everett loved raspberry thumbprint cookies, but Tricia was getting a little tired of them. They needed something different—and celebratory. Perhaps cupcakes? They were decorated with gorgeous lifelike roses in a multitude of colors, or topped with a mountain of white frosting and an avalanche of fluffy coconut, or with towers of rich, dark chocolate, for those with an extra-sweet tooth. Maybe she'd get a selection.

Nikki breezed through the saloon doors that separated the shop from the bakery itself. "Hello, Tricia," she said in rather a snide tone—or perhaps Tricia had just imagined it.

"Hi."

"What can I get you today? Another gross of thumbprints?"

No, her imagination was not at all involved. "Uh, is something wrong, Nikki?"

"Wrong? What could possibly be wrong?"

"You seem . . . a little angry?"

"Angry? Why should I be angry?"

"Let me guess. Because Russ is running for Chamber president and somehow you blame me?"

"Of course I blame you," she snapped.

"Why?"

"Because he's only doing it to keep *you* from having the job." Which Tricia already knew.

"Do you think he's got a chance of winning?" Since she hadn't seen or heard of him actively campaigning, it was still more likely she'd prevail. That is, if the organization's female members voted for her and the men split their votes between Russ and Chauncey—at least, that was her hope.

"Of course, he's the only sane choice. You and Chauncey are both at the far end of the spectrum. Chauncey wants the Chamber to do nothing and you want them to do too much, which is asking a lot of those of us who are chained to our businesses."

Nikki never lost an opportunity to drive home the point that she had wanted to be a stay-at-home mom and resented the fact her child had been placed in day care since six weeks after his birth.

"Did you talk about this before Russ threw his hat in the ring?"

"No."

And *that's* why she was so angry. But did she have to take it out on Tricia?

"Now, hurry up and order. I've got things to do in back."

Tricia shook her head. "Sorry, but I think I've lost my appetite." And without another word, she exited the shop.

The breeze was stiff and cold, blowing up and under her heavy wool cloak, and Tricia walked to the crosswalk, looked both ways, and traversed Main Street, heading for the Coffee Bean. She turned and saw that Nikki was watching her. Well, when you're treated with rudeness, there's no reason to support one business when another will be happy to serve. And Alexa was behind the counter, only *too* happy to sell Tricia some cupcakes that she had made just that morning. They weren't as pretty as Nikki's, but Tricia had a feeling eating them would be far more satisfying.

She returned to Haven't Got a Clue, hung up her cloak, and was setting the cupcakes on a dish when Pixie breezed through the door in her big faux fur coat, carrying her purse and a large shopping bag.

"You brought the scrapbook?" Tricia asked by way of a greeting.

"You bet your booty," Pixie said, and laughed. She set the bag on the reader's nook coffee table and went in back to hang up her coat and don her Haven't Got a Clue apron. Mr. Everett arrived just seconds later.

"Good morning," he called, but his face looked careworn.

"I wasn't expecting you in this early. Did you take Charlie to the vet?"

He nodded, looking sad. Pixie came up to stand in front of them.

"Something wrong, Mr. E?"

"It's Charlie." Tricia could tell it wasn't going to be good news.

"Why don't we all sit down," she suggested. "Hang up your coat, and then we'll have a cup of coffee. I got cupcakes for us."

"Aw, that's awfully sweet of you," Pixie said, but she looked almost as downhearted as Mr. Everett.

When he returned, Mr. Everett took a seat, and Tricia passed around the coffee. "What did the vet say?"

"That Charlie has had a long life, and that we should enjoy him during his last days." His voice broke, his lips trembling.

"Oh, Mr. Everett, I'm so sorry." Tricia reached across the table to rest her hand on top of his. His fingers curled around hers ever so gently.

"Did she talk about putting the little guy to sleep?" Pixie asked, and seemed to cringe as the words left her lips.

Mr. Everett shook his head. "No. She doesn't think Charlie is in any pain, just . . . tired."

"Did she tell you how long he's got?" Pixie asked.

"If we're lucky, a couple of weeks. If not . . ." His eyes shone with unshed tears.

"Do you need a hug?" Pixie asked shyly, knowing that Mr. Everett was not fond of emotional scenes, but surprisingly enough, he nodded.

Then Pixie and Tricia were right at his side, their arms wrapped around him, and they all had a good cry. Tricia was glad she kept a box of tissues on the big coffee table, because they all needed more than one once the group hug dissolved.

"You've done a wonderful thing, Mr. Everett. You took in poor old Charlie from the shelter and gave him a loving home, making his last days on earth perhaps his happiest. I applaud you for your bravery."

"Bravery?" he asked.

"Yeah," Pixie agreed. "You knew you'd only have the little guy for a short time, and that it would be hard to lose him, but you and Grace did it anyway. If I had a medal, I'd pin it on your sweater—for both of you."

"I would, too," Tricia agreed.

Miss Marple seemed to appear from out of nowhere and jumped on Mr. Everett's lap, nuzzling his chin and purring loudly. Mr. Everett petted her and she turned around twice before settling onto his lap.

"Why don't we all have a cupcake? That might cheer us up, if only for a few minutes," Pixie suggested.

"Yes," Tricia agreed, glad for a change of subject. "I thought we could celebrate the wonderful video you made yesterday."

"Do you want me to send it out right now?" she asked.

Tricia shook her head. "Why don't we enjoy our cupcakes and coffee, and if no customers come in for a while, we could look through your scrapbook. I missed so much of the party, I'd love to catch up."

Pixie gave a shy smile. "This is just the bridal shower scrapbook. I coulda brought the wedding ones, but figured this was enough for today."

She had more than one for the wedding?

"You get it out, and I'll get the cupcakes and napkins," Tricia said.

Moments later, they had peeled the paper wrappers from their cupcakes and enjoyed them before wiping their hands and carefully handling Pixie's pride and joy. It was pleasant to think about a happier time, and even Mr. Everett smiled at the costumes and the cake and the apparent fun that Tricia and he had missed.

But Tricia couldn't help watching as Mr. Everett paged through the book, sitting rather awkwardly so as not to disturb Miss Marple. For years he hadn't allowed himself to own a pet for fear of losing it, and now that he had brought Charlie into his life, and obviously loved him, he would soon be without him.

She couldn't help feeling sorry for both of them and the wasted years.

It wasn't a customer who opened the door accompanied by the jingling of a bell overhead and interrupted their little coffee klatch, but the mailman.

"Hi, Randy. I hope you brought more than bills," Pixie said, rising from her chair and without her usual enthusiasm.

"Don't kill the messenger," he said, and handed her the small stack of envelopes. "See you tomorrow."

"We'll be here," Pixie said.

She took her seat again and handed the pile to Tricia, who didn't bother to look at it.

"I'm so impressed with that scrapbook, Pixie. I wonder if you'd be willing to put something together that shows our author signings. I'd be more than happy to pay for everything you need, and it would be a showpiece we could share with our customers who aren't able to come in for the events."

"Sure. That'd be fun to put together."

"And, of course, I wouldn't expect you to do it on your own time. Maybe you could do it in January when things are slow."

"I'd love to."

That was, of course, if Angelica didn't recruit her for Nigela Ricita Associates before that.

Miss Marple chose that moment to jump down from Mr. Everett's lap. "I'd best get my lamb's wool duster and attack those shelves in the back. The forced air from the heat register leaves them terribly dusty. But perhaps first I should go down to the basement and change the furnace filter."

"Oh, you don't have to do that."

"It would be my pleasure, Ms. Miles," he said, and it would probably also be good for him to have something else to do to keep his mind off Charlie for just a little while.

"Thank you."

Pixie packed up her scrapbook and replaced it in the bag. "I'll go put this in the back so it doesn't get damaged."

Tricia nodded and turned her attention to the pile of envelopes still in her hand. As she shuffled through them, she saw that one had been delivered in error. It was addressed to Mary Fairchild at the By Hook or By Book shop. Holding it up to the light, she saw that it seemed to contain a check.

"Oh, my. This is for Mary down the block. It looks important. I think I'll pop on down the way and give it to her. I wouldn't want it to get lost."

She once again donned her cloak and left her shop in Pixie's capable hands.

The temperature hadn't risen a degree since her earlier foray outside, and the wind was just as stiff, messing up her hair despite the felt hat she wore.

By Hook or By Book was just as devoid of customers as Haven't Got a Clue, but Mary was already occupied on the phone, with her back to the door. She covered the receiver, but didn't turn. "Be with you in a moment," she called, and went back to her conversation.

"No, I'm telling you, she jinxed me!"

Tricia felt her cheeks color. There was only one person in the village who bore that reputation: herself!

"Yes, she told me to 'break a leg,' and gosh darn it—the very same day I *did* break my leg. Yes, she's got *that* kind of power, and if she used it for ill once—she's *bound* to do it again."

Tricia cleared her throat, but Mary just waved a hand in annoyance.

"No, and that's why you've got to vote for Chauncey tomorrow at the Chamber of Commerce meeting. It's for the good of the entire organization, not to mention the entire village." She paused. "Uh-huh. Uh-huh. Yes. Thank you. Okay. I'll see you tomorrow. Good-bye." And she hung up the phone. Then she turned—and her mouth dropped open.

Mary gave a feeble laugh. "Hi, Tricia. I didn't know you were standing there."

"Obviously," Tricia managed, barely able to keep the fury from her voice.

Mary laughed again, but looked like she might also be sick. "Hee-hee. I was having a little fun with . . . with one of the . . ."

"Chamber members?"

Mary's blush was fever-bright. "I've got a perfectly good explanation," she said defensively.

"Oh?"

"Yes, you see . . ." She let out a breath and frowned. "No, I don't, and I should level with you. I don't blame you for my broken leg. That maniac who plowed into me with his scooter was totally responsible—not you."

Tricia well remembered—she'd been only one of hundreds of witnesses to the assault. "That wasn't how it sounded just now."

Mary's expression seemed to crumple, and she looked like she might cry. "I have to break it off with Chauncey."

"And bad-mouthing me will help you do that?"

"Of course not. But I need an excuse, and . . . if he wins the Chamber presidency, he'll be too busy to juggle his shop, the Chamber, and a marriage."

"Mary, just hand him the ring, say, 'Sorry, it's over,' and walk away."

"That's easy for you to say. You don't know Chauncey like I do."

Oh, yes she did. From past events she knew exactly what Chauncey was capable of—including battery.

"What do you think would happen if you broke it off?"

"What happened to you when you and Russ Smith called it quits—and I don't want to be stalked. It's bad enough his shop is directly across the street from mine. I've even thought about relocating my store when the lease runs out next year. But in the meantime, I know he watches me like a hawk. He doesn't like me talking to other people, or even my own family members."

"Those are all red flags for domestic violence," Tricia pointed out.

"And don't I know it. That's why I need to ease myself out of this relationship. He's been pressuring me to get married, and it's just not going to happen."

"Have you thought about going to couples counseling?"

"I have. I've suggested it a number of times, but he won't hear of it. The truth is—I'm scared of him, Tricia. I don't know what he's liable to do to me if I flat out say we're through."

Tricia's emotions had run the gamut of anger to sympathy in less than five minutes.

"There are organizations that help battered women."

"Yeah, and he hasn't lifted a hand to me."

"Yet," Tricia pointed out. "Their mission is to help abused women. It couldn't hurt to contact one of them."

Mary merely shrugged, looking trapped.

"I'm sorry, Mary. I do feel sorry for you, but it isn't fair for you to paint me as the villain here. I didn't hurt you, and what you're telling people could be considered slander. I have to live in this village—whether I get the job of Chamber president or not. I understand you have problems, and I'm sorry I can't help fix them, but you can't go around telling people lies about me."

"I'm sorry," Mary said contritely. "I promise, I won't do it again."

Would she instead make up something about Russ?

"Why did you come here, anyway?" Mary asked.

Tricia had almost forgotten. "Randy delivered an envelope to my shop instead of yours. I thought it might be important and came down as soon as I discovered it." She handed the envelope to Mary.

Mary's face lit up. "Oh, I've been waiting for this. It's the check from the cruise line's insurance company. This could help me escape from Chauncey. Please don't tell him it's arrived—he's been hounding me about it ever since I told him about the settlement."

"I definitely wouldn't say a word to anyone." Except Angelica, who was famous for keeping secrets. "You should cash it immediately and put it in an account that Chauncey can't touch."

"Don't worry. I've got a contingency plan for this money." Was she planning on leaving the village and abandoning her shop? Tricia wasn't sure she cared to know.

There didn't seem to be anything more to say . . . except—"Will you be at the Chamber meeting tomorrow?"

"You better believe it. And I'll be casting my vote for Chauncey—and if you're any kind of a friend, you will, too."

"Mary!"

"If things were different, I'd vote for you in a heartbeat, but in this instance, it's self-preservation."

Tricia guessed she could understand that, but she also hoped that when Mary could think clearly, she would realize how outrageous her request really was.

"I'd better get going. I have a shop to run."

"Thanks for bringing the check. And I'll see you tomorrow morning at the meeting."

"Good-bye," Tricia said, civilly, if nothing else.

She left the shop and headed back up Main Street, wondering what else could go wrong that day.

TWENTY-FIVE

Pixie was waiting behind the sales counter ready to pounce when Tricia walked through the shop door. "Are you ready to send out that e-mail?"

It took Tricia a moment to remember that Pixie was referring to the video she'd created the day before. "Oh, yes. Let's send it out now. Mr. Everett, would you mind the shop while Pixie and I use the computer in the basement office?"

"Not a bit," he said affably.

There was a joyful bounce to Pixie's step as she preceded Tricia down the steps to the basement, turning on the lights as she went. "Is the computer on?"

"Yes. And I've written the e-mail and saved it to the draft folder. I split the list of Chamber members into four sections so it wouldn't be considered spam. All we have to do now is attach the video, and they're good to go."

"Let's watch it one more time. I wouldn't want you to have sender's remorse if it went without one last tweak."

The truth was, Tricia had watched the video three times that morning, but couldn't think of any changes she'd like to make.

Pixie read through the e-mail to make sure there were no typos, and then crossed her fingers as Tricia hit the send button.

"Well, it's off into the big, wide world!" Pixie said excitedly.

Yes it was, and just like Pixie had predicted, Tricia immediately wished she could hit unsend. What was she thinking, sending out such a promotional message? Didn't it just prove how needy she was? Would she look too ambitious? A lot of men were threatened by ambitious, capable women. Would she be accused of tooting her own horn—and way too loudly?

Then she thought again. If a man had sent it, everyone would think he was great at marketing, and smart to take advantage of whatever technology had to offer to get his message across to win the election.

It wasn't a bit fair that women weren't held to the same standard—and in just about every aspect of life.

"Do you want to hang around to see if you get any comments?" Pixie asked.

"I think I'll wait awhile for that in case some of the members aren't happy with the reminder to vote." *And for me,* she thought to herself.

Pixie nodded. "Then I guess we'd better head upstairs. Isn't today the day when the bus of pre-Christmas shoppers comes in from Portland?"

"Yes," Tricia said, and it had been much anticipated by the Main Street business owners.

"We should have put up our decorations," Pixie hinted, not for the first time. "Why don't we do that later?"

"We can plan it today and perhaps put them up tomorrow after the Chamber meeting."

"But you'll have too much to do tomorrow, won't you?"

"I wouldn't start the job until the first of the year, and I pretty much know everything there is to know about it. And if I don't, I can always bend Angelica's ears."

"Great. I can't wait to start decorating. The holidays are my absolute favorite time of year."

"Do you have a scrapbook for that?"

Pixie's smile faded. "I haven't actually had a lot of happy Christmases," she admitted, "but I'm sure that's going to change this year now that Fred and I are married. I can't wait to put up our tree. I might even do it this weekend to get a jump on the season."

Tricia wasn't nearly that eager. But maybe she'd put a tabletop tree on the new washstand—if she could figure out a way to keep Miss Marple off it.

In the meantime, she needed to get ready for that busload of shoppers and hope they liked vintage mysteries.

By the time Tricia and Pixie made it back up the stairs to the shop, the phone was already ringing. Mr. Everett answered it. "Why, yes, she's right here; just a moment." He handed the phone to Tricia.

"This is Tricia; how can I—?"

"Tricia? It's Joyce over at Have a Heart romance. I just got your e-mail and I think it's absolutely darling."

"Thank you, Joyce."

"I just wanted to let you know that you've got my vote, and I can't wait to see where you take the Chamber."

As she hung up the phone, Tricia's smile couldn't have been wider.

The next call was from Jason Evanston, who owned the tire store down near the highway. He wasn't quite as complimentary, and Tricia had to hold the phone away from her ear during his tirade.

"I don't think I need to take any more calls for a while," she announced after she'd hung up.

"Talk about a poor sport," Pixie muttered, but she took the lead when it came to answering the rest of the calls—and there were only six more—telling each person she'd pass along the message. And she did—for four of the calls. Tricia didn't ask about the others.

The bus dutifully arrived at about eleven o'clock, and it almost felt like the summer tourist season once again. The riders had three hours to kill in the village, and they spread out among the shops and eateries. Tricia and Pixie held the fort while Mr. Everett went to lunch, and then Tricia and Mr. Everett took care of the customers when it was Pixie's turn. The hours went quickly with so many eager shoppers browsing through the merchandise, and Tricia was happy to note that they would have to restock some of the shelves later.

The bus was just about to take off on its return trip when Tricia exited Haven't Got a Clue and headed over to Booked for Lunch to meet Angelica.

Once again, Angelica was seated at the back booth, and Molly was hard at work busing the tables, which had obviously been quickly vacated.

"What a day," Tricia said as she removed her cloak and settled in across the table from her sister.

"Almost as good as summer."

"I'll say," Molly chimed in. "If this keeps up through the holiday season, I'll be able to buy presents for all my kids and grandkids."

"It will," Angelica assured her. "Can I have a warm-up when you've got a minute?" she asked, proffering her nearly empty cup.

"Sure thing," Molly said. "Can I get you a cup, too, Tricia?"

"Yes, please."

She continued to clear off the tables, and Angelica leaned forward. "So, what's the skinny on your e-mail? Did you get any feedback?"

"Yes. Some people like it, and some don't."

"That was to be expected," Angelica said realistically.

"Yes, but the positives do seem to outweigh the negatives."

Angelica's expression sobered even more. "I meant what I said the other night. I'd really like to offer Pixie a better job than just salesperson. She's sharp, and she's dedicated, and I know you wouldn't want to stand in her way when it comes to a career opportunity."

Tricia felt like she'd been punched in the gut.

"She wouldn't have to interview until January—you need her for the holidays—but the winter months are so slow it would benefit your bottom line if you shed one paycheck. Besides, you and Mr. Everett could handle everything alone. You did it before Pixie came to work for you."

"Yes, but . . . I've come to rely on her. And it took months to replace Ginny. I wouldn't look forward to doing that again."

"Which is why winter is the perfect time to try to find someone else. If they don't work out—it wouldn't be a hardship."

Tricia frowned, unhappy that she couldn't refute Angelica's logic except for one tiny thing. "If I win the Chamber election tomorrow, I'll need her more than ever."

Angelica sighed. "All right. Then let's make it contingent on what happens tomorrow. If you win, we won't speak of this again—and I'm pretty sure you will win," she said with authority. "But if you lose, then Pixie should be given an opportunity to do more with her life than just sell old mystery books."

When she put it that way, it made Tricia feel very selfish to even suggest the alternative.

"All right. You win."

"No, an opportunity like this gives *Pixie* the chance to win."

Yes, but it was also just one more thing to feed the anxiety that seemed to be growing within Tricia.

TWENTY-SIX

It was after three when Tricia returned to Haven't Got a Clue and found that, despite a bulging cash register, there was no hint that the store had accommodated more than a dozen customers just hours before. The shelves were once again brimming with books, a fresh pot of coffee had been brewed, and the wastebasket full of customers' discarded paper coffee cups had been emptied. Pixie and Mr. Everett had more than proved their worth once again.

"Is everything okay?" Pixie asked once Tricia had hung up her cloak. "You seem kind of down."

Tricia forced a smile. "Just considering how many changes there'll be to my life should I win the election tomorrow." And just as many if she didn't.

"We'll manage, won't we, Mr. E?" Pixie asked cheerfully.

"We certainly will," he agreed, and even conjured up one of his rare smiles.

Tricia nodded.

Pixie grabbed a scrap of paper from the top of the cash desk. "I almost forgot. Antonio called while you were out. He wants you to call him back. He sounded kind of antsy."

Oh, dear.

"Maybe I'd better call him from the office downstairs," Tricia said, accepting the note.

She headed for her office and sat down in her desk chair, picking up the phone with trepidation. She had a pretty good idea of what he wanted to discuss, and she wasn't looking forward to the conversation. She punched in the number on her cell phone. Antonio answered almost immediately.

"Ah, Tricia. Thank you for getting back to me so soon."

"I take it you and Ginny have made a decision on what you want Angelica to do about her blackmailer."

"There can be only one decision. She must go to the *polizia*, if only for herself. We believe that is the best course of action, and I know you do, too."

"Yes, but—" She didn't voice the rest of the thought. Angelica was going to be furious with her, no matter what Antonio said. But there was more at stake than just her relationship with her sister—especially when it came to Sofia's safety.

"When do you intend to speak with her?"

"Tonight."

"What time?"

"After I get out of work. It is my turn to pick up Sofia at day care. I will probably arrive at her home about seven."

"Okay, that'll give me time to prepare her for what's to come."

"You do not have to do that."

"I feel obligated to do so."

"Very well. Then I guess I will see you this evening?"

"I'll be there." *Unless Angelica shoves me down the stairs.*

"See you then," Antonio said, and ended the call.

Tricia hung up the phone, sat back in her chair, and let out a long breath. The idea of the impending conversation felt like just another brick on her already sagging shoulders.

Unlike the early part of the day, the hours until closing seemed to drag, making the sense of dread Tricia felt seem even more debilitating. She'd gone over various conversational openings and hadn't come up with one that she felt would quell Angelica's anticipated ire. But she had come to one conclusion and wasn't sure how she felt about it. No matter what, they were going to have a very difficult conversation.

Tricia had donned her cloak and was ready to leave when the phone rang. The store was officially closed, but maybe it was one of the shoppers from earlier in the day. Mr. Everett had found a pair of gloves on one of the back shelves. Tricia answered the call on the third ring. "Haven't Got a Clue. This is Tricia."

"Hey, Trish. It's Marshall."

Marshall? Good grief! She'd completely forgotten they had a dinner date. Now what was she supposed to do?

"I'm sorry, but I'm going to have to cancel our date tonight."

Thank goodness!

"Oh?"

"Yeah, something's come up and I've got an appointment with my attorney in half an hour. I'd cancel that, but I've been waiting two weeks to get in to see him to finalize a deal. Who knew the guy would be open to seeing me outside of regular hours?"

Tricia gave a little laugh. "Who knew?"

"Can I get a rain check?"

"Of course."

"Great. But I'll see you at the Chamber meeting tomorrow."

"Oh, you're going to be there?"

"I wouldn't miss it."

"All right. I'll see you there."

"And, again, I'm really sorry to cancel on you at the last minute."

"It's not a problem."

"Okay. Bye."

"Bye."

Tricia hung up the phone and let out a breath, grateful for the reprieve and wondering what kind of a deal would make Marshall so excited. Could it have something to do with the arrest Baker had mentioned? That didn't seem likely. Perhaps she'd find a way to bring the subject up tomorrow at the Chamber meeting—or was that too public a place? Probably, but she had other things to think about just then.

Tricia locked up and walked next door, still unsure how to approach the ensuing conversation. She let herself into the Cookery, like she had more than a thousand times before, and trudged up the stairs. Sarge barked happily, belying her melancholy, and she opened the door. "Good boy," was all she could muster as she hung up her cloak and followed the deliriously happy dog through the apartment and into the kitchen.

"There you are," Angelica said cheerfully as she skewered two queen olives on a frill pick. "What a day I've had. I am so ready for this drink. How about you?"

"Oh, yeah," Tricia muttered.

Angelica set the olives in the stemmed glasses, poured the drinks, and handed one to Tricia. "Let's drink to your victory tomorrow."

"Isn't that a little premature?"

"Nonsense. It's the power of positive thinking." They clinked glasses, and Tricia took a fortifying slug from hers.

Angelica smiled, but then her expression changed to one of puzzlement. "Correct me if I'm wrong, but didn't you say you had a date tonight?"

"Marshall canceled."

"Oh?"

"He needed to see his attorney."

"After office hours?"

Tricia nodded.

"Did you believe him?"

"Why wouldn't I?"

Angelica shook her head and took another sip of her drink. "Men!"

But Tricia had other matters to attend to. She set her drink down, grabbed the little jammer from off the counter, and switched it on.

"I have something to tell you, and you're not going to like it."

"Oh?" Angelica asked, sounding wary—her cheerful mood immediately evaporated.

"Antonio came to talk to me on Sunday afternoon just before dinner."

Angelica's eyes widened—already blazing—and she seemed to gain an inch or more as she straightened to her heels-assisted full height. "And you told him?"

"He'd already guessed. He just came to me to ask for confirmation."

"Why? Why did you talk to Antonio when I specifically asked you not to?" Angelica hollered, and Tricia sure hoped the jammer was doing its job. As far as Tricia could remember, her sister had never been so angry with her. Even as children, when they hadn't gotten along, Angelica had never once raised her voice to Tricia.

"If you recall, I never actually promised I wouldn't speak to him about this."

Angelica's glare could have started a five-alarm fire.

"I've been thinking about it all afternoon, and I could only come to one conclusion: you wanted me to tell him."

"Are you delusional?"

"No, I'm not. Think about it. You kept secrets from me for decades. If you hadn't wanted me to know, you would have kept the blackmail letters to yourself. You told me because you wanted Antonio to know. Maybe it was an unconscious decision, but in your heart you know it's the truth."

Angelica looked away, her lower lip trembling.

"But that's not all that's been going on. There's something you haven't told me, bigger than the blackmail, and much bigger than just being outed as Nigela Ricita. What is it?"

Angelica turned away. "Oh, yeah—I'm going to tell you. You'd just run off to someone else and spill my secrets."

"Then I'm right—there *is* an even bigger secret you've been keeping."

Angelica wouldn't look at her, but Tricia grabbed her arm, pulling her forward and forcing her sister to look at her. "What is it, Ange? What could possibly be so terrible that you'd risk so much?"

And then suddenly it occurred to Tricia just what that secret might be.

Was it worth saying the words aloud? Was it worth possibly alienating her sister forever?

"You aren't Antonio's stepmother. You're his birth mother, aren't you?"

Angelica's head whipped around, her mouth dropping open in horror. "How could you say that? I'm much too young to have a child that old."

"No, you're not," Tricia countered.

Angelica glared at Tricia, just as fiercely as before, but then her eyes filled with tears. She sagged, and Tricia grabbed her with her good arm, bracing her against the kitchen island before she could fall, and then plunking her onto a stool.

It was then that Angelica began to cry. Not silent tears, but loud, wrenching sobs. Tricia bent down and wrapped her good arm around her sister's shoulder.

"Don't cry, Ange. It's nothing to cry about. You love Antonio, and you know he loves you."

"Yes, but his life is based on a lie. He would never trust me again if he knew the truth."

"Do Mother and Daddy know about this?"

Angelica wiped her eyes and shook her head. "Just me. Everyone else who knew is dead."

"Who was Sofia—the woman Antonio thought was his mother?"

"His father's sister."

"So Rod Perry wasn't his biological father?"

"No. That rat bastard. I thought I could trust him. He promised when we married I could bring Antonio to live with us."

"But he did visit you from Italy. I remember Daddy telling me so."

"Yes, he came for six months, but he had no idea why he'd been brought here to live with people who were virtual strangers to him. Rod was horrible to him."

"Did he hit Antonio?" Tricia asked, appalled.

"No, nothing like that. But he'd make snide remarks. Make fun of Antonio's limited English. The poor kid was miserable. He wanted to go back to his home in Italy and be with the woman he thought was his mother."

"What about Sofia?"

"She never married. She was content to play the *madre* role."

"But you kept visiting him. You kept supporting him."

Angelica nodded miserably. "Sofia concocted the story about her being his mother. She told him Rod was his biological father—that they'd had an affair. I let Antonio believe that."

"What did Antonio's real father say about all this?"

"Nothing. He died before Antonio was even born. A motorcycle accident. In those days, there were no helmet laws. The back wheel of his bike slid on a wet road."

"He was killed instantly?" Tricia asked, hoping it was true, but Angelica shook her head.

"He died three days later. We were going to be married." Her eyes filled with new tears, and she began to sob again. "He was the love of my life . . . until Antonio came along."

Had such a loss driven Angelica into a series of bad marriages and unhappy relationships?

And now Tricia had to ask the hardest question of all. "Why did you leave him?"

"Because I was twenty. I was stupid. I knew exactly what Mother would say if I came home from my year in Europe with a baby in my arms. She would've made my life miserable—told me I'd ruined it. Made me give him up."

"But you *did* give him up."

Angelica shook her head. "I stayed in touch. I bought his clothes. I paid for him to go to school. I'd go to Firenze every chance I got. I learned to speak fluent Italian."

"Antonio *is* grateful for everything you've done for him. He's told me so many times. Why do you think he couldn't accept the truth?"

"Because I know I would never forgive our mother if she'd perpetrated such a lie."

As far as Tricia was concerned, their mother had done far worse by her treatment of Tricia after her infant twin brother had died.

"I don't think you give Antonio much credit."

Sarge suddenly let out a sharp yelp and bolted upright in his bed. Then he jumped out of it and ran toward the door that led to the stairwell, barking his doggy head off. Tricia knew she had locked the door to the Cookery after her when she'd arrived. She hadn't known Antonio, too, had a key.

Sure enough, Antonio entered, his coat damp with melted snowflakes, and again Sarge went berserk with happiness at the sight of another person who was sure to give him a biscuit. Antonio picked up the wiggling dog and allowed it to smother him with kisses. "Sarge, Sarge, calm down, *ragazzino*."

"Oh, no!" Angelica cried. "What is he doing here?"

"I suspect he wants to help you deal with this blackmail plot in any way he can. He loves you. And he deserves to know the truth."

"I can't tell him, I can't—" But she didn't have an opportunity to finish the sentence, because Antonio put Sarge down and walked down the corridor and into the kitchen. He stopped at the biscuit jar on the counter, tossed Sarge a treat, and then walked over to the island.

Antonio looked down at Angelica, who still sat on the island stool, then bent down and kissed her on the forehead. "*Cara Matrigna*, we have a lot to talk about."

Angelica said nothing as more silent tears cascaded down her cheeks.

Antonio reached for her hand. "And the first thing you must know is that I know you are my *madre*. I have always known it."

Tricia winced, and Angelica burst into sobs once more.

Tricia moved aside as Antonio bent down and wrapped his arms around his mother, letting her cry on his shoulder.

Tricia looked away, embarrassed to intrude on their private moment. She saw Sarge sitting, head cocked, watching the human drama, and stooped to pick him up. "Sarge and I are going for a walk. We'll be back in a little while," she said, and marched out of the kitchen. She grabbed her cloak and Sarge's leash and then quietly closed the apartment door behind her.

TWENTY-SEVEN

**Tricia wasn't** sure it was a good idea to take a prolonged walk along the empty streets of a village that was no longer identified as the "safest" in the state, but she figured with Sarge acting as a barking alarm, she could at least draw attention to herself should someone attack. Still, she confined herself to Main Street, walking up and down the block. If she had to make a run for it, the Dog-Eared Page was open, and she knew she could find someone to help. But . . . not only was she being just a little paranoid, she was getting *cold*!

Tricia picked Sarge up. "If you don't want to freeze your little paws off, we can go inside. You've just got to hide under my cloak and be quiet. Got it?"

Sarge looked up at her with inquisitive eyes. Well, if he made a noise, they'd just have to leave. She decided to take a chance.

With Sarge tucked away, Tricia entered the Dog-Eared Page. The place was hopping, with the jukebox playing a jaunty tune with fiddles, bagpipes, and goodness only knew what else, while two couples played darts. There wasn't an empty seat at the bar, where Chauncey Porter stood—his back to her—with what looked like a glass of ginger ale. As far as she knew, he was a teetotaler and had never set foot inside the pub before that night. He was regaling the others, who seemed to be looking anywhere but in his direction, or ignoring him altogether. He'd chosen the wrong crowd to pontificate to—Tricia didn't see a single Chamber member in sight.

The table nearest the door was empty—no doubt because of the draft every time someone came in—but that would be just perfect for her and Sarge. She slid into the booth and rearranged her cloak to ensure that the little dog wasn't in danger of suffocating.

Bev, the waitress, approached. "Tricia! Great to see you here at the Dog-Eared Page."

"I heard you love working here."

"I enjoyed my time at Booked for Lunch, but I really am loving it here. I'm a night person, so this suits me. What can I get you?"

Back at Angelica's, Tricia hadn't finished her martini, but she had no idea when she was likely to have dinner, so she decided she'd order something simple. "How about a gin and tonic?"

"A G and T it is," Bev said. "Would you like some popcorn or chips to go with that?"

"Chips, please."

"You got it."

Tricia watched as Bev put her order in at the bar, and then as the new bartender, Hoshi Tanaka, made her drink. And, of course, she couldn't help but hear Chauncey bellow.

"She's no good for the village. She cost us the title of Safest Village in New Hampshire, and she caused my fiancée's injury back in January when we were on that author cruise. Everything she touches is jinxed. Everywhere she goes, trouble follows."

That old blowhard—spreading lies far and wide. At least Tricia had been able to get Mary to stop.

Bev approached with a tray that held her drink and a small bowl. "Here you go. Enjoy."

"Thanks. Do you have a minute?"

"A few seconds," Bev said, her gaze raking over the crowd in case someone wanted another drink.

"How long has Chauncey been here talking me down?"

Bev frowned. "About twenty minutes. As you can see, no one's interested in what he's got to say."

"Yes, but unfortunately he keeps on saying it."

"Want me to call Shawn out to make him shut up?"

Tricia shook her head. She didn't need to look like a poor sport, even if it was to people who probably had no interest in the Chamber election or even knew her name.

Someone signaled Bev. "Duty calls."

Tricia nodded and watched her go. Then she reached for one of the chips and heard a whimper from beneath her cloak. "Shhh!" she told Sarge, who was a warm little bundle of fur stretched across her lap. She looked around, then snuck him a chip. "Whatever you do, don't tell Angelica," she whispered, relatively sure that their secret was safe from her sister.

Tricia sipped her drink and tried not to listen to Chauncey prattle on and on, but his booming voice seemed to cut through the rest of the patrons' quiet discussions.

"Yessiree, when I'm the new president of the Chamber of Commerce, things will be different around here."

Did he think the job would entail enacting new laws?

"I'm going to bring back prosperity!"

Actually, Nigela Ricita Associates had almost single-handedly done that, which made Tricia feel terribly proud of her sister.

"Stoneham will be the star of Southern New Hampshire."

And was he going to pull off world peace and cure cancer, too?

Tricia snuck another chip under her cloak, encountering a little dry nose.

"I'll show him tomorrow," she whispered to Sarge, and crossed her fingers.

Tricia continued to sip her drink, share her chips, and wish Chauncey would Just. Shut. Up. After about ten minutes of this abuse, her ringtone sounded. She pulled her phone out of her cloak's pocket, punched the talk icon, and answered, "Hello."

"You can come back now," Antonio said. "We wouldn't want you—or Sarge—to get frostbite."

"Thank you," Tricia said, although after sitting in the cozy bar, she was anything but cold. She signaled Bev and paid her tab. "Good night."

"Good night, Tricia. And—good night to you, too, Sarge."

Tricia frowned. She thought she'd pulled off the old disappearing dog act.

By the time she and Sarge made it up the stairs to Angelica's apartment, Antonio was at the door ready to leave. He kissed Angelica on the cheek and they embraced one last time.

"We will talk again tomorrow, *Madre*."

Angelica nodded and watched him until he reached the bottom of the stairs and closed the door to the shop behind him.

"Are you okay?" Tricia asked.

Angelica rubbed her red-rimmed eyes. "Yes. Much better." Then her mouth trembled. "For the first time in my life I can say it aloud. I'm a mother."

Tricia laughed. "Yeah, I guess you are." Then she reached over and hugged her sister. "How about another drink? I never got to finish my martini."

"I could sure use one," Angelica said wearily. "But I'm too exhausted for spirits. How about a glass of wine?"

Tricia hung up her cloak and went back to the kitchen, where she took two fresh glasses down from the cupboard. Grabbing the opened bottle from the fridge, she poured for both of them and handed one glass to her sister. They clinked the rims and sipped.

"So, what happens next?" Tricia asked.

"I guess I have to go see Chief Baker. Antonio said he'd come with me."

"Do you want me to come, too?"

"No. I've already involved you in far too much. I agreed to speak to the chief after the Chamber meeting tomorrow morning, although I've been thinking—I'd really rather not go to the police station. Do you think Grant would meet us at some neutral location? Like maybe the Brookview?"

"I'm sure he would. Would you like me to arrange it?"

Angelica nodded, wiping her bloodshot eyes with the back of her hand.

"I'll see what I can do." She sipped her wine. It was far too late to think about making dinner. "Is there any pizza left from last week?"

Angelica offered a wan smile. "Not a chance."

"I thought maybe you'd frozen the leftovers. Okay, then let's order one."

Angelica nodded. "And let's get the works."

"Okay, but *no* anchovies."

"Anchovies are good for you. Full of fish oil."

"It's a deal breaker," Tricia said.

"Oh, all right," Angelica acquiesced, but the barest hint of a smile graced her lips. Things weren't perfect—not by any means—but they just might improve.

Tricia crossed her fingers and hoped with all her heart.

After a day filled with so much turmoil, it wasn't surprising that Tricia had a hard time falling asleep. Angelica had calmed down and looked absolutely exhausted when Tricia left her apartment at close to eleven o'clock, and she was grateful that Chief Baker had answered her call shortly after, agreeing to meet with Angelica and Antonio at the Brookview the next morning. With her work over for the day, Tricia finally turned in for the night, intending to read for only a couple of minutes.

That was the plan, at least. Unfortunately, she'd closed her book and turned the light off at least three times, and still sleep wouldn't come. She wondered if she should get up and make herself a mug of hot milk and Ovaltine. Her grandmother had made that for her when she was a child. It always seemed to do the trick. But she was feeling lazy and lay there, staring at the ceiling, willing herself to drift off to Neverland when she heard the sound.

At first, she wasn't sure just what it was. Stones pelting the brick wall below her bedroom window? Throwing back the covers, Tricia got out of bed and padded to the window overlooking the alley. She peeked through the blinds and saw the silhouette of a man below—and yes, he *was* throwing rocks at her building, but lower than her window—like he was aiming to break the glass on the big lamp in the alley outside of her shop that had caused her injury some five days before. It had only just been replaced.

Anger drove her to savagely yank the cord on the blinds, and then throw open the window. "Hey!" she hollered.

For a moment, the silhouetted man just stood there, looking up at her, and then he turned and ran.

"Stop! I'm calling the police!"

But, of course, he just took off down the alley heading north.

Not bothering to shut the window, Tricia flew across the room and grabbed the phone on her nightstand, punching in 9-1-1.

"I want to report a vandal!" she announced in no uncertain terms once the call was answered.

But, as there was no actual damage to her home, she was told she couldn't file a report for that, though trespassing was a possibility. She could come in the next morning to file a complaint. In the meantime, they would have the officer on patrol drive down the alley several times during the night.

Tricia wasn't happy.

Crossing the room, she closed the window and blinds—and shivered in the now-cold room. Then she climbed back into her bed and yanked the covers up to her chin.

So, the vandal was a man.

She tried to remember exactly what she'd seen, and her anger flared. Although the man's face had been in shadows, she thought she knew without a doubt who had tried to inflict the damage.

Russ Smith.

She had a suspect, but with nothing in the way of proof, was Baker liable to take her claim seriously?

She doubted that.

It was a long—a very long—time before Tricia finally dropped off to sleep.

TWENTY-EIGHT

In the grand scheme of things, Tricia would never have thought the Chamber of Commerce election would have brought out such a high level of anticipation within her. But as she drove to the Brookview Inn the next morning, she found herself feeling as nervous as she'd felt on her wedding day way too many years before. Should she win, it wouldn't be as life-altering an event as holy wedlock, but at this time of her life, it was almost as exciting. Or had her life become so dull that anticipating the possibility of a new dimension held such appeal?

That enthusiasm waned considerably when she got in her car, turned the key, and nothing happened. Nothing. Not a thing. Just what she needed on that of all days. But then she remembered what Ginny had told her days before.

Getting out of the car, she walked to the back of the vehicle and crouched down. Sure enough, a medium-sized russet potato had been stuffed into her Lexus's tailpipe. Unfortunately, steadying herself with her left hand sent her stitches into red-alert mode while she tugged on the tuber with her right hand. What she needed was something to help her pry the vegetable out. Should she go all the way back to her apartment to obtain a knife, or would the metal nail file in her purse do the trick?

It took some doing, and gouging the spud bent the file to an almost forty-five-degree angle, but she was able to pull it out without breaking the file. She bent it back into position and walked over to a nearby trash can to toss the potato, then got back in her car, which thankfully started right up, and off she went.

Angelica had already arrived at the inn, as evidenced by her car, parked in the farthest corner of the parking lot, and Tricia entered the inn through the back door. The lobby was tastefully decorated for Thanksgiving, as was the dining room. The inn was known for its fabulous holiday dinner, and she knew it had been booked solid since September.

Tricia checked her cloak and stepped into the dining room, which was brimming with Chamber members. Far more were present than had attended the week before when the candidates for the Chamber presidency had been announced. Was it her promotional efforts or Mary's phone calls disparaging her that had predicated the turnout? She guessed the voting outcome would reveal that answer.

The Chamber's receptionist, Mariana, stood by the door, handing out ballots and indicating the white linen–clad table just inside, where a big box with a slit in the top awaited and many pens stood erect in metal holders.

"Hi, Tricia. Here's a ballot. Please fill it out and put it in the box."

Tricia tried not to look at what her fellow members were checking as she added an X next to her own name and stuffed the ballot into the box before turning to take in the rest of the room. Once again the inn had provided a lavish continental breakfast spread, but Tricia found she was too nervous to partake of the Danish and other sweet rolls, settling instead on a cup of coffee—not that she needed the caffeine. Her nerves were already jangled enough. She caught Angelica's eye and then crossed the room to join her.

"Yes, I'm sure there's precedent," Angelica was telling Leona Ferguson, "but it's something the next Chamber president will have to deal with. As of today, I'm a lame duck."

"Very well," Leona said, and without even acknowledging Tricia, turned and walked away.

"What's her beef?" Tricia asked, and sipped her coffee.

"She wants to change our charter and forgo the campaigning for Chamber president. She said she felt harassed by your e-mail and Mary's phone calls on Chauncey's behalf."

"One e-mail and one call?" Tricia asked, skeptically.

"Apparently Mary called her several times."

That made sense. Tricia looked around and saw Mary sitting at one of the tables for eight, with Chauncey standing nearby boasting about his upcoming win. Mary looked bored, and Tricia could hardly blame her. Chauncey really was an incredible old gasbag.

It was then that Tricia saw Marshall Cambridge. "Marshall said he'd be here today, and there he is."

Angelica turned to look. "A man of his word is to be appreciated."

Oh? Angelica hadn't seemed as forgiving when Tricia had first told her she was going to meet the man socially.

"I'm going over to say hello."

"Well, don't be too long. I'm going to call the meeting to order in about ten minutes."

Tricia didn't wait and started off to intercept her new friend. "I'm happy you were able to make it here this morning."

"I had to cast my vote for you, didn't I?"

She smiled. "I'm flattered."

He shrugged. "You're the best person for the job. How's the arm doing?"

Tricia raised it just a little. "Much better. I'm probably going to ditch the sling tomorrow. If all's well, the stitches will come out on Friday." She noted he had no coffee and didn't seem to have found a place to sit. "Did you have breakfast?"

"I'm a ham and eggs kind of guy. I ate breakfast before I came here. There're too many carbs on that buffet table."

"I must admit, I'm too nervous to eat."

"Eh, you're a shoo-in," he said rather cavalierly.

Tricia shook her head. "I sure hope you're right. Would you like to join my sister and me at our table?"

"Would she mind?"

"If she did, she'd never say so."

He smiled. "All right. Lead the way."

By the time they made it back to the table, Angelica was conversing with Toni Bennett. Tricia was glad she'd jotted down her ideas for recruiting a candy shop to come to the village to be part of her acceptance speech. Well, it wasn't really a speech—just an outline—but it was in her purse and ready to be read as soon as the announcement was made. And if she wasn't chosen as the next president . . . well, no one had to know it was there.

They sat down at the table, and a nervous Tricia looked around the room, wondering which members she could count on to vote for her.

Russ had arrived, looking just a little seedy in a plaid flannel shirt and a pair of well-worn jeans, and seemed to be hanging around the buffet table, scarfing down sticky buns and drinking coffee rather than mingling with his potential constituents. He looked tired, too, no doubt from his nocturnal wanderings the night before. Tricia turned away, unable to stand the sight of him.

Meanwhile, Chauncey seemed a bit red-faced as he lectured Boris Kozlov about some matter. Boris looked ready to bolt if given the chance.

"So," Marshall said, drawing Tricia's attention back to him. "Sorry about canceling dinner last night. But we're good to go for dinner tonight, right?"

"As it turned out, my sister needed me, so I'm glad I was able to be there for her."

Marshall looked quizzical, but didn't ask questions.

"Where are we going?" Tricia asked.

"A country club just outside of Nashua. I figured since there was just too much gossip after our Sunday lunch here in the village that it might be nice to go someplace where we'd have a little anonymity."

"True enough. How else are people supposed to get to know each other? But we live in a small village, and that's what happens; everybody seems to know everybody else's business."

"The hazard of living here," he agreed.

"But there are a lot of nice things, too," Tricia said. "The flowers along Main Street in the summer. The Wine and Jazz Festival last June was fun." Except when someone tried to kill her. "The Dog-Eared Page is welcoming." *Except when someone spends the better part of an hour disparaging you,* she thought. "And I do love this inn. I've stayed here twice. The food is very good—and the staff is wonderful."

"You sound like you're ready to be Chamber president."

"I hope so."

"But won't that cramp your style?"

"I don't think so. I enjoyed volunteering for them after my store burned. I made a lot of new acquaintances."

"Not friends?"

She shook her head, and her mouth drooped. "Acquaintances, but one never knows."

"As a matter of fact, you first met *me* at a Chamber meeting," he reminded her.

She nodded. "Yes, I did."

They looked at each other and smiled. Tricia even felt a little flutter in her stomach, which hadn't happened for quite some time. And yet . . . Marshall sold porn. She liked him, but that was an awfully big hurdle to overcome.

The loudspeaker overhead issued a squawk as Angelica tested the sound system at the front of the room. "Testing, testing." She tapped the microphone several times and seemed satisfied it was working correctly. "Attention, everyone!" She waited for those milling around the fringes of the room to quiet down and take their seats before speaking once again.

"Welcome, Chamber members. I'm so pleased to see so many of you here today to choose your next leader. We have three very qualified candidates." And here she looked right at Tricia and smiled. "And if you haven't already done so, it's now time to place your ballots into the box at the other end of the room. Mariana and Leona Ferguson will retreat to the conference room down the hall and will tabulate the results. It should only take five or ten minutes, and then we'll announce the outcome. In the meantime, let's polish off the wonderful breakfast the Brookview has set up for us. Thank you."

She switched off the mic and headed straight for the table where Tricia and Marshall were seated, looking exhausted.

"Is everything okay?" Tricia asked.

"As you know, I have other things to do this morning, and as soon as I can adjourn the meeting, I'm going to do so. I probably won't be available for lunch today."

"I'm a big girl. I can handle it," Tricia said. "And I've got dinner plans," she reminded her sister, "but I want you to call me this afternoon."

"Of course I will," Angelica promised. Then she seemed to notice the other person seated at the table. "Oh, hello, Marshall. Thank you for coming this morning."

He nodded. "My pleasure."

Tricia looked toward the back of the room, but Mariana and Leona had already removed the ballot box and were nowhere in sight. She flexed her fingers, her nerves getting the better of her. "Were you this antsy when you ran for election?" she asked Angelica.

"Of course not. I knew I'd win."

Tricia wished she felt as confident.

"Maybe I will have another cup of coffee," Marshall said. "Can I get you ladies anything?"

"No thanks," Tricia said. Angelica merely shook her head.

Marshall left them, and Tricia again let her gaze roam the dining room. Russ still hadn't moved from his spot at the buffet table, while Chauncey was speaking into Mary's ear. She seemed tight-lipped and perhaps as anxious as Tricia felt. She felt sorry for Mary and her predicament. But still, Tricia wanted to *win*.

The murmur of voices seemed to quiet and Tricia saw that Mariana and Leona had returned to the dining room, both staring straight ahead, their expressions rigid, and not making eye contact with anyone.

"The moment of truth has arrived," Angelica said, and stood. She patted Tricia's shoulder before she turned and strode to the front of the room, where she consulted with the official ballot counters. Tricia leaned forward, trying to interpret just what Angelica's rather stoic expression meant. Bottom line, it wasn't encouraging.

Angelica turned to the lectern, switched the microphone back on, and cleared her throat before speaking. "The ballots have been counted, and it is now my duty—"

Tricia cringed. She would have said *pleasure* if the news were good.

"—to announce that your new Stoneham Chamber of Commerce president is Chauncey Porter."

A ripple of applause broke out through the room, and Tricia felt heat rise up her neck to color her cheeks, her stomach doing a belly flop. She glanced across the room. Mary looked absolutely elated. Turning her head, Tricia saw Russ shrug. After all, he hadn't even wanted the job.

"Tough luck, kid," Marshall said close to her ear, sounding sincere.

"The official tabulation is Chauncey Porter: twenty-five; Russ Smith: twenty-three; and Tricia Miles: twenty."

It had been a close race, but Tricia had still come in last.

Jinxed again.

"Chauncey, will you please approach the lectern?" Angelica asked.

Chauncey got up from his seat and slowly walked to the front of the room. He was sure milking the moment. Angelica's smile was absolutely rigid as she handed her gavel to Chauncey and took a step back.

Chauncey moved up to the microphone and took a long look around the room, as though taking in all of their faces. And then his mouth dropped open and he seemed to sag against the wooden stand, until suddenly it fell forward, and Chauncey dropped like a stone to the floor.

A loud gasp echoed through the room and Angelica was immediately at his side. She felt for a pulse before ordering, "Call nine one one!"

Here we go again, Tricia thought, as suddenly everyone in the room seemed to pull out their cell phones and stab the numbers onto their keypads.

Tricia watched as the paramedics whisked Chauncey's gurney out of the dining room. He'd been in full cardiac arrest when they'd arrived, and the first responders seemed grim, since they hadn't been able to restart his heart before taking him away.

Mary looked shell-shocked, once again sitting at the table she'd shared with her fiancé only minutes before. Tricia went over to face her. "Are you okay, Mary?"

Mary looked up. "Well, this certainly could change everything."

For better or worse? Tricia wondered.

"Would you like me to drive you to the hospital?"

Mary straightened and suddenly seemed to pull herself together. "No, that won't be necessary. I'm fine to drive. And who knows how long I may need to be at the hospital. I wouldn't want to leave my car here in the parking lot and be stuck."

"You didn't come with Chauncey?"

"I drove," she said flatly, as though it hadn't been her idea.

Other concerned Chamber members milled nearby. "Did Chauncey have a heart condition?" asked Mindy Weaver, easing forward.

Mary shook her head. "Not that I know of." She stood. "I'd better get my coat."

"I'll walk you to your car," Mindy offered, and the two women set off for the coatroom.

"Call me if you need anything," Tricia called.

Mary waved a thank-you, but didn't turn.

Tricia pivoted and headed back to the front of the room, where Angelica was talking to Antonio, who, as Brookview's manager, had shown up only moments after Chauncey's collapse.

Tricia halted before them. "Well?"

"It doesn't look good," Angelica said grimly—but was she thinking about Chauncey or her impending conversation with Chief Baker?

Suddenly Russ Smith was standing beside Tricia, and she made a point to step aside. "What happens if the old geezer dies?" he asked Angelica, his voice oddly fierce.

"Then you're our next duly elected Chamber president," she said sweetly, knowing he didn't want the job.

Russ turned an angry glare on Tricia. "You *are* a stinking jinx." And with that, he turned and left the room.

"Did I miss something?" Antonio asked. "Or did he seem upset by that news?"

"Oh, he's upset all right," Tricia said.

Angelica reached out a hand and touched Tricia's good arm. "I'm so sorry you lost, Trish. In fact, I'm absolutely astounded."

"Easy come, easy go," she said, but she felt anything but accepting of the situation. That would take a couple of days—maybe a week—to happen.

"Angelica," Antonio said. "We have a meeting in five minutes," he prodded.

Angelica sighed, looking depressed. Just another dark cloud hanging over their heads. "I'll call you later," she again promised Tricia, and then she and Antonio headed out of the dining room.

Marshall still sat at the big round table. Tricia resumed her former seat, and it was her turn to feel exhausted.

"So, is he going to die?" Marshall asked, his voice devoid of emotion.

"I don't know, but it doesn't look good," she said, repeating Angelica's assessment.

"How do you feel about that?"

"Terrible."

"Even though the guy treated you like crap?"

"Yes," Tricia admitted.

Marshall shook his head. "You're a nice person, Tricia. Maybe *too* nice."

"And nice people always finish last," she lamented.

He gave her a quirky smile. "How about I make *you* first?"

"What do you mean?"

"I mean instead of going out to dinner tonight, let's go out to lunch. Maybe a *liquid* lunch where you can drown your sorrows."

"But it's barely nine thirty."

"So it'll be brunch. Do you like mimosas?"

"I have a store to run, and so do you."

"You've got a couple of employees who are perfectly capable of taking care of it. I'm only liable to miss one customer, if that. Most of my business is later in the day."

Tricia sighed. "Brunch sounds awfully good. But instead of a mimosa, make it a martini."

"Maybe two," he promised.

She smiled. "Let's go."

And they both rose and headed for the coatroom.

TWENTY-NINE

Marshall Cambridge was a man of many surprises. Since his shop looked rather shabby, she was surprised that he owned a late-model Mercedes that appeared to have every bell and whistle available. The porn business paid well, indeed.

After dropping her car off at the municipal parking lot, she joined him in the Mercedes and they headed north out of town. They made small talk until they passed St. Joseph Hospital in Milford. That was where the paramedics had taken Chauncey. Tricia recognized Mary's car in the parking lot and forced herself to look away. She was tired of bad news.

"Does this radio work?" she asked, pointing to the dashboard, which could have passed for the control panel of an Airbus.

Marshall switched it on, and mellow jazz from a subscription music station poured out of the hidden speakers. "Is that okay?"

She gave him a weak smile. "Perfect."

Tricia had never once played hooky while in school, and so she felt guilty leaving Haven't Got a Clue in Pixie's and Mr. Everett's more than capable hands while she moped over her election loss. However, she also did *not* feel guilty. She deserved a completely fat-filled, alcohol-laden brunch and was determined to have one.

The Mercedes pulled up in front of the stately clubhouse on the outskirts of Nashua, and a valet stepped forward. "Welcome back, Mr. Cambridge."

"Thanks, Pete." He handed over his keys, and then offered his hand to Tricia. She accepted it and they steered toward the grand entrance with its massive columns. It must have looked magnificent on a sunny summer's day. Like the Brookview, the lobby was decorated for the upcoming holiday. They paused at the hostess station, where a pert young woman awaited.

"Do you have a reservation?"

"I'm sorry. We came on the spur of the moment. But I am a member," Marshall said, and gave his name.

Tricia turned to look at him. The membership fee for this place must cost a small fortune.

"Ah, yes. We're so glad you and your guest could join us, Mr. Cambridge. I'd be glad to take your coats"—which she did, and then handed Marshall the check slips. "If you'll step this way."

They were taken to a table that overlooked a big pond. Several geese paddled along the edges, stragglers who hadn't gone south for the winter. Even though the trees nearby were bare, there was a stark beauty about the grounds that Tricia found enticing.

"Ben will be taking care of you this morning."

"Thank you," Marshall said, giving the young woman a toothy smile before she nodded and retreated.

"Nice place," Tricia said.

"It works," Marshall agreed.

"So, are you any good?"

Marshall blinked. "At what?"

"Golf."

Marshall shook his head and laughed. "About average. I should try to get here more often."

"And your business keeps you away?"

"You could say that."

Tricia picked up her napkin, shook it, and placed it on her lap. "How did your meeting go last night?"

"Very well."

"Tell me about it."

He shook his head. "You wouldn't be interested."

"I wouldn't have asked if I wasn't interested."

Their eyes met. "No, I don't suppose you would have," he said, amused. "I've been in negotiations for months trying to obtain what's left of Dale Talbot's art collection."

Tricia's eyes opened wide. Dale had been Carol Talbot's husband. "Do tell."

"Sometimes when dealing with an estate, you can get things for a bargain."

"And that isn't happening with his things?" After Carol Talbot's sudden death, Marshall had shown her the kinds of items that made up such an assemblage. Some of them turned her stomach.

"Her attorney is a hard bargainer."

Ah, so he knew Carol Talbot's attorney's name—possibly useful information when it came to returning Carol's jewelry to the estate. "Really? Who is he?"

"She. Cassandra Logan."

Tricia instantly memorized the name for future reference. "Has she seen what she's negotiating for?"

"Yes. And she's done her homework. But I lucked out, because like

Carol, she wasn't able to get what she thought the items might be worth at auction."

"I suppose she gets a certain percentage of the estate for her trouble."

"As per usual."

"And who gets the rest? I didn't think Carol had any heirs."

"She didn't. She left it to some animal rescue place in Milford."

Tricia nodded. The very place where Mr. Everett and Grace had adopted Charlie. "I know of it. I'm glad Carol left a legacy for good."

Marshall cocked his head, giving her a sidelong glance. "Being a little judgmental there, eh, Tricia?"

"Possibly. We can't forget that Carol once took a life and was never truly repentant."

Marshall nodded. "Touché."

"Are estates a common place for you to find merchandise?" Tricia asked. What did families do with porn collections once someone died? Toss them—would be her first instinct.

"Sometimes. My goal now is to make my business more attractive to a potential buyer."

Tricia blinked. "You're thinking of selling Vamps?"

"Until recently, no. But I've been approached by a chain."

"There are chains of porn dealers?" she asked.

"Of course."

"What would you do instead?"

He shrugged. "Whatever I do, I'll research it thoroughly before I make a commitment."

"Would you leave the area?"

"I don't know. I have no ties here. Since April died, I let the wind take me where it will. But I do like this part of the state." He gave her a wistful smile. "There are certain attractions."

The waiter arrived, bringing with him two leather-clad menus. "I'm

Ben, and I'll be serving you today. Would you like to start your brunch with a cocktail?"

Marshall nodded toward Tricia.

"I'd like a dry gin martini, up, with olives."

"And the gin?"

"Hendrick's."

"And you, sir?"

"The same."

It was Tricia's turn to smile.

Despite two very strong martinis, Tricia felt totally, one hundred percent sober when Marshall pulled the Mercedes into an empty parking space in front of her store—something that would have been impossible during high summer.

"Thank you for the lovely lunch," Tricia said.

"The food was good," Marshall agreed. "But the company was better."

Tricia gave him a smile but then turned to stare at the front of her pretty little mystery store. "I don't want to go inside. I'm sure I'll only hear more bad news, and I feel like I've had enough for one day."

"Pull up your big girl panties and face it," Marshall advised, grinning.

Tricia shook her head. "It's more than just losing the election and Chauncey keeling over. It's knowing that the majority of villagers just don't like me. The Chamber election only reinforced that fact."

"Self-pity doesn't suit you," he chided.

"I don't usually allow myself to feel this way, although I may let myself sulk for another few hours or so while I wait for happy hour and another couple of martinis."

"Big girl panties," Marshall advised once more.

"Oh, all right," she acquiesced. And then Marshall suddenly

leaned closer and kissed her on the lips. Nothing romantic; just a nice soft kiss.

"Can I call you?"

Tricia couldn't help the smile that crept across her mouth. "You've got my number." And with that, she reached for the door handle.

A cold wind blew all around her, and she didn't look back as Marshall's car took off. And when she opened the door, a cold shiver ran up her back when she saw Pixie's wide-eyed stare.

"The old geezer bought the farm," she said without preamble.

"What?" Tricia asked.

"Chauncey Porter. He's dead," Pixie said.

Tricia sighed and closed the door—the little bell above it sounding ridiculously cheerful. "I take it you heard what happened at the meeting."

"Oh, sure—Frannie called me right after Angelica got back. Said your sis was so upset she had to go lie down. I didn't think she was *that* friendly with the old coot."

"Angelica made it her business to know all the Chamber members," Tricia said neutrally. "That, and he was the second person she recently tried to help who died."

"Damn, I wish I'd gone to that meeting—not to see the old geezer keel over, mind you. I thought about showing up as moral support," Pixie said. "But then I figured they might not let me in, thinking I was there to pinch a free breakfast or something. As it turns out, it was a good thing I didn't go."

Tricia looked around the store, noting Mr. Everett's absence.

Pixie noticed her noticing.

"Don't tell me—" Tricia said, dreading more bad news.

"Yeah, Charlie bought the farm overnight. Mr. E called in and said he and Grace were taking him to the vet to drop him off to be cremated and that he might not be in today."

Tricia sagged. "Oh, poor Mr. Everett. What a terrible, terrible day."

So many people's lives had been disrupted for so many reasons, and none of them good. Of course, what was Mary Fairchild thinking, now that all her problems had died along with Chauncey? No wonder she hadn't wanted to be driven to the hospital. She might have wanted to leave there and go straight to a bar to celebrate her good fortune in avoiding marriage to a man with abusive tendencies.

"What do you think we should do for poor Mr. E?" Pixie asked.

"I don't know. I'll call him later to see how he's doing, but first I need to talk to Angelica. I think I'll do that up in my apartment. This could be an epic call."

Pixie nodded, and probably figured the sisters would commiserate.

But then Tricia noticed the clock on the wall. It was almost two. "Oh, Pixie—you haven't had your lunch yet."

"I'm good," she said with a shrug.

"No, I insist. I just assumed Mr. Everett would be here and . . . Go. Please go. The Bookshelf Diner is still open."

"Well, if you insist. I'll get my coat. Give me yours and I'll hang it up."

Once Pixie was out the door, Tricia picked up the phone and called Angelica's number.

"Are you okay?" she asked when Angelica answered.

"Yes. I tried to call you earlier, but there was no answer—and you didn't answer your cell phone, either."

"I turned it off. Marshall took me out to brunch at an exclusive country club outside of Nashua."

"You'll have to tell me all about it—but not right now, please."

"Can you talk?" Tricia asked.

"Yes; the jammer is on. I assume you heard about Chauncey?"

"Apparently Frannie's been calling all over the village. She got to Pixie, and Pixie delivered the bad news."

"Mary must be dancing a jig," Angelica commented. Tricia had told her over pizza the night before about the conversation she'd had with Mary earlier that day. "She wasted her vote."

"I still would have lost," Tricia lamented. "And you won your bet."

"Bet?" Angelica asked.

"About Pixie."

"Oh, yeah. I'd forgotten all about it."

Maybe for the moment—but Angelica had a sharp mind, and she wouldn't have forgotten it for long. Tricia changed the subject. "How did your meeting with Chief Baker go?"

"Well, my phone will be tapped. They'll be looking at the mail—before I do—and I hope they catch the bastard who's been threatening my family."

"Did he say anything about the crime wave?"

"Only that there's no evidence to link my problems with the outbreak of vandalism."

"Why?"

"Because all the businesses along the alley behind us got hit—not just me."

"He may have something there. With all that's gone on, I never had a chance to tell you that I saw someone throwing rocks at my light last night."

"What time was this?"

"After one. I opened the window and yelled to scare him off. I think it was Russ Smith."

"Why would he do that?"

"Maybe to make it look like I wasn't being singled out?" Tricia suggested.

"He couldn't have known you'd fall and get hurt the last time it happened."

"No, that was probably a bonus."

"But he smashed the light at the Patisserie, too."

"He probably wanted to spite his wife as much as me," Tricia offered.

"Did you report this to the police?"

"Yes, but not that I thought it was Russ. I guess I should tell Chief Baker—not that he'll do anything about it."

"At the very least, he should talk to him."

"I agree." Tricia remembered what else Pixie had told her. "Mr. Everett called. Charlie died last night."

"Oh, no!" Angelica lamented. "The poor dear. He and Grace must be heartbroken."

"They knew Charlie was living on borrowed time—I just wish they'd had more than a few days with their sweet boy."

"I hope they're not sorry they adopted him, but I can understand if they were. It was years after I lost my little Pom-Pom that I was brave enough to love another pet."

As though he knew what she was talking about, Tricia heard Sarge bark somewhere in the background.

"You tell her, Sarge," she encouraged.

Angelica sighed. "I'm sorry, but I have tons of things to do before the end of my workday—which is fast approaching. Come to my place for dinner. I've brought leftovers from the café."

"Soup?" Tricia asked. After her large lunch, that was about all she thought she'd need.

"Among other things."

"Okay. I'll see you just after six."

No sooner had Tricia put down the receiver than the door to Haven't Got a Clue opened and Russ Smith staggered inside.

"What do you want?" Tricia said, none too friendly.

"You." He lurched toward her, and she could see that he was drunk.

"Get out of my store."

He didn't bother to look to see if anyone else was present; he must have waited for Pixie to leave before he made his move. And what was he interested in?

"That's not a very friendly way to greet an old friend—or should I say lover?"

"Get out of my store," Tricia repeated.

Russ staggered closer, and Tricia was glad to have the big glass display case/cash desk between them. He leaned closer, and she could smell the sour stench of Scotch on his breath.

"You screwed me."

"What?"

"*You* were supposed to win the damn election. *Why* didn't you win it?" he demanded.

"I thought that was your plan—to sabotage my chances. Isn't that why you wrote that horrible story about me in your terrible little rag?"

"Yeah, but *I* wasn't supposed to come in second. Three votes. I got three lousy votes more than you, and now I'm stuck."

"'You reap what you sow,'" Tricia quoted, not feeling at all bad about it.

"Nikki's furious with me. She said she's going to leave me."

"Why don't you try counseling?" Tricia suggested, trying to sound sympathetic—not that she truly felt that way.

"It's all your fault," Russ grumbled.

"Russ, I think you need to leave. Now, please."

"Or what are you gonna do? Call your little cop friend? The one who took my place in your bed?"

"Please leave. Now! Or I *will* call the police."

Russ reached over and grabbed the cord on the vintage telephone that sat beside the register, giving it a vicious yank, pulling it from the wall socket. Tricia instinctively backed away, and Russ grabbed the phone's heavy receiver, brandishing it at her like a weapon. It wouldn't take much force for it to cause serious injuries.

"Come on, Russ—go home. Sleep it off. Things will look better tomorrow."

"How can they? My wife is leaving me, you don't love me—"

This wasn't the time to mention that she was pretty sure she never had.

The door opened and Pixie walked into the shop holding a brown paper bag that no doubt held her take-out lunch. "Uh, am I interrupting something?" she asked, sounding uncertain.

"Get out of here. Tricia and I are talking," Russ slurred. He yanked hard on the receiver's cord, pulling it from the body of the phone, and threw the receiver at her.

"I'm out of here," Pixie said, tossing the bag on the floor and high-tailing it out of the store, the door slamming behind her.

"Pixie!" Tricia called, but her assistant was gone.

Russ turned back and grabbed what was left of the phone, glaring at Tricia. "Now, let's have a nice li'l talk, shall we?"

Tricia didn't want to talk to him at all, but she knew Pixie would be on her cell phone calling 911, and then trying to find someone—anyone—to help.

"All right. What do you want to talk about?" Tricia said, hoping her voice sounded soothing instead of terrified. She wasn't sure what she should expect from the lout.

"The future. We can go back to where we were before you dumped me. I'll take you back," he said, sounding maudlin.

If anything, Tricia never wanted to see his red, sweating face again, but she needed to stall him until help arrived.

"Put the phone down, and then we'll go sit in the reader's nook and talk."

Russ gave her a calculating look. "No."

"Then no deal."

"Why? Don't you trust me?"

Tricia eyed him. Of course she didn't! "It's hardly a romantic gesture to threaten the woman you love with a weapon."

He looked at the business end of the phone still in his hand and seemed to have trouble focusing on it. "This—a weapon?"

"Well, it's not a bouquet of roses. Have you forgotten how to sweet-talk a woman?"

Russ seemed to ponder the question before answering. "Maybe I have." He set the phone back on the top of the case. "Come out from behind there."

Tricia eyed him. "Only if you back off."

He laughed. "Why? Do you think I'd hurt you?"

Yes!

"That's the deal."

Russ swayed as he took a step back.

"One more step," Tricia said.

He complied, and she moved around the end of the case.

Russ held out his arms. "Come to Poppa."

"Shouldn't you be saying that to your son?"

"What do I care about that brat? I never wanted him."

As Tricia had always suspected.

"Come on, Tricia. Come and give me a little kiss and tell me all is forgiven."

Boy, he really *was* drunk. But Tricia did take a tiny step forward.

"Close your eyes."

"Why?" he asked suspiciously.

"Because a kiss is always better when you close your eyes."

"You wouldn't play a trick on me, would you?"

"Me?" she asked innocently, slowly slipping her arm out of her sling.

"You don't like me," he said petulantly.

"I thought we were friends," Tricia said, and she meant it—as in the *past* tense.

"We could be more—*should* be more. I never loved anybody like I love you, Tricia."

Yes, and that's why he had stalked her. He didn't want her to be with anyone else, and he'd obviously held on to that assertion.

"Close your eyes, Russ," she said softly, and took another tiny step forward.

Again he scrutinized her face, but then he did close his eyes.

Tricia pounced, shoving him backward, knocking him off balance. Despite her sore arm, she managed to roll him over onto his stomach, haul his left arm behind his back, and kneel on his buttocks, effectively pinning him. He bucked and wriggled, but Tricia wasn't about to let him up.

Just then, Pixie and one of Stoneham's uniformed police officers burst through the door and practically skidded to a halt.

"You got him!" Pixie hollered.

"Yes, and I could sure use some help."

The officer motioned for Tricia to get up, and Pixie leapt forward to give her a helping hand.

"Get up!" the officer demanded of Russ, who'd stopped wiggling but made no move to obey the order. "Sir, get up!" But Russ didn't seem to have the strength to raise himself.

The officer grabbed one of Russ's arms and hauled him to his feet. As though in reply, Russ threw up all over the officer and the carpet.

"Uggh!" Tricia and Pixie cried in unison.

Russ doubled over and threw up again, then he fell to his knees and vomited again and again, until he was left with the dry heaves.

Without comment, the officer peeled off his jacket and tossed it out the door.

"I take it you've been through this before," Tricia said.

"Way too many times," he said wearily. "Do you want to press charges?"

"I don't know," Tricia answered honestly.

"If nothing else, I can drag him in for being drunk and disorderly."

"If you would, please."

"I'll say," Pixie chimed in, eyeing the sick on the carpet and wrinkling her nose at the stench. She hurried to get the door and hold it open as the cop dragged Russ out into the street. The cold, fresh air must have hit him like a brick wall, and Russ doubled over and vomited once again.

"Glad he did that outside. Much easier to clean up," Pixie said.

They looked at each other, then at the stained carpet, then at each other again.

"It's my store; I'll clean it up," Tricia said.

Pixie shook her head. "Nah. Back in the day I was a janitor at an elementary school for a while. Kids barfed on almost an hourly basis come flu season. I'll get this."

"And you'll get a nice fat bonus for it," Tricia said.

Pixie merely grinned.

THIRTY

After Russ had been dragged away, Tricia phoned Chief Baker, leaving a message that she was pretty sure it had been Russ who had thrown the stones at her light the evening before. She left it up to him to follow up—or not—on the information. And then it was back to work.

While Pixie took care of the shop, Tricia went to her office and logged onto the Internet. It took less than a minute for her to find Cassandra Logan, Esquire's address in Milford. Grabbing one of the padded envelopes they used for shipping stock, she wrote the address down with a black marker. She quickly typed up a note, detailing what the items were and to what estate they belonged, and hit the print button. She donned a pair of plastic gloves and folded it, hoping that Ms. Logan wouldn't be too inquisitive. Tricia's fingerprints had been taken more than once. She would just have to hope that the return of the jewelry would be seen as good fortune, and not an opportunity to go after the person who had returned it.

Next, Tricia went up to her apartment, removed Carol Talbot's jewelry from her closet, and cleaned and dried it. Still wearing gloves, she stuffed the items into the envelope and sealed it before heading back down to the basement. She kept a variety of stamps in her desk, so she weighed the package and then added stamps to it. Since it was only being mailed to the next town over, she didn't dare bother with insurance and would just have to hope the good old post office would deliver the package safely.

It took only a few minutes for her to walk to the nearest blue USPS mailbox and drop the envelope in it, heaving a sigh of relief that she'd been able to return the stolen items to the estate—and that at least one thing that day had gone in her favor. And it gave her a feeling of peace to know that the money obtained from the sale of the jewelry would go to take care of abandoned pets just like Charlie, giving them a secure place to live until they found their forever homes.

The sky was darkening, and Tricia had just finished cleaning the beverage station when Pixie looked up from her book. "Hey, look—there's Mary Fairchild."

Mary passed the shop's big display window with her head held high, apparently heading for her store, which had been closed all day.

"I think I'll go offer her my condolences for Chauncey," Tricia said.

"Sure thing," Pixie said.

Tricia grabbed her cloak and ventured out into the deepening twilight. By the time she reached By Hook or By Book, the lights were on inside, but the blinds hadn't been drawn and a CLOSED sign still hung from the door. She tried the door, but it was locked. Pounding on it drew Mary's attention, and she soon came and unlocked it.

"Goodness, Tricia, what are you doing here?"

"I came to check up on you."

Mary shrugged and walked deeper into her store, heading for the stool behind the counter. Tricia closed the door and ventured closer. "So . . . ?"

Mary picked up a skein of pastel pink yarn and a crochet hook, and began working on what looked like a baby blanket. "I followed the ambulance to the hospital. Of course, as I wasn't Chauncey's next of kin, nobody wanted to tell me anything. I guess they worked on him for about an hour before he was pronounced dead. At least, that's when someone finally came out and told me." She kept her eyes on the yarn, giving it a yank every so often.

"What happens next?" Tricia asked, noting that Mary had spoken without emotion and remained dry-eyed. In fact, it didn't look like she'd cried at all, which wasn't much of a surprise.

"As it happens, it turns out I inherit Chauncey's entire estate."

"And how do you feel about that?"

Mary's hook stopped moving. "Weird."

"How did you find out about it?"

"I went to his apartment right after I left the hospital. I knew where he kept his important papers—not that he ever actually told me. So I went through them. I mean, at the very least I needed to find out about who was responsible for making burial arrangements for him—and it turns out to be me."

"What will you do?"

"I've already spoken with VanArsdale's in Milford. He'll be cremated tomorrow."

"Will you hold a memorial service?"

Mary shook her head. "He wasn't religious and he didn't have any close friends. As he'd just won the Chamber presidency, I thought perhaps Angelica might devote a few minutes of the next meeting to celebrate his life."

"I'll speak to her about it," Tricia promised. "And what about you?"

"I'm sorry he's dead. I never wished that on him, but I'm not sorry he'll be out of my life, which you well know."

Tricia nodded. "What about his store?"

"I'd like to talk to Angelica about that—she's thrived while juggling multiple businesses. Chauncey wasn't all that successful until he took advice from the two of you, but he did manage to get out of the red, and there's enough money to take care of his affairs. As his heir and executrix, I have the authority to keep the business running, and I intend to do so."

"Wow. You've made a lot of decisions in a short period of time."

"Yes, and the biggest one is that I'm never going to rush into a relationship again."

Something Tricia had also decided upon. But then she thought about Marshall. They'd shared two meals, although unlike Frannie, Tricia didn't intend for her third date with Marshall—should there be one—to be the deciding factor for intimacy. What she wanted more than anything else was friendship. She'd thought she'd had that with Russ, but she'd been wrong. She never wanted to be that wrong again.

"Why did you come back to your store this evening instead of going home?"

"What for? This is my home away from home. I'm going to put some music on, make myself a mug of cocoa, finish this blanket, and think about the future."

"What would you like to do?"

Mary looked thoughtful for a few moments. "I'd like to be more like you and Angelica."

"In what way?"

"First of all, I'm going to sell my house. Now that Chauncey won't be moving in, it's far too big for just me. The lease on the apartment upstairs runs out in a few months. Alice Jones, who lives there, is going to move out, and I'm going to ask my landlord if I can have it. That way I can be close to my shop—and be around people more. I really don't like living so isolated."

"No doubt about it, something is always happening here in Stoneham," Tricia said.

"And I do apologize for telling people you're responsible for the bad things that have occurred here in the village. I admit I was feeling desperate."

"Let's not get into that again," Tricia advised.

Mary nodded and set down her crocheting. "Would you like to join me and have some cocoa?"

Tricia glanced at the clock on the wall behind Mary. "Thanks, but no. Dinnertime is sneaking up on me, and I've got plans."

Mary turned to have a look. "Sorry. I didn't realize it was so late. I'm probably going to stop at the Bookshelf Diner before I head home. Or maybe," she said rather thoughtfully, "I might stop at the Dog-Eared Page and soak in some of the conviviality."

Obviously she knew nothing about Chauncey's visit there the evening before—or that he'd done nothing but slander Tricia during his visit. Well, if nothing else, that would never happen again.

"Pixie's probably wondering where I've gotten to. Have a good evening, Mary."

"You, too."

"I'll talk to you soon," Tricia said, and headed for the door. Mary followed, locking it behind her.

Tricia started down the empty sidewalk toward her store. Poor Mary. But she sounded like she knew what she wanted in her new life without Chauncey, and Tricia wished her well.

Now, if she could just figure out her own short-term plan for happiness.

* * *

The last forty-five minutes of the workday were quiet. Maybe too quiet, giving Tricia far too much time to think about the terrible events of the day. There'd been virtually no foot traffic all afternoon, and the day's take in the till was not worth the time and effort it would take to walk to the bank to make the night deposit.

Despite the hectic day, it was Pixie who seemed restless as darkness settled in and it was almost time to close the store.

"Have you got any plans for the evening?" Tricia asked.

"No. Well, maybe just a discussion with Fred about moving. My place seemed pretty big—until he brought all his stuff over. It's been five months and I don't have room to fa—" She stopped, and Tricia suspected she had been about to say something mildly vulgar. "To turn around," Pixie amended. "We've got to look for a bigger place."

"A house?" Tricia asked.

"I wish. There's no money for that—not that we're big spenders. We've been saving for a rainy day, and I guess that day is coming up fast."

Tricia remembered Angelica's desire to liberate her assistant. And she remembered that the house that had temporarily been home to the Chamber the year before was ready to go on the market. Angelica hadn't done so, because she worried about finding just the right owner. Perhaps Pixie and Fred would fill the bill. Tricia mentioned the property, where Pixie had worked during the months before the Chamber had found its present home.

"That would be a real pipe dream."

"If you could afford it, would you like something like that?"

"You bet."

Tricia sighed. "I think you could more than swing it if you went to work for Nigela Ricita Associates."

"Why would I want to do that?"

"Because . . . someone in the organization contacted me and asked about it."

Pixie frowned. "Why didn't they call me directly?"

"They wanted to know what I thought of you and your abilities."

"And you said?" Pixie asked, sounding wary.

"That often I think your talents are wasted here. That you have a world of experiences and an abundance of creativity and that I want only the best for you."

Pixie was quiet for several long seconds, then her eyes filled with tears. "You want to get rid of me?"

"No! Not at all. But I don't want to hold you back, either. I didn't do that to Ginny, and look where she is now."

"Yeah, but she's just a kid," Pixie said bitterly.

"And that's one thing I really admire about Nigela Ricita Associates. They don't discriminate; not by race, not by gender, not by sexual orientation, and not by age."

"And not by a criminal record," Pixie added. She knew about Jake Keenan, who'd had a record for assault. He'd been a short-order cook at Booked for Lunch and now worked as the head chef at the Brookview Inn.

"That's right," Tricia affirmed.

"This Nigela chick seems to be the real thing," Pixie said.

"Yes. She is," Tricia agreed.

Pixie said nothing, and Tricia felt she had to tell the truth—at least to a certain extent.

"If I had won the Chamber presidency, I was prepared to have you take on a lot more responsibility here at the store. I know you would have excelled. Unfortunately, I lost."

"I may not have said it aloud, but I'm real sorry that happened. You would have done a great job for the Chamber and its members."

"I like to think so. But it is what it is."

"Yeah." Pixie let out a long breath. "I'd like to think about this for a while. I mean, I couldn't walk out on you during the holidays. The store's about to see its best sales of the year. And I'd need to talk this over with Fred. It's a big, a really *big* decision."

"Take all the time you need. As I understand it, the offer is pretty open-ended."

Pixie nodded. "Okay. But I was wondering . . . you had your heart set on that Chamber job. You've been thinking about it for months. Isn't there something else you'd like to do? Devote time to a hobby or something?"

"I don't know. I used to repair old books, and I'm pretty good at it, but a lot of the books we see are paperbound. We don't see a lot of damaged books worth saving."

"That's true," Pixie agreed. "But I thought you said a time or two that you might like to work with or start a pet rescue."

Tricia thought about Carol Talbot and her legacy. "Yes, but . . . like you said, it's kind of a pipe dream. Angelica has urged me to start a second business."

"The area could use another shelter. Mr. E had to go to Milford to get Charlie—God rest his kitty soul. And even if you didn't open a shelter, you could always give your time or donate to that shelter. The world is full of crappy people who abuse animals—and just as full of nice people who want those dogs and cats to have a better, happy life."

That was true.

"It's something to think about," Tricia said. "Are you sad that you didn't find it feasible to open a tailor shop?"

Pixie shook her head. "Nah, I'm not like Frannie."

"Frannie wants to open her own furniture repair shop?"

Pixie shook her head. "But she's thought about selling her own brand of wood gunk."

"What do you mean?" Tricia asked.

"I guess her father was into making wood finishes. He left the recipes for his concoctions to Frannie. She cooks them up on her kitchen stove—when the weather is fine. I guess the fumes can be kind of nasty, so she only does it during the summer when she can have the windows open and run a fan."

"Really?"

"Oh, yeah. She goes out along the highway and picks all kinds of wild stuff to cook up. Stuff like poison sumac and other leaves and bark."

"Sumac?" Tricia asked, remembering what Chief Baker told her about Ted Harper's allergy to one thing: the sap from a sumac plant. "I thought it only grew here in the Northeast."

"Apparently not. Frannie's into all kinds of natural crap. I asked her if it wasn't a lot of trouble to cook that crap and risk your lungs rather than buy a can of the ready-made stuff, but she said there was no comparison."

No comparison? Maybe. But deadly lethal to ingest, at least for someone like Ted Harper. Would putting something like that in a canapé have been just worth a tummy upset to someone who *wasn't* allergic to the poisonous substance? Would a small dose of the stuff merely make the average person ill, but not kill? And why—why would Frannie want to pull such a stunt at Tricia's party? The idea turned her stomach. Frannie's actions had caused a man's death—a man she professed to care about, and yet she hadn't acted guilty in the least.

"Are you okay?" Pixie asked, studying Tricia's face. "You look kind of pale."

Tricia shook her head. "It's been a very long and troubling day."

Pixie nodded and glanced at the clock. "It's almost time to go home."

"We may as well close up shop for the night," Tricia agreed, and they went through their end-of-day routine.

It was still only five fifty, but Tricia had had more than enough for one day, turned the OPEN sign to CLOSED, and pulled the blinds on the front window before giving Pixie a good-night wave as she left for home.

And Tricia pondered what she should do with the knowledge of what Frannie had done.

THIRTY-ONE

Like most of the businesses in Stoneham—at least during the off season—the Cookery closed its doors at six o'clock. Tricia usually left her own store to go to Angelica's for dinner about five minutes later—but that day she waited ten. There was no way she wanted to run into Frannie.

Tricia dithered, waiting for the big hand on the clock to make its way to the ten-minute mark before she grabbed her cloak. Despite her tussles with Russ, her arm was feeling much better, and she decided to leave her sling on the hook. She'd take it upstairs and put it away. Then she thought better of that idea. She'd toss it out. If she ever hurt her arm again, she'd be given a new sling.

She wasn't sure what she would say to Angelica about Frannie. She wouldn't want to believe her assistant—the woman she trusted to run the Cookery—could be so callous, so reckless, and so damnably unrepentant.

Tricia lowered the lights and locked her shop door. But as she swung around to enter the Cookery, she noted that though the blinds had been pulled, the lights were still blazing behind them. She pushed the shop's door and found it unlocked. The first thing she noticed was that the plate had been taken off the light switch and that bare wires hung from it. The floor below it was sopping wet. As she stepped inside, she saw Frannie standing behind the cash desk—the last person she wanted to run into.

"Hello, Frannie. You're here late tonight," Tricia said, feeling uncomfortable. She shut the door and moved off of the saturated carpet.

"I've been waiting for you," Frannie said, none too friendly.

A bigger twinge of unease gave Tricia a shudder. She moved farther into the store. "Why's that?"

"Because you figured it out. Somehow you always do," Frannie said bitterly.

"I don't know what you're talking about."

"Pixie told you not twenty minutes ago."

Tricia swallowed. There was only one way Frannie could have known that. She must have bugged Haven't Got a Clue, too. But when? Tricia hadn't seen the woman in the shop in quite some time—but then she often worked in her office in the converted basement. She and Angelica had an agreement that if their stores needed change, either Pixie or Mr. Everett could pop next door to get it—and Frannie could do the same. She must have planted one of her little listening devices during just such a visit.

"The question is," Frannie asked, her voice deadly calm, "what are you going to do about it?"

"I don't know what you mean," Tricia bluffed.

"Of course you do. Chief Baker told you about Ted's allergy—he tells you *everything*," she said snidely.

"As he must have told you," Tricia added.

"Yes."

"Why didn't you say something?"

"And get arrested for murder? I didn't mean for anyone to die—just to get a little sick."

"And who was your intended target?"

Frannie smiled. "Guess."

And then everything seemed to slip into place, and Tricia knew. "Angelica."

Frannie's smile widened and she nodded.

"That doesn't make sense."

"She almost always takes the last of anything," Frannie practically growled. "And what did it matter who got sick? Damn Ted for having a sumac allergy, anyway."

"But why would you want to hurt Angelica? She's treated you with nothing but kindness, respect, and most of all, trust."

"Like hell. If she respected me so much, why am I still working in retail when she's got about ten businesses and hires people with a lot less experience than me? She'd even hire Pixie—an ex-prostitute—for one of her high-and-mighty Nigela Ricita businesses."

Again Tricia swallowed. Despite the obvious trap of water and electricity, which she'd stepped well away from, as far as she could see, she was in no immediate danger, although she couldn't see Frannie's hands. Did she have a gun behind the counter?

The prudent thing was to get the heck out of there—but what about Angelica? Would Frannie go right upstairs and threaten—harm—her sister?

Stall for time. Keep her talking.

"Did you ever ask to interview for another job?"

Frannie's lip curled. "I wasn't supposed to know about her double life."

Frannie, the eyes and the ears of Stoneham, was known for ferreting out secrets—and blabbing them to the world at large. Why hadn't she told *that* tale?

"It's you who's been blackmailing her," Tricia accused.

Frannie shrugged. "So what?"

"You threatened a child," Tricia pointed out.

"But I would have never gone through with it."

"You poisoned your own boyfriend," Tricia said, as though to belie that statement.

"That was an accident."

"But you would have been okay with poisoning Angelica."

"*She* wouldn't have died."

"You don't know that."

Again Frannie shrugged.

Tricia's gaze wandered to the clock. Angelica would soon be wondering why she hadn't arrived upstairs for their predinner drink.

"Was it you who vandalized my store? My car?"

"And Ginny's car—let's not forget about *her*."

"But why?"

"The people who work for Nigela Ricita have all had chances to move up—to make a better living—all except me."

"For instance?" Tricia asked, still stalling.

"Jake moved from Booked for Lunch to the Brookview Inn—with a hefty increase in salary. Bev moved from Booked for Lunch to the Dog-Eared Page. And of course we can't forget dear, sweet *Ginny*." She said the name with utter disgust.

"What do you mean?"

"She went from shopkeeper to management—nepotism at work," she practically spat.

"Excuse me, but Ginny is tremendously capable. It took me months to replace her. And she proved her mettle with last summer's Wine and Jazz Festival." Frannie's lip curled, and Tricia changed tacks. "Did you ever tell Angelica you wanted that kind of opportunity?" she pressed again.

"I'm over fifty. Who in the world would hire me for anything other than retail?"

"You'd never find out without asking. And, by the way, *I* hired someone over the age of fifty to take Ginny's place at Haven't Got a Clue."

"That's *you*—not Angelica."

"Don't be ridiculous. Michele Fowler, at the Dog-Eared Page, was over fifty when she got the manager's job. Bev is over fifty. The innkeepers at the Sheer Comfort Inn are over fifty. If nothing else, Angelica *and* Nigela Ricita Associates are well known for hiring people by their abilities, not their race, not their age, but by their qualifications."

Frannie's sneer deepened. What was her *real* beef? Or was she just playing victim because it was easier?

"Why did you bug my apartment?" Tricia demanded.

"To find out more about Angelica's business dealings. She only talks about it to *you*. She could have confided in *me*. She could have used *me* as a sounding board. She could have done so much more for *me*!"

"What about Ted?" Tricia had believed that Frannie's tears had been real the night Ted Harper died.

"How was I supposed to know he was allergic to sumac?"

"Why did you pull all those pranks?"

"Not all. There's a copycat somewhere in the village."

Yeah; Russ Smith.

Frannie shrugged. "It was Bob Kelly's idea."

"Bob? But you and he weren't friends. After how he treated you at the Chamber for all those years, you vowed you'd never speak to him again."

"Yeah, well, it's hard to put your ex-lover completely out of your life—no matter what they've done to you."

Ex-lover?

"When were you and Bob lovers?"

"Early on in my tenure at the Chamber. I've been visiting him in jail—when they let me. He only gets to see someone every other month—and *you* made sure he was sentenced to life in prison. Now we can never be together."

Bob used people. He was using Frannie. In her present state of mind, she'd never be able to see that. "That's a better outcome than he gave my husband."

"*Ex*-husband," Frannie corrected.

"Christopher didn't deserve to die."

Frannie moved around the counter, and Tricia noticed how sturdily she was built. She must have had forty or fifty pounds on Tricia. She advanced, her gaze hard.

"I think it's time you joined him."

Tricia backed up, crashing into a display of kitchen utensils that hung on the wall, sending a number of them clattering to the floor. Tricia ducked right, straight into the puddle, as Frannie lunged for her.

She bobbed to her left, just missing Frannie's outstretched arms.

"Angelica!" Tricia hollered as Frannie grabbed hold of her, yanking her off balance and toward the door once more. Younger and faster, Tricia dipped lower, but then Frannie's clenched fist came around, smashing into Tricia's face, sending her reeling.

"What on earth?" came a muffled voice.

Frannie grabbed Tricia by her cloak and hauled her upright, but Tricia knew what was in store if she didn't move quickly—get away. She twisted around, giving Frannie a mighty shove, which sent her stumbling backward, smashing into the wall.

A bloodcurdling scream cut the air as Tricia lost her balance and fell to the floor.

So did Frannie.

"Tricia!"

Angelica dodged the bookshelves and displays and was suddenly there, grabbing Tricia's sore arm and hauling her to her feet. "What happened?"

"I think Frannie just electrocuted herself."

Angelica took in the crumpled figure on the floor behind the door, the bare wires and the sodden carpet.

"Call nine one one!"

Tricia did as she was told, while Angelica jumped into action once again.

"She's not breathing." Angelica felt for a pulse, and then immediately started CPR.

"Frannie poisoned Ted. She's the vandal. She's the one who was blackmailing you!" Tricia cried, but Angelica was not to be deterred. She kept up the chest compressions.

"Then it's . . . in my best interest . . . to make sure she lives . . . to go to jail . . . where she can rot!"

THIRTY-TWO

"I guess the third time was the charm," Chief Baker said, closing the shop door behind the EMTs. He'd just gotten off the phone after calling in the state police crime scene team to come to take care of things at the Cookery.

A disheartened Angelica sat on the stool behind the Cookery's sales counter. "Charm?"

"He's right," Tricia piped up. "You gave CPR to Ted Harper and Chauncey Porter without success, but your efforts tonight saved Frannie's life."

Angelica sighed. "She was my very first employee," she said, watching as the lights of the ambulance disappeared—with a police escort—up Main Street toward Milford and St. Joseph Hospital.

Frannie had regained consciousness and hadn't been at all grateful that she now owed her life to Angelica—a fact she'd railed about to the police and the EMTs, who had arrived only minutes after Frannie's near death from electrocution. And she didn't go quietly, either—shouting and hollering abuse at Angelica and Tricia for "ruining my life!"

"That's not entirely true," Tricia said, remembering that when Angelica had first taken over the Cookery, she hadn't been able to keep any of her hired help. Whether that was Angelica's fault or the fault of the workers who hadn't lasted, Tricia wasn't sure. There was no denying that Angelica had honed her hiring skills and now seldom if ever made a mistake in that regard.

"Well, she was my first employee who stuck," she amended, and shook her head ruefully.

Chief Baker went back to looking at the cell phone he'd picked up from the sales counter, scrolling through the apps. "There's no doubt about it. Frannie was definitely listening in on both your conversations, and doing it with this phone."

"The last few times I saw her, she did have on earbuds. I thought she was listening to music while she worked," Tricia said.

"We'll get a warrant and search her home. I'm betting we'll find evidence on her computer to build a case against her for blackmailing you, Angelica. Especially after we take a look at her bank accounts. And, of course, she'll be charged not only with Ted Harper's murder but for attempting to kill you, too, Tricia."

The thought that she'd come very close to being electrocuted made Tricia shudder.

"I just don't understand how she could do this to me. What did I do to her?" Angelica asked.

"You didn't offer her a better job. She was furious to know that you wanted to hire Pixie."

"For what?" Baker asked. "Clean rooms at the B and B you're part-owner in? Wait tables at Booked for Lunch?"

Angelica covered her face with her hands.

"You're going to have to come clean and publicly confess," Tricia said, not unkindly.

"Confess what?" Baker said.

"That I'm Nigela Ricita."

"Oh, yeah," Baker said. "I guess I forgot about that."

No doubt Angelica had told him everything that morning when he'd met her and Antonio at the Brookview Inn after the Chamber meeting—which now seemed like weeks instead of hours ago.

"But you know, I don't think it's all that big a secret," Baker said.

Angelica removed her hands from her eyes. "It's not?"

Baker shook his head. "Not really."

"You knew?"

"Half the village knows. I mean—Ricita *is* an anagram for Tricia—and everybody knows the two of you are practically joined at the hip."

"But Nigela is *not* an anagram for Angelica," Angelica asserted.

"So you're a lousy speller."

"Who else knows?" Tricia asked.

"That I know of?" Baker looked thoughtful. "A couple of my officers. Boris and Alexa Kozlov. Joyce Widman. Jim Stark." He bit his lip, thinking. "Toni Bennett, Shawn at the Dog-Eared Page—"

"Is there *anybody* who didn't know?" Angelica asked, sounding frustrated.

"Russ Smith," Baker guessed. "Otherwise he would have blown your cover a long time ago." He leveled a gaze at Tricia. "He's not the nicest man in the world."

"You don't have to tell me that."

"Did you want to press charges against him for trespassing in your store earlier today?"

"A part of me would love to say yes. He told me that Nikki's leaving him—and for some reason he seems to blame me. I'm worried about him trying to stalk me again."

"You could get a restraining order."

"How is that going to work when our businesses are so close and he's going to be the Chamber of Commerce president?"

"Do you really think he's going to go through with that?" Angelica asked.

"I do," Tricia said. "Once Nikki leaves him—and Russ is convinced she's going to bleed him dry—what else will he have to do to occupy his time?"

"I thought he didn't want the job," Baker said.

"I'm sure he doesn't, but he isn't going to allow me to have it, either," Tricia said.

"Spiteful jerk. What did you ever see in him?" Baker asked.

"I have no idea—and I certainly don't want to revisit those memories."

"When can I get my light switch fixed?" Angelica asked. "I can't open the shop tomorrow with live wires hanging out."

"Do you really want to do that?" Tricia asked.

"I'll call June to see if she'd like to take Frannie's hours, at least temporarily, until I can find some other help."

"If she can't, I can offer you Pixie."

Angelica's eyes lit up.

"You can't have her—at least not in a retail position," Tricia said firmly.

"It was just a thought, and it would only be temporary. And anyway, that would be up to Pixie."

"Yes, it would," Tricia grudgingly agreed.

Angelica looked up at Baker. "Chief, do we have to sit here and wait for the crime team?"

"Yes, there's a pitcher of martinis waiting upstairs, and I, for one, could use one," Tricia said.

"So could I," Angelica said, sounding exhausted.

"Sure, go ahead. If I need you, I know where to find you," Baker said. "And I'll call Jim Stark to see if he can send someone over to fix the switch."

Angelica rose to her feet. "Thank you, Chief."

Tricia followed her sister up the stairs to her third-floor apartment. As promised, Angelica took out the pitcher of martinis and poured. "What do we drink to?"

Tricia stared at her glass. "How about the good and the bad?"

"What do you mean?"

"Take Chauncey. The good for him was that he won the Chamber election. The bad was that I lost. The bad for him was that he worked himself into a massive heart attack over the job. But the good was that Mary won't have to marry a tyrant."

"That is good, but the truth is Mary never *had* to marry him. It was her choice to accept his proposal."

"And one she'd come to regret."

"Anything else?" Angelica asked.

"Mr. Everett and Charlie. The bad was losing Charlie. The good was that he gave Charlie almost two weeks of happiness. Otherwise, Charlie would have died in a cage at the shelter, where he'd spent far too many of his kitty lives."

"That would have been bad," Angelica agreed. "Any more good? I'd rather hear that than the bad."

"The best of the good? Your blackmailer was caught and Sofia is safe."

Angelica managed a small smile. "That is the best of the best."

They clinked glasses and drank.

THIRTY-THREE

White fairy lights twinkled on the Christmas tree at the far end of Tricia's living room. She had never hosted a holiday celebration, but this one was looking to be a big success, as evidenced by the pile of wrapping paper and ribbons that littered the floor that Christmas Eve.

"We must open presents on *vigilia di Natale*," Antonio had insisted, and so they had—with an even bigger extravaganza planned for the following day.

Their little family had enjoyed a Thanksgiving turkey dinner, with all the trimmings, at the Brookview Inn, with Angelica promising that next year it would be in her revamped home. Tricia had made all the food for December 24, and Angelica was all set to cook a prime rib of beef for the gang in Tricia's kitchen come Christmas Day.

Between Frannie's arrest and the holidays, it had been a rough six weeks. Pixie and Mr. Everett pitched in at the Cookery until Angelica could find part-time help, and June was only too happy to take over as the manager of the shop.

Mr. Everett hadn't wanted to speak about Charlie's loss, and Tricia knew he'd been devastated. But the hustle and bustle of the season had considerably cheered him, and he was almost his old self once more.

Baker had wrung a promise from Russ not to bother Tricia—under threat of arrest. But Tricia wasn't sure she trusted that oath. Nikki and Russ had separated, and as she'd promised, Nikki was determined to get what she could from their union. As far as Tricia knew, Russ hadn't bothered to seek joint custody of his son and hadn't even visited the boy.

And best of all, Angelica's secret hadn't gone public. Yet. Of course, once Frannie went to trial, it was sure to come out. Angelica was considering hiring a PR firm to help draft an announcement. But she felt she still had time.

The phone rang, and Tricia hurried into the kitchen to pick up the extension. "Hello. Merry Christmas."

"Tricia? Hi, it's Pixie."

"Oh, hi. What's up? I thought you and Fred had another party to go to."

"We did. But it broke up early. Since we were in the neighborhood, I wondered if I could drop off a little present. Could you come down and get it?"

"That is so sweet of you, Pixie. You've got a key. Why don't you come on up? Is Fred with you? Bring him, too. We've got tons of food, and I know everybody would love to have you join us."

"Oh, no. It's getting late."

"It's not *that* late," she said, looking at the clock.

"Well. Okay. But just for a few minutes. We'll be right up."

Tricia hung up the phone. "Hey, everybody. Pixie and Fred are coming up."

"That's nice," Angelica said.

"I haven't seen her since—" But then Ginny stopped; it had probably been the night of Tricia's cocktail party almost two months before.

"I'm so glad she could be here," Mr. Everett said. He wore a silly green and red polka-dot bow tie that had been a gift from Sofia. When you pressed a button, it played "Jingle Bells," which delighted the baby to no end.

"I'm glad she could join us, too," Grace said.

Seconds later, Pixie knocked before opening the door to Tricia's apartment. "Merry Christmas," she called as she entered, with Fred right behind her.

A chorus of "Merry Christmas" greeted them.

Tricia took their coats and directed them to sit in the living room—which no longer was rife with listening devices. When the professionals had done a sweep, they'd found two more, which Frannie must have planted the night of the cocktail party.

Pixie looked rather embarrassed. "I'm sorry, I only brought one gift."

Just about everyone looked from Pixie to Tricia and seemed surprised when instead she presented it to Mr. Everett.

"For me?" he asked, surprised.

"Uh-huh. I thought you might like it."

The large, rectangular gift box was exquisitely wrapped in gold-and-red-striped metallic paper, with a jumbo scarlet bow fastened on the top.

"I don't know what to say," Mr. Everett said.

"Open it, open it, Mr. E," Ginny encouraged. She herself was wearing a bow taped to the top of her head.

While Mr. Everett fumbled with the wrapping, Angelica swooped in with a tray of glasses filled with wine, offering them to Fred and Pixie, who graciously accepted. Antonio had his cell phone out and was furiously snapping photos.

Mr. Everett lifted the box lid and pulled aside the white, sparkly tissue paper. "Oh, my," he said as the rest of the room crowded around to see what was inside.

"It's a scrapbook," Pixie said as Mr. Everett extricated the gift from the box and his eyes filled with sudden tears.

The front of the book featured a picture of a big tabby cat, and across the cover, in what looked like gold leaf, was the word *Charlie*.

"Grace raided your cell phone and sent me the pictures. I hope you like it," Pixie said quietly, while Grace beamed and reached for her husband's hand.

There were oohs and aahs as Mr. Everett reverently turned the ten or so pages. The photos all had captions, and they showed Charlie sitting on Grace's and Mr. Everett's laps, eating, sleeping, and playing with his toys—and the very last one was of Mr. Everett with Charlie nuzzling his chin. He tapped the picture. "This is my favorite. It's how I shall always remember my first boy."

"First?" Tricia asked.

Mr. Everett squeezed Grace's hand. "Hard as it was to lose Charlie, we've decided we cannot be a cat-free family."

"That's right," Grace piped up. "It broke our hearts to lose him, but we know Charlie's last days were happy and that he knew he was loved. We'd like to give another older cat the same experience."

Mr. Everett nodded, and then turned to Pixie. "Thank you for such a thoughtful gift. I will treasure it."

Pixie bent down and kissed him on the cheek. "Merry Christmas, Mr. E."

Mr. Everett blushed, but seemed extraordinarily pleased.

"I don't know if you remember," Tricia began, "but I know of a cat who could use a loving home."

Mr. Everett looked up.

"But it's a girl—not a boy."

Everyone looked puzzled.

"Her name is Penny. She's an orange and white tabby. Frannie's cat. She's been sitting in a cage at the shelter for the past six weeks just waiting and hoping for a new forever home."

"How old is she?" Grace asked.

"Three."

Grace and Mr. Everett exchanged glances. "I suppose we could have two cats."

"Yes," Grace agreed, smiling. "What's to stop us?"

The whole group broke into cheers and applause.

"This calls for another round," Tricia said, and headed toward the kitchen to get another bottle of wine.

"I'll help," Pixie volunteered, and Mr. Everett passed the scrapbook to Ginny and Angelica so that they could admire it.

Tricia grabbed another chilled bottle from a cooler on the floor and opened it. "There's a tray full of canapés in the fridge. Would you get them out, please?"

"Oh, sure," Pixie said. She placed the tray on the counter and took off the plastic wrap. "I wanted to let you know that I've thought long and hard about working for Nigela Ricita Associates."

If Pixie knew Angelica was behind the company, she hadn't mentioned it.

"And?" Tricia asked, dreading the answer.

"I can't do it."

"What?"

"I can't leave you and Mr. E. You're like family to me—better than anybody I'm actually related to. I couldn't bear to be away from you guys."

"Are you sure you don't even want to interview for a job?"

Pixie nodded. "Yeah, me and Fred have talked about it a lot. Why should I give up a job I know I love, with the two greatest people on the planet—besides Fred—for the unknown? Maybe that makes me kind of a jerk, afraid to leave my comfort zone, but these past couple of years have been the best of my life, and I sure don't want to blow it."

Tricia smiled and remembered what Pixie had told her about the possibility of losing the race for the Chamber presidency. *"Would it make you happy to work yourself into an early grave without a minute to sit back, relax, read, and pet your cat?"*

No. It wouldn't have.

"I've been thinking a lot about what we talked about, too. I'm ready for new challenges. I'm not giving up Haven't Got a Clue—but I am going to try something new, and if you're willing, I would like for you to take on some new responsibilities at the store when I do."

Pixie smiled. "I'd sure like to try."

"I'm so pleased." Tricia gave her friend and assistant a hug, then pulled back. "Now, let's get this food and drink out to that hungry mob."

"You got it, boss," Pixie said, and picked up the tray.

The phone rang, and Tricia grabbed it. "Hello! Merry Christmas."

"Merry Christmas, Tricia."

"Marshall?"

"It's me."

"Long time, no hear."

"I'm sorry about that. With all the trouble you and your sister have been through—and the Christmas rush and all—I thought I'd give you some space."

He was right. She'd been so caught up in depositions and juggling work schedules and shopping, cooking, and everything else that went with the holidays that, while she'd thought of Marshall, it hadn't been all that often or too intently.

"I've been busy, too. I finalized the deal to sell Vamps."

"Oh?" Tricia wasn't sure how she felt about that. She was happy that he was getting out of a business that so demeaned women, but did that mean he was going to leave the area for good?

"Yeah. But I've also been looking for another business opportunity, and I found one right here in Stoneham."

"That's nice—what is it?"

"The Armchair Tourist."

"Mary Fairchild sold it to you?" Tricia asked, surprised.

"Yeah, and for a good price. I've spent the past few weeks learning about the travel industry and talking to the people at Milford Travel about cross promotion."

"When will you take over?"

"As of the first of the year. Which is kind of why I called. What are you doing New Year's Eve?"

Tricia smiled. "I haven't made any plans at all."

"Then maybe you might like to have dinner with me."

"Dinner only?"

"I don't tap, but I do dance," he said.

"Okay," she said, and laughed.

"All right. I'll call you between now and then to firm things up."

"Okay. Until then . . . Merry Christmas."

"Merry Christmas to you, too."

Tricia hung up the phone.

"Hey, where's the wine? We want to toast," Angelica called.

Tricia grabbed the bottle and headed for the living room filled with the people she loved best.

It was a very Merry Christmas indeed.

ANGELICA'S *EASY-DOES-IT COOKING* RECIPES

Salmon-Cucumber Rosettes

8 ounces cream cheese, softened
1 tablespoon fresh dill, chopped
3 ounces smoked salmon (in thin slices)
1 large cucumber
Toothpicks

Combine the softened cream cheese, chopped dill, and smoked salmon into a smooth spread. Using a large-scale vegetable peeler, peel the cucumber into thin strips. Spread the smoked salmon spread onto each strip and roll up. (Toothpicks help keep them together.) Serve chilled.

Yield: approximately 30

Crab Stuffed Mushrooms

7 ounces crabmeat
5 green onions, thinly sliced
¼ teaspoon dried thyme
¼ teaspoon dried oregano
Black pepper to taste
⅓ cup mayonnaise
¼ cup grated Parmesan cheese
1 pound fresh mushrooms
3 tablespoons grated Parmesan cheese
Paprika to taste

Preheat the oven to 350°F (175°C). In a medium bowl, combine the crabmeat, green onions, herbs, and black pepper. Mix in the mayonnaise and ¼ cup Parmesan cheese until well combined. Refrigerate the filling until ready for use.

Wipe the mushrooms clean with a damp towel. Remove the stems. Spoon out the gills and the base of the stem, making deep cups. Discard the gills and stems or use for another purpose. Fill the mushroom caps with rounded teaspoonfuls of the filling and place them in an ungreased shallow baking dish. Sprinkle the tops with additional Parmesan and paprika.

Bake for 15 minutes. Remove from the oven, and serve immediately.

Yield: 6 servings

Mini Spinach Quiches

½ cup butter or margarine, softened
1 (3-ounce) package cream cheese, softened
1 cup all-purpose flour
3 slices bacon
¼ cup chopped green onion
2 eggs
½ cup half-and-half cream
¼ teaspoon salt
⅛ teaspoon ground nutmeg
½ cup grated Parmesan cheese
1 (10-ounce) package frozen spinach, thawed and well drained (use your hands to squeeze out the water)

In a small mixing bowl, cream the butter and cream cheese. Add the flour; beat until well blended. Shape into 24 balls. Press the balls into the bottom and the sides of greased mini muffin cups.

Preheat the oven to 350°F (175°C). In a skillet, cook the bacon until brown and very crisp; drain. Sauté the onions in the same skillet with the bacon drippings and cook for 5 minutes, or until tender, stirring constantly; drain. Place the onions in a medium bowl. Crumble the bacon into small pieces, and add in with the cooked green onion. Add the eggs to the bacon and onions; beat well. Stir in the cream, salt, nutmeg, and Parmesan cheese. Add in the squeezed spinach; mix well to combine. Divide the mixture into the crust-lined cups (do not overfill).

Bake for 25 to 30 minutes, or until puffed and golden brown. Cool in the pan on a wire rack for 5 minutes. Serve warm or cool. Store the leftovers in the refrigerator.

Yield: 24

Spanakopita

½ cup olive oil
2 large onions, chopped
2 (10-ounce) packages frozen chopped spinach, thawed, drained, and squeezed dry
2 tablespoons chopped fresh dill (or 2 teaspoons dried dill)
2 tablespoons all-purpose flour
1 (8-ounce) package feta cheese, crumbled
4 eggs, lightly beaten
Salt and pepper to taste
1 (24-ounce) package phyllo dough
¾ pound butter, melted

Preheat the oven to 350°F (175°C). Heat the olive oil in a large saucepan over medium heat. Slowly cook and stir onions until softened (do not overcook). Mix in the spinach, dill, and flour. Cook for approximately 10 minutes, or until most of the moisture has been absorbed. Remove from the heat and mix in the cheese, eggs, salt, and pepper. Lay the phyllo dough flat and cut into long strips (about 2 inches wide); brush with the melted butter. Place a small amount of spinach mixture at the bottom of each piece of dough. Fold the phyllo into triangles around the mixture. Place the filled phyllo dough triangles on a large baking sheet. Brush with butter. Bake for 45 minutes to 1 hour, or until golden brown.

Yield: Varies